SPIDER-MAN
SPIDER-VERSE
MILES MORALES

ULTIMATE COMICS SPIDER-MAN (2011) #1-2

WRITER: BRIAN MICHAEL BENDIS
ARTIST: SARA PICHELLI
COLOR ARTIST: JUSTIN PONSOR
LETTERER: VC'S CORY PETIT
COVER ART: KAARE ANDREWS
ASSOCIATE EDITOR: SANA AMANAT
EDITOR: MARK PANICCIA

ULTIMATE COMICS SPIDER-MAN (2011) #5

WRITER: BRIAN MICHAEL BENDIS
LAYOUTS: SARA PICHELLI
FINISHES: DAVID MESSINA
COLOR ARTIST: JUSTIN PONSOR
LETTERER: VC'S CORY PETIT
COVER ART: KAARE ANDREWS
ASSISTANT EDITOR: JON MOISAN
ASSOCIATE EDITOR: SANA AMANAT
EDITOR: MARK PANICCIA

SPIDER-MAN (2016) #1-2

WRITER: BRIAN MICHAEL BENDIS
ARTIST: SARA PICHELLI
INKING ASSIST: GAETANO CARLUCCI
COLOR ARTIST: JUSTIN PONSOR
LETTERER: VC'S CORY PETIT
COVER ART: SARA PICHELLI & JUSTIN PONSOR
ASSISTANT EDITOR: DEVIN LEWIS
EDITOR: NICK LOWE

SPIDER-MAN CREATED BY STAN LEE & STEVE DITKO

COLLECTION EDITOR: JENNIFER GRÜNWALD ASSISTANT EDITOR: CAITLIN O'CONNELL
ASSOCIATE MANAGING EDITOR: KATERI WOODY EDITOR, SPECIAL PROJECTS: MARK D. BEAZLEY
VP PRODUCTION & SPECIAL PROJECTS: JEFF YOUNGQUIST SVP PRINT, SALES & MARKETING: DAVID GABRIEL
BOOK DESIGNER: JAY BOWEN WITH ADAM DEL RE

EDITOR IN CHIEF: C.B. CEBULSKI CHIEF CREATIVE OFFICER: JOE QUESADA
PRESIDENT: DAN BUCKLEY EXECUTIVE PRODUCER: ALAN FINE

SPIDER-MAN: SPIDER-VERSE — MILES MORALES. Contains material originally published in magazine form as ULTIMATE COMICS SPIDER-MAN #1-2 and #5, and SPIDER-MAN #1-2. First printing 2018. ISBN 978-1-302-91416-5. Published by MARVEL WORLDWIDE, INC., a subsidiary of MARVEL ENTERTAINMENT, LLC. OFFICE OF PUBLICATION: 135 West 50th Street, New York, NY 10020. **Printed in Canada.** DAN BUCKLEY, President, Marvel Entertainment; JOHN NEE, Publisher; JOE QUESADA, Chief Creative Officer; TOM BREVOORT, SVP of Publishing; DAVID BOGART, SVP of Business Affairs & Operations, Publishing & Partnership; DAVID GABRIEL, SVP of Sales & Marketing, Publishing; JEFF YOUNGQUIST, VP of Production & Special Projects; DAN CARR, Executive Director of Publishing Technology; ALEX MORALES, Director of Publishing Operations; DAN EDINGTON, Managing Editor; SUSAN CRESPI, Production Manager; STAN LEE, Chairman Emeritus. For information regarding advertising in Marvel Comics or on Marvel.com, please contact Vit DeBellis, Custom Solutions & Integrated Advertising Manager, at vdebellis@marvel.com. For Marvel subscription inquiries, please call 888-511-5480. **Manufactured between 9/7/2018 and 10/9/2018 by SOLISCO PRINTERS, SCOTT, QC, CANADA.**

10 9 8 7 6 5 4 3 2 1

ULTIMATE COMICS SPIDER-MAN (2011) #1

MILES MORALES HAS BEEN HIDING HIS AMAZING ARACHNID-LIKE
ABILITIES FOR MONTHS. BUT WITH THE ULTIMATE UNIVERSE
SHAKEN BY THE DEATH OF PETER PARKER, WILL HE RISE UP
TO TAKE THE MANTLE OF SPIDER-MAN?!

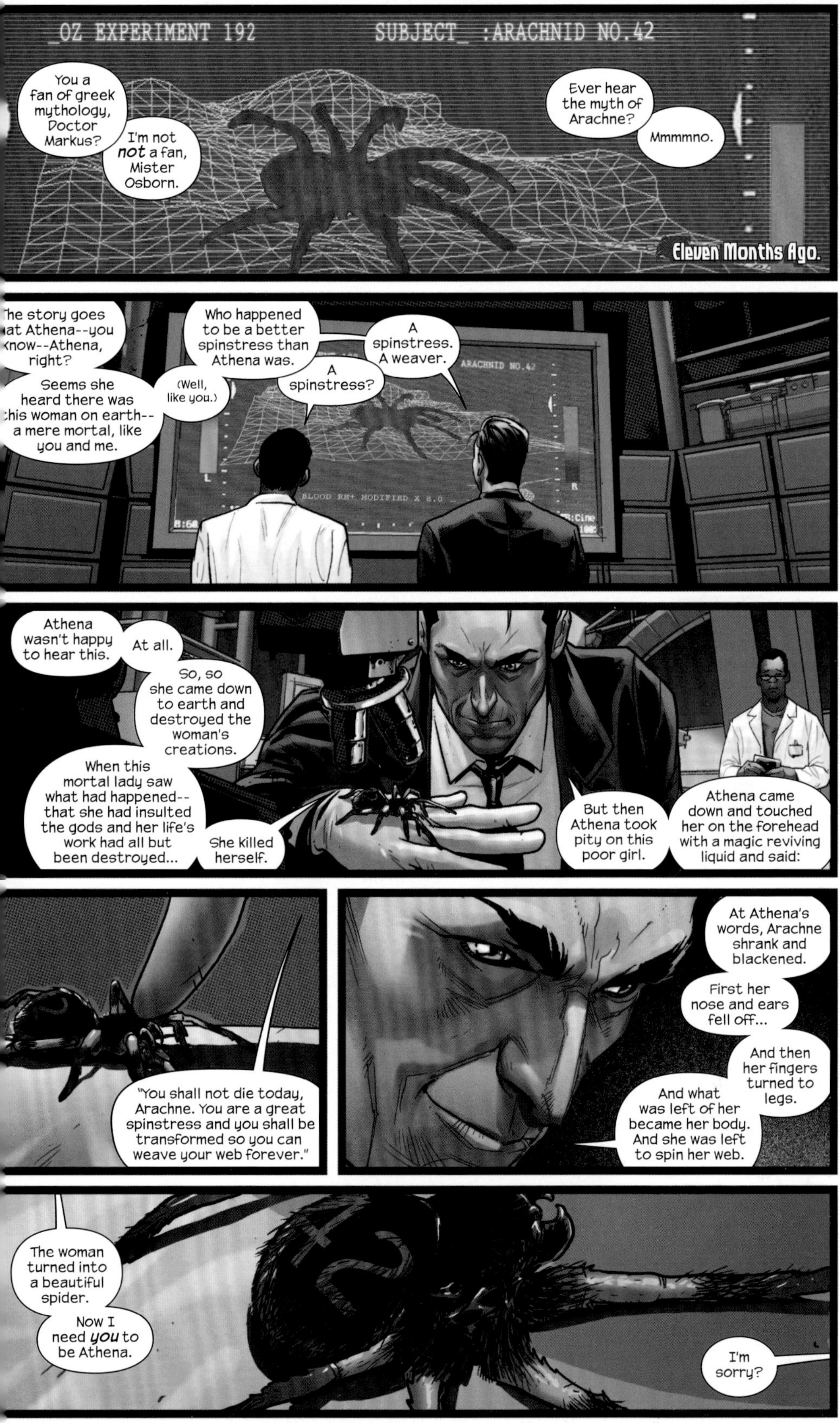

_OZ EXPERIMENT 192
SUBJECT_ :ARACHNID NO.42
You a fan of greek mythology, Doctor Markus?
I'm not *not* a fan, Mister Osborn.
Ever hear the myth of Arachne?
Mmmmno.
Eleven Months Ago.
The story goes that Athena--you know--Athena, right?
Seems she heard there was this woman on earth--a mere mortal, like you and me.
Who happened to be a better spinstress than Athena was.
(Well, like you.)
A spinstress?
A spinstress. A weaver.
ARACHNID NO.42
BLOOD RH+ MODIFIED X 8.0
Athena wasn't happy to hear this.
At all.
So, so she came down to earth and destroyed the woman's creations.
When this mortal lady saw what had happened--that she had insulted the gods and her life's work had all but been destroyed...
She killed herself.
But then Athena took pity on this poor girl.
Athena came down and touched her on the forehead with a magic reviving liquid and said:
"You shall not die today, Arachne. You are a great spinstress and you shall be transformed so you can weave your web forever."
At Athena's words, Arachne shrank and blackened.
First her nose and ears fell off...
And then her fingers turned to legs.
And what was left of her became her body. And she was left to spin her web.
The woman turned into a beautiful spider.
Now I need *you* to be Athena.
I'm sorry?

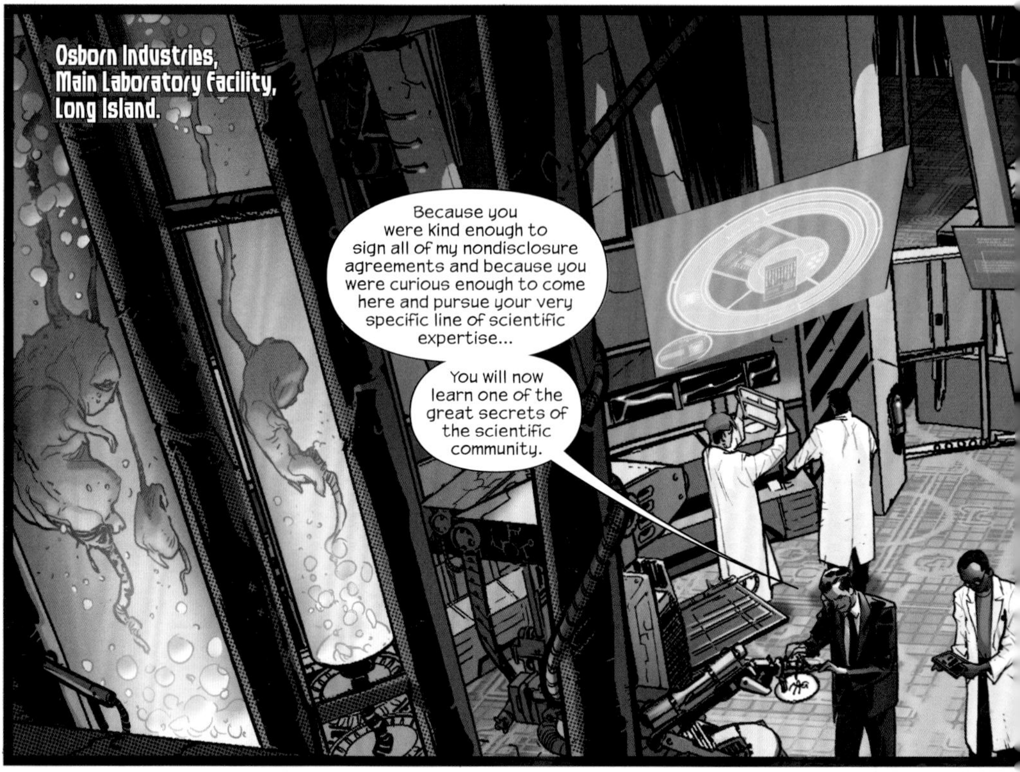

Osborn Industries, Main Laboratory Facility, Long Island.
Because you were kind enough to sign all of my nondisclosure agreements and because you were curious enough to come here and pursue your very specific line of scientific expertise...
You will now learn one of the great secrets of the scientific community.

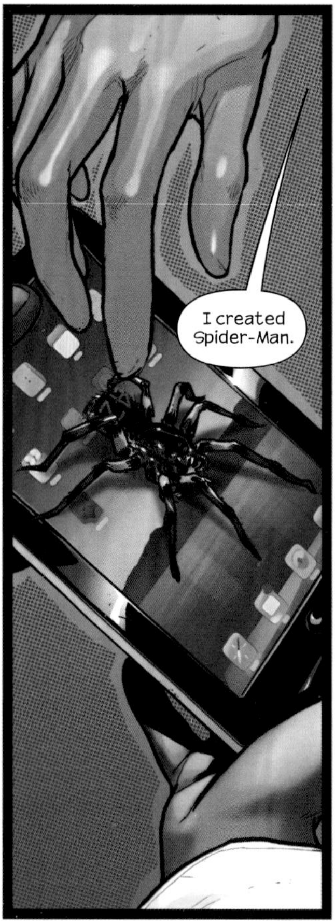

I created Spider-Man.

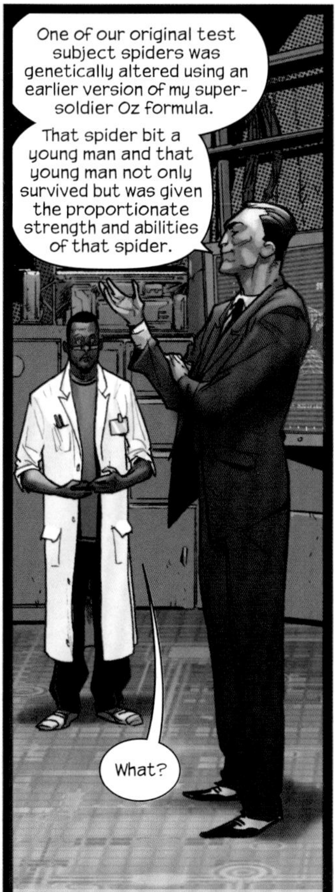

One of our original test subject spiders was genetically altered using an earlier version of my super-soldier Oz formula.
That spider bit a young man and that young man not only survived but was given the proportionate strength and abilities of that spider.
What?

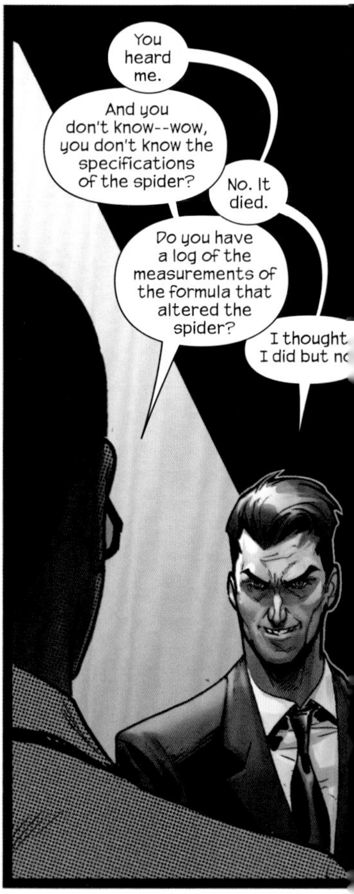

You heard me.
And you don't know--wow, you don't know the specifications of the spider?
No. It died.
Do you have a log of the measurements of the formula that altered the spider?

an we
blood
ples of
e boy?

We have
them.

And you
weren't able
to reverse-
calculate
the--?

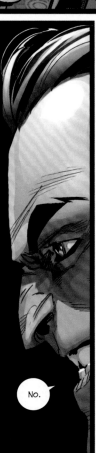

No.

But now we have *you!!*

SLAP

And now I know why you were so crazy to buy out my contract from the Roxxon Corporation.

You're the expert in the field, Doctor Markus.

Actually Otto Octavius is the real expert in the--

We don't talk about *that* man in *this* laboratory.

I said I will beat you to death with my bare hands.

You have four doctorates... which one of those words do you not understand?

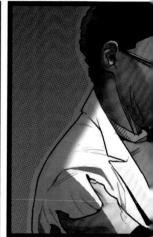

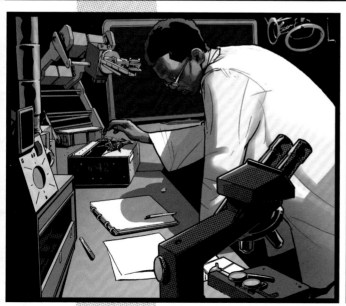

You created Spider-Man.

And I hope you understand that if this information leaves this building I will *kill* you.

Excuse me?

But if you solve this problem for me I will reward you to the point where I reinvent your life on every conceivable level.

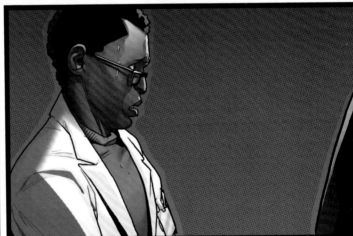

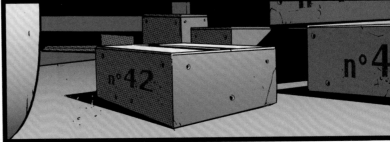

74° • LOG IN • REGISTER • ARCHI

DAILY BUGLE

| LOCAL | INTERNATIONAL | ARTS & ENTERTAINMENT | OPINION | SPORT

NORMAN OSBORN IS
THE GREEN GOBLIN!

CONTROVERSIAL INDUSTRIALIST IS REVEALED TO BE GENETICALLY ALTERE MONSTER NOW IN TH CUSTODY OF S.H.I.E.L.

Reporting by Frederick Fosswell

Agents of the world peacekeeping task force S.H.I.E.L.D. have confirmed to the Daily Bugl that controversial industrialist Norman Osborn had infected his own bc with one of his experiments altering himself into what one of our S.H.I.E.L.D. sources are referring to as the Green Goblin.

Sources also confirm tha this Green Goblin is the same one that attacked Midtown High School a few month ago, shutting the school down for weeks. It is also referred to as the public debut of the mystery man called Spider-Man. Whether or not there is a connection between Spider-Man and Norman Osborn's double life has yet to be revealed.

Speculation continues as to why Norman Osborn would break one of the cardinal rules of science by experimenting on himself. Sources close to Norman say that certain pressures to create a workable version of his experimental "super-soldier" formula led him to use the formula on himself.

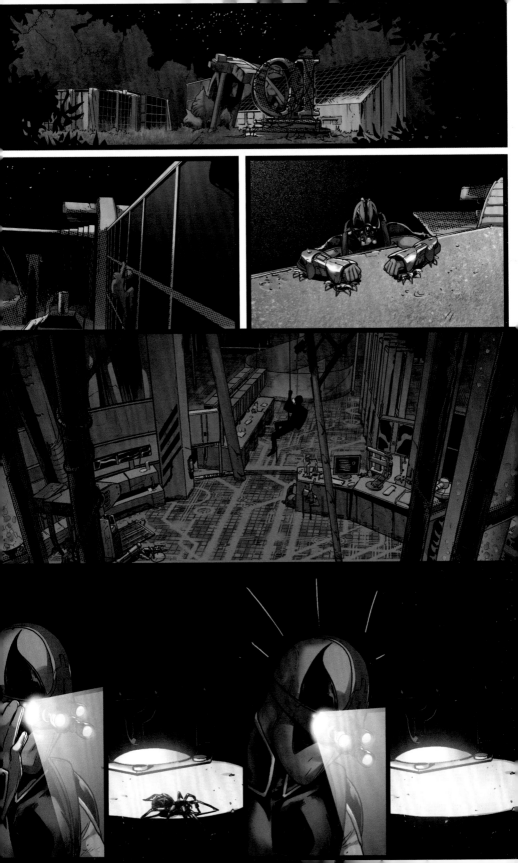

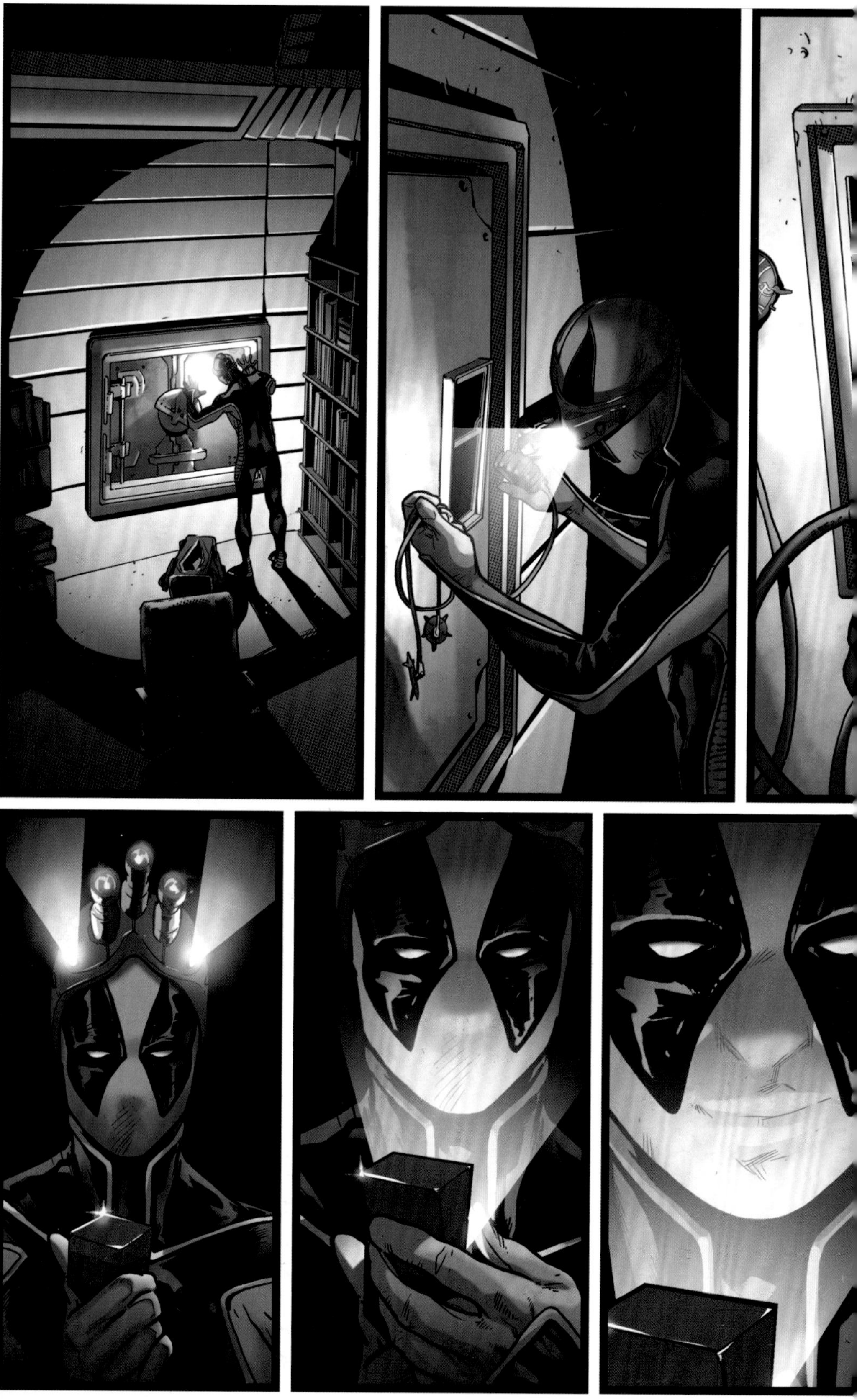

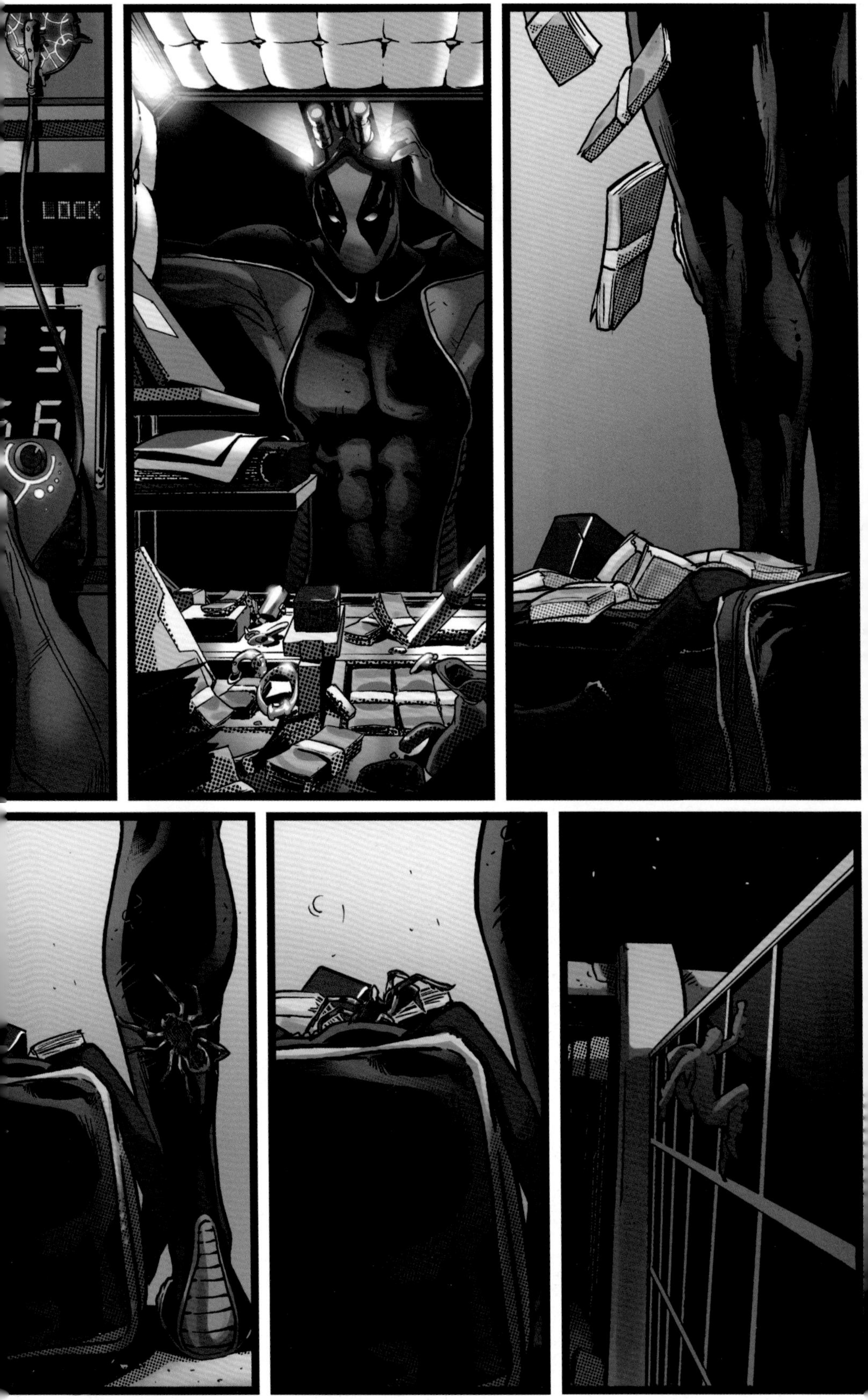
LOCK

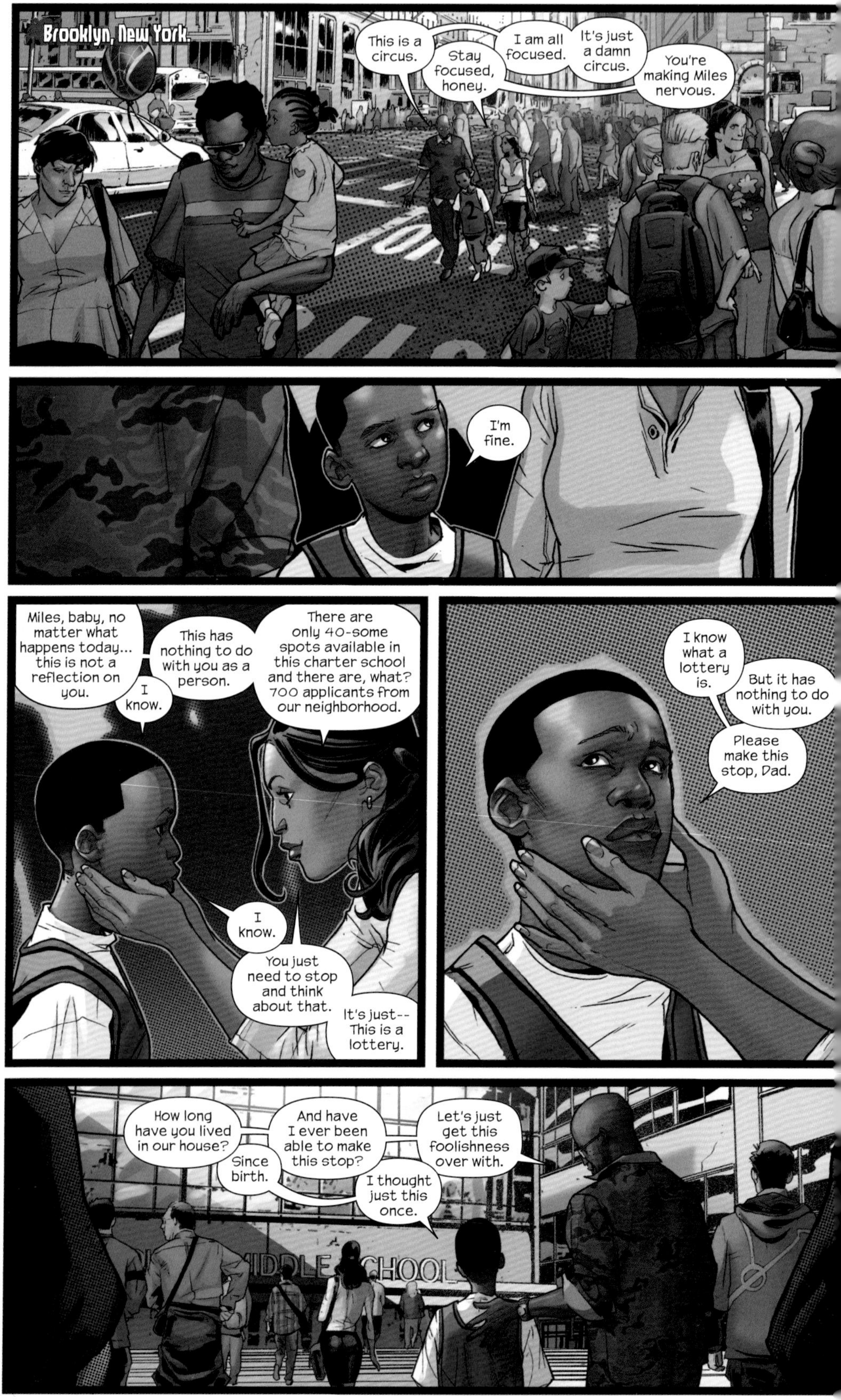
Brooklyn, New York.
This is a circus.
Stay focused, honey.
I am all focused.
It's just a damn circus.
You're making Miles nervous.
I'm fine.
Miles, baby, no matter what happens today... this is not a reflection on you.
This has nothing to do with you as a person.
I know.
There are only 40-some spots available in this charter school and there are, what? 700 applicants from our neighborhood.
I know.
You just need to stop and think about that.
It's just-- This is a lottery.
I know what a lottery is.
But it has nothing to do with you.
Please make this stop, Dad.
How long have you lived in our house?
Since birth.
And have I ever been able to make this stop?
I thought just this once.
Let's just get this foolishness over with.
MIDDLE SCHOOL

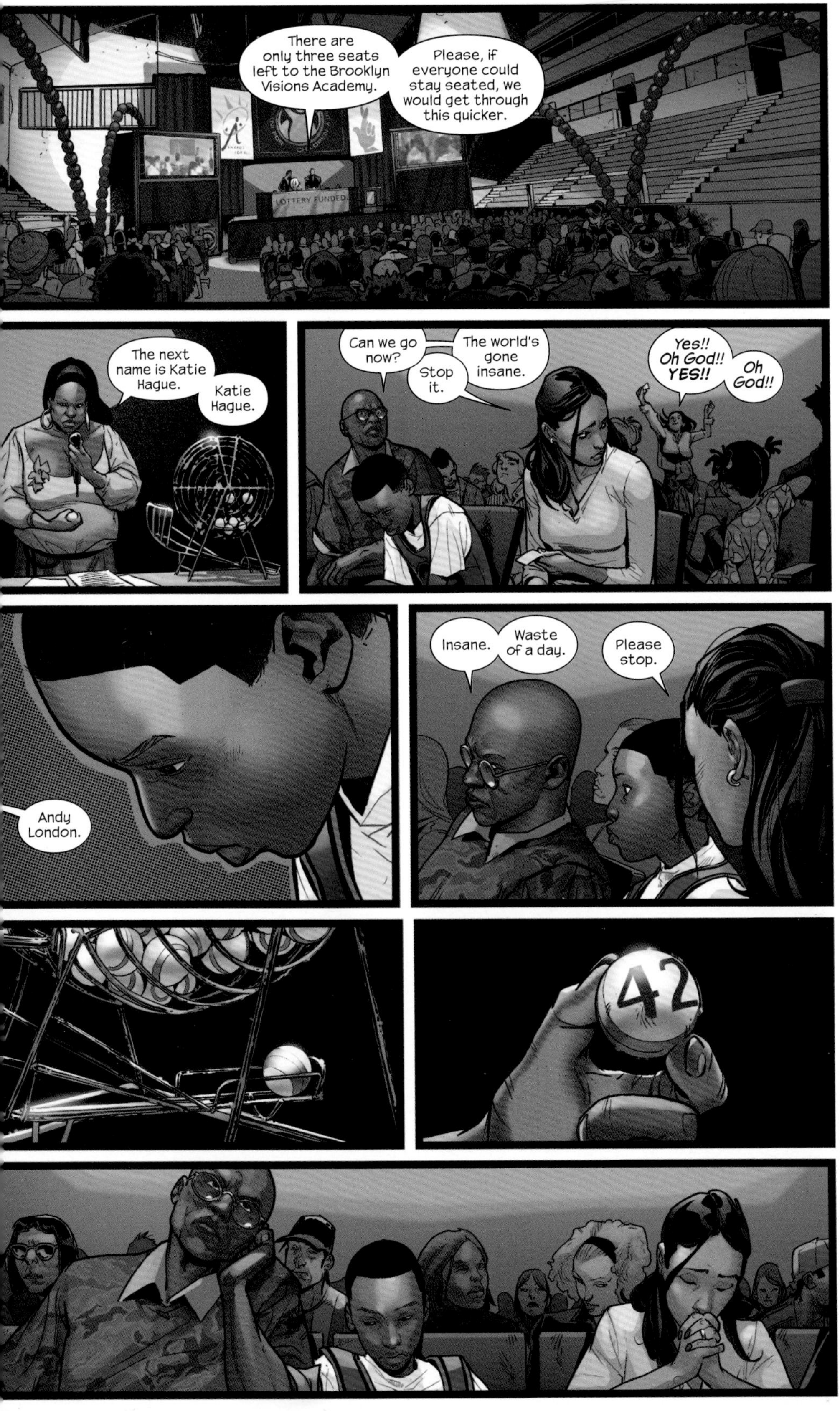
There are only three seats left to the Brooklyn Visions Academy.
Please, if everyone could stay seated, we would get through this quicker.
LOTTERY FUNDED
The next name is Katie Hague.
Katie Hague.
Can we go now?
The world's gone insane.
Stop it.
Yes!! Oh God!! YES!!
Oh God!!
Andy London.
Insane.
Waste of a day.
Please stop.
42

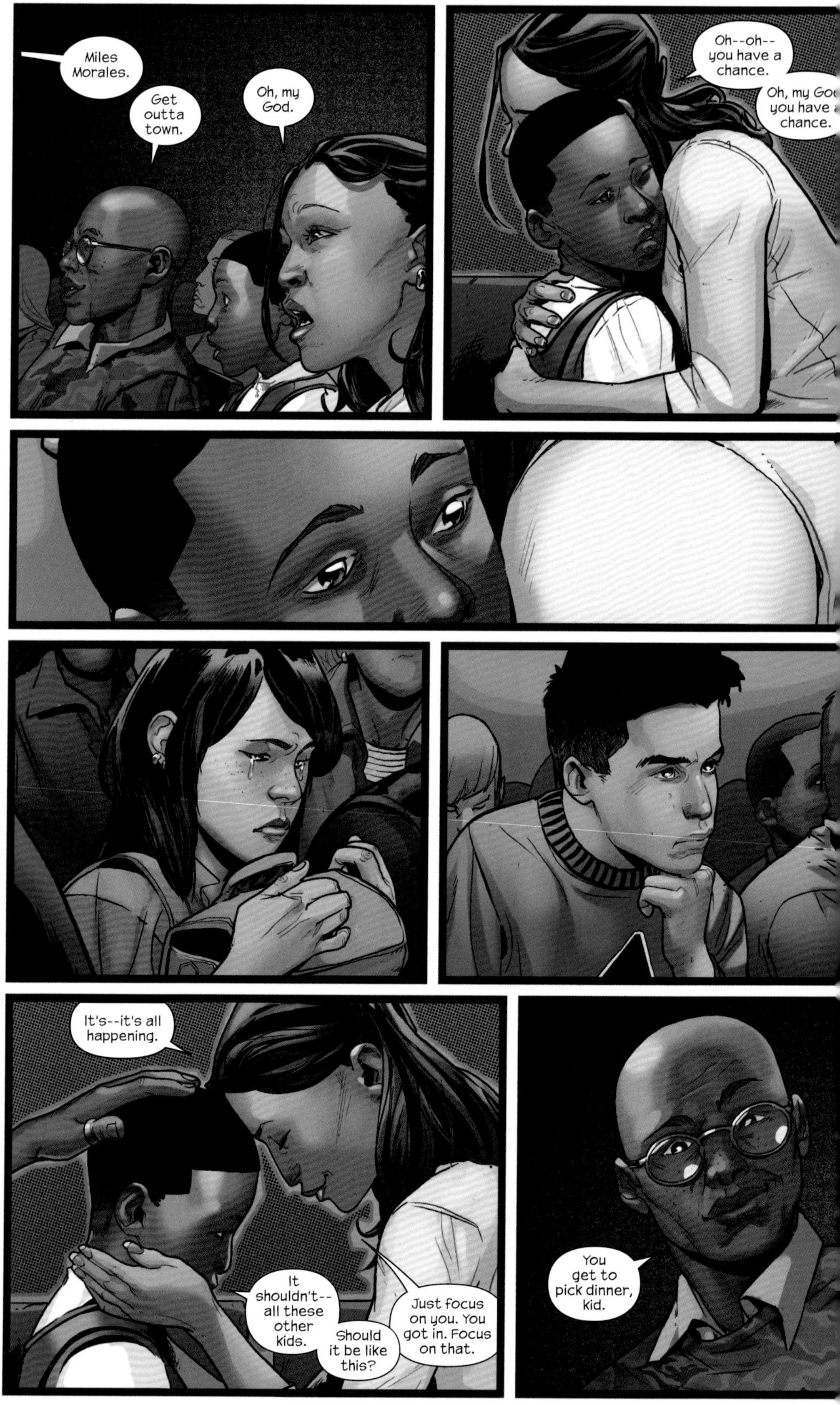

Miles Morales.
Get outta town.
Oh, my God.
Oh--oh--you have a chance.
Oh, my God, you have a chance.
It's--it's all happening.
It shouldn't--all these other kids.
Should it be like this?
Just focus on you. You got in. Focus on that.
You get to pick dinner, kid.

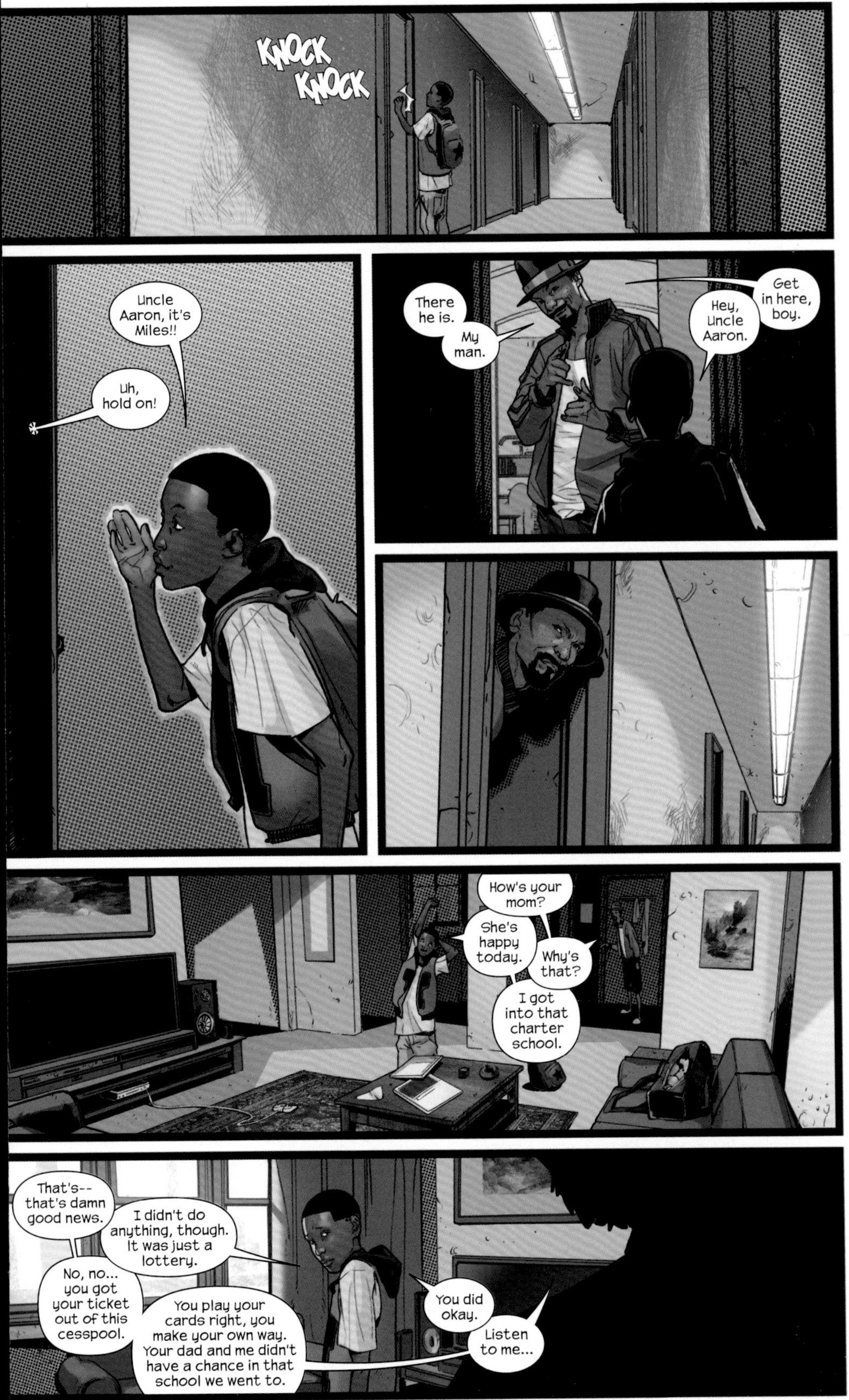
KNOCK KNOCK
Uncle Aaron, it's Miles!!
Uh, hold on!
There he is.
My man.
Hey, Uncle Aaron.
Get in here, boy.
How's your mom?
She's happy today.
Why's that?
I got into that charter school.
That's-- that's damn good news.
I didn't do anything, though. It was just a lottery.
No, no... you got your ticket out of this cesspool.
You play your cards right, you make your own way. Your dad and me didn't have a chance in that school we went to.
You did okay.
Listen to me...

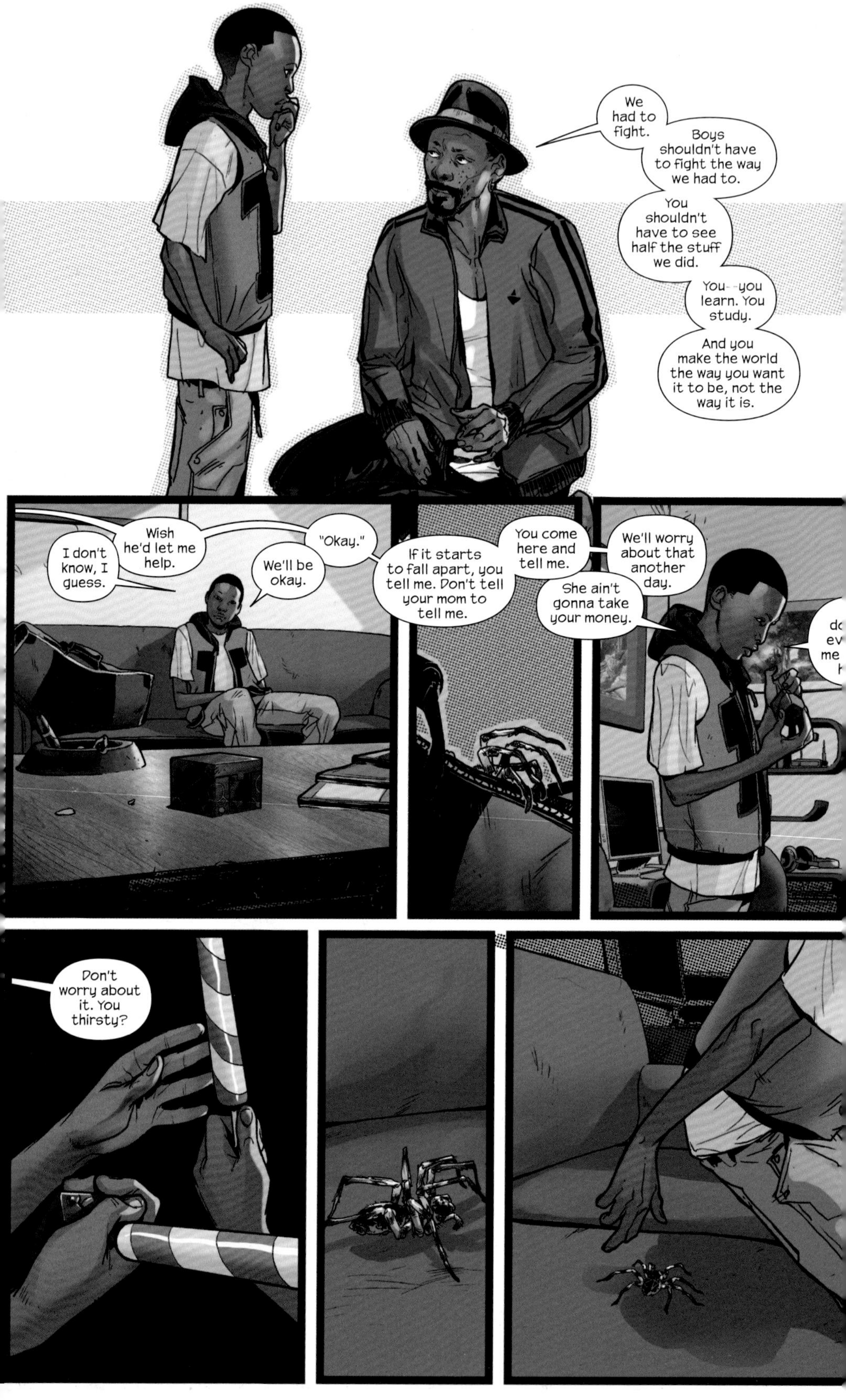

We had to fight.
Boys shouldn't have to fight the way we had to.
You shouldn't have to see half the stuff we did.
You--you learn. You study.
And you make the world the way you want it to be, not the way it is.
I don't know, I guess.
Wish he'd let me help.
"Okay."
We'll be okay.
If it starts to fall apart, you tell me. Don't tell your mom to tell me.
You come here and tell me.
We'll worry about that another day.
She ain't gonna take your money.
Don't worry about it. You thirsty?

You make it.

Don't let people make it for you.

This is a good thing. This-- this calls for popsicles.

Right?

Yeah.

Your daddy gonna be able to pay for it?

What's this?

Oh hey no. That is something else--that is something for work.

What is it?

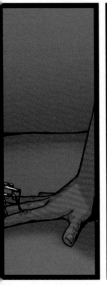

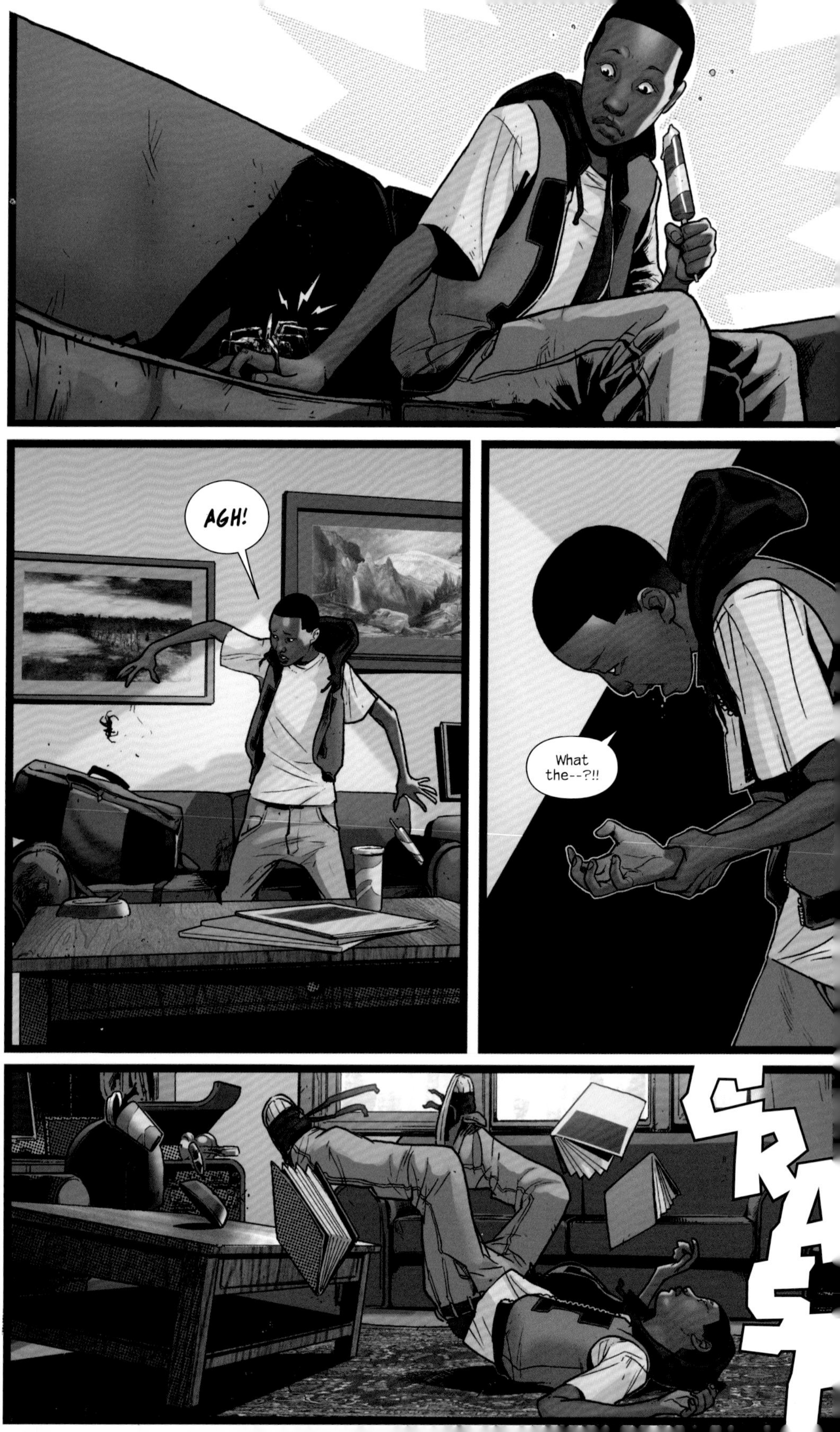

AGH!
What the--?!!
CRASH

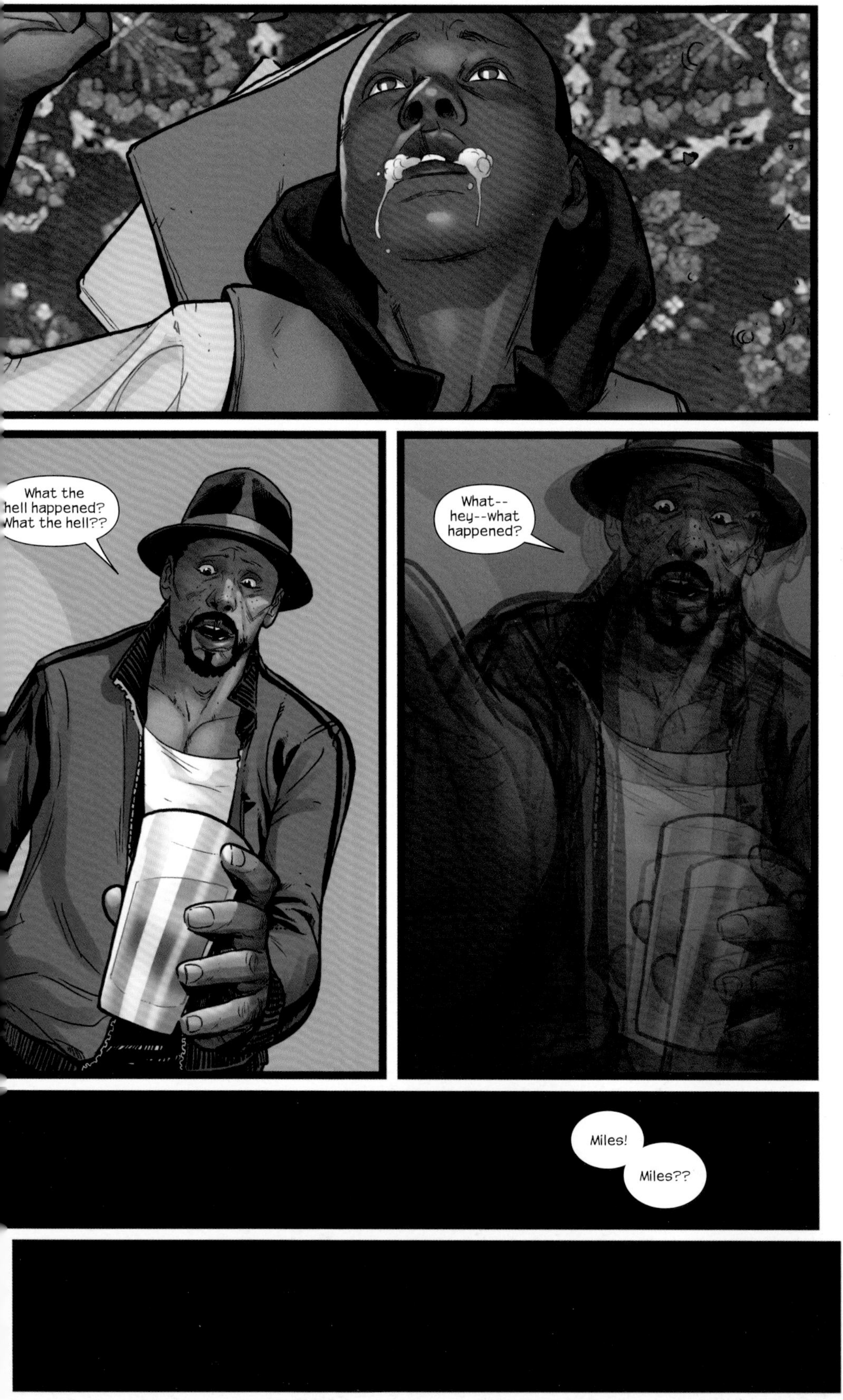
What the hell happened? What the hell??
What-- hey--what happened?
Miles!
Miles??

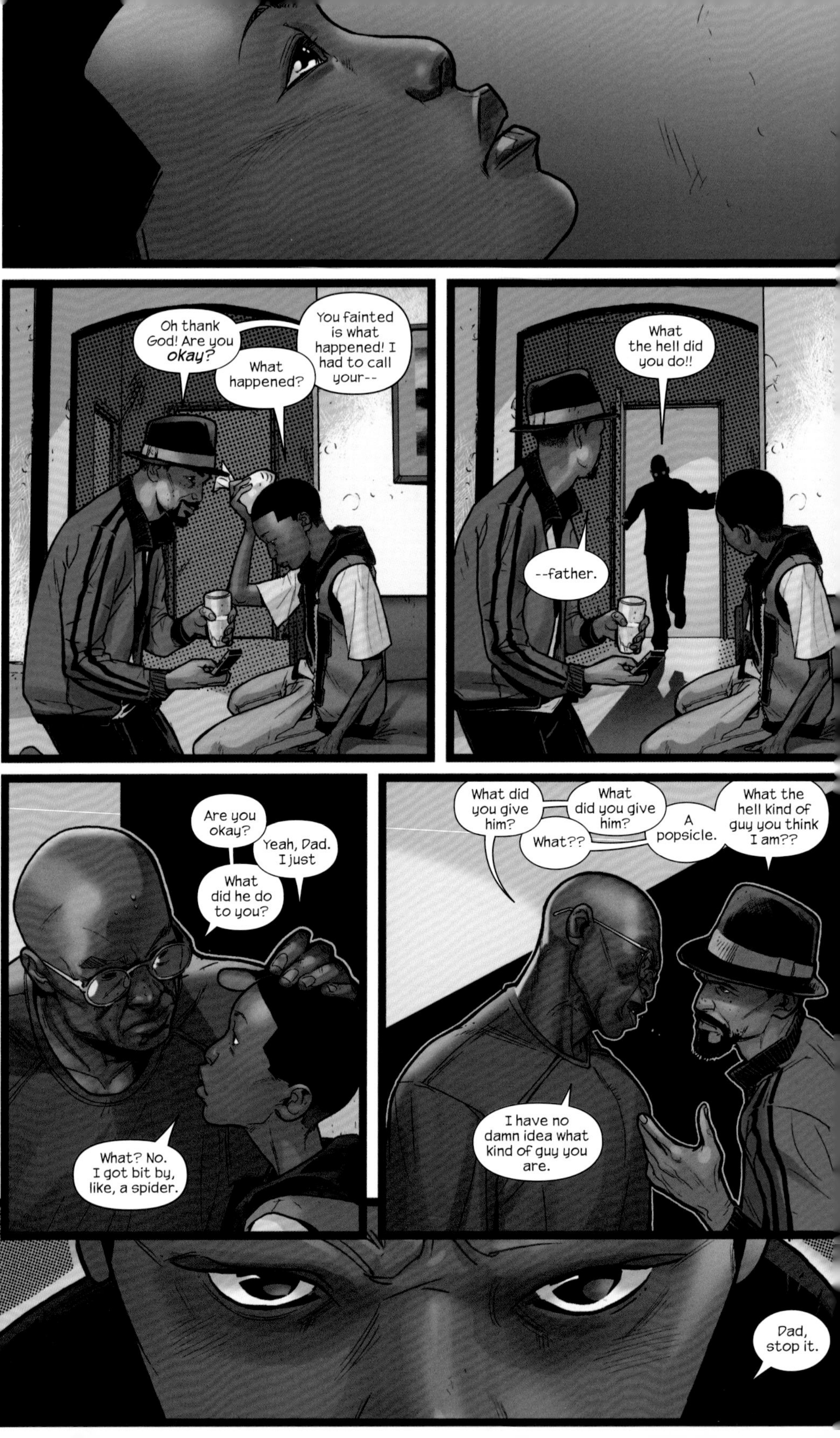
Oh thank God! Are you okay?
What happened?
You fainted is what happened! I had to call your--
--father.
What the hell did you do!!
Are you okay?
What did he do to you?
Yeah, Dad. I just
What? No. I got bit by, like, a spider.
What did you give him?
What??
What did you give him?
A popsicle.
What the hell kind of guy you think I am??
I have no damn idea what kind of guy you are.
Dad, stop it.

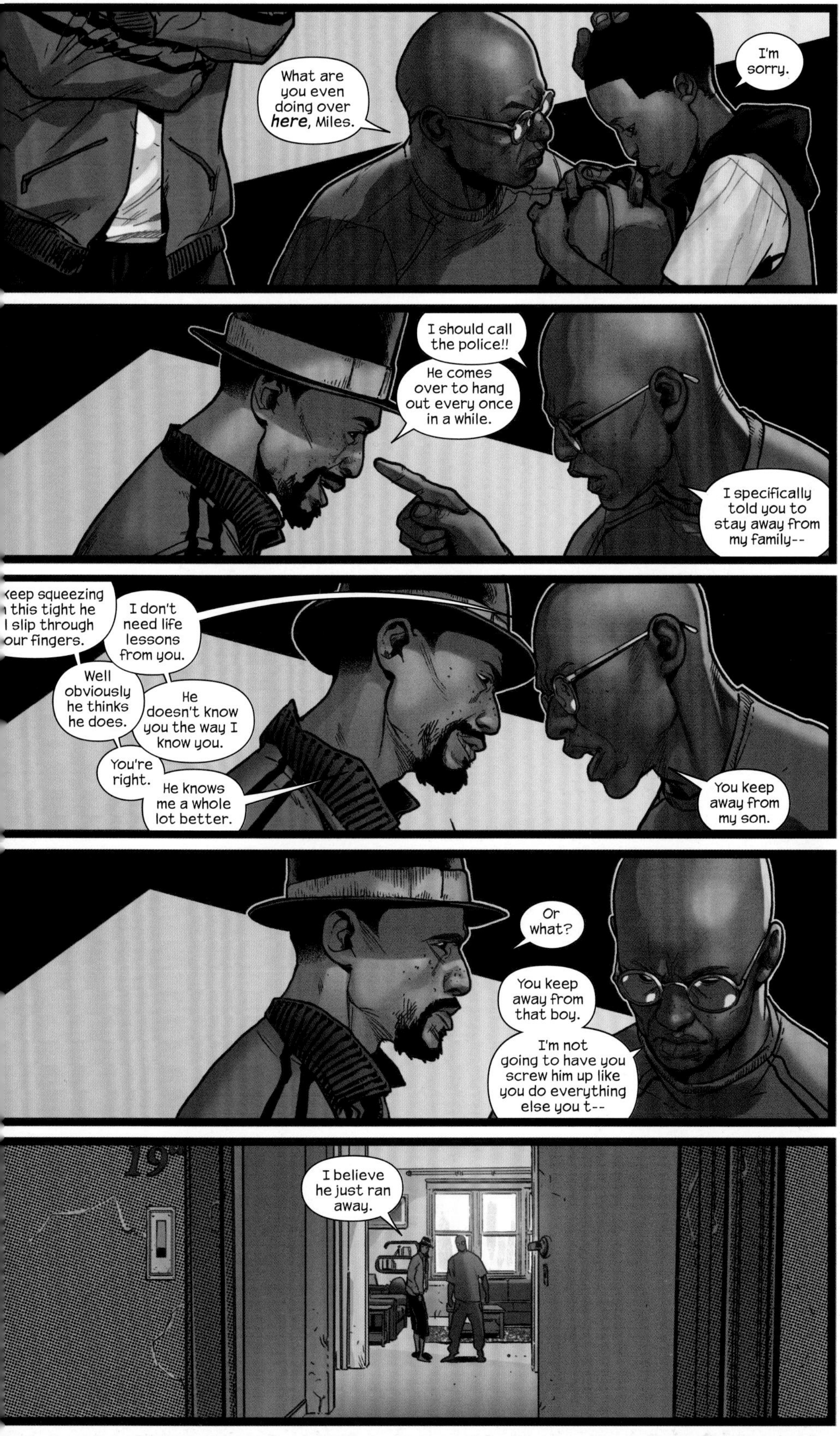
What are you even doing over *here*, Miles.
I'm sorry.
I should call the police!!
He comes over to hang out every once in a while.
I specifically told you to stay away from my family--
eep squeezing this tight he slip through our fingers.
I don't need life lessons from you.
Well obviously he thinks he does.
He doesn't know you the way I know you.
You're right.
He knows me a whole lot better.
You keep away from my son.
Or what?
You keep away from that boy.
I'm not going to have you screw him up like you do everything else you t--
I believe he just ran away.

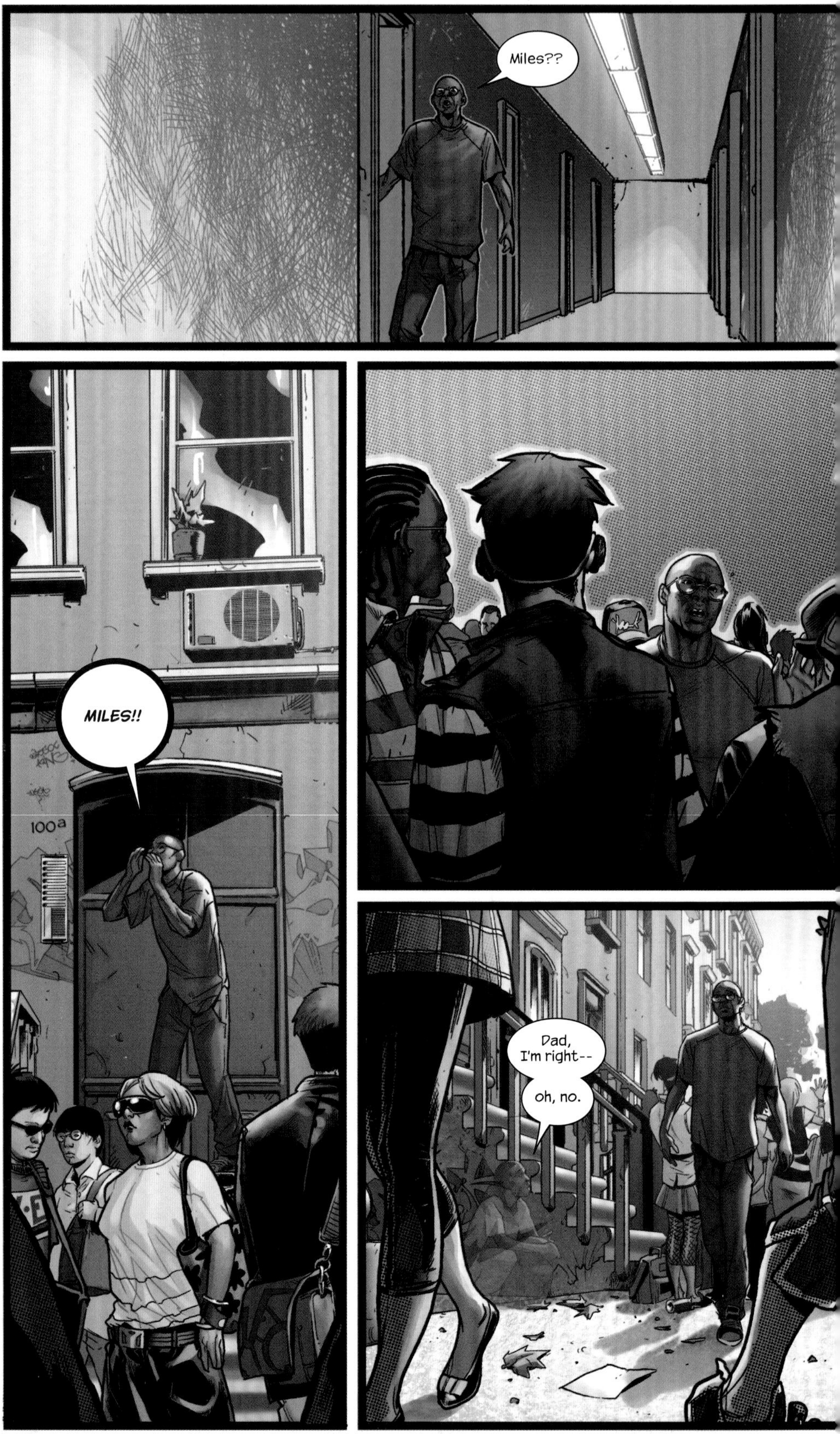
Miles??
MILES!!
Dad, I'm right--
oh, no.

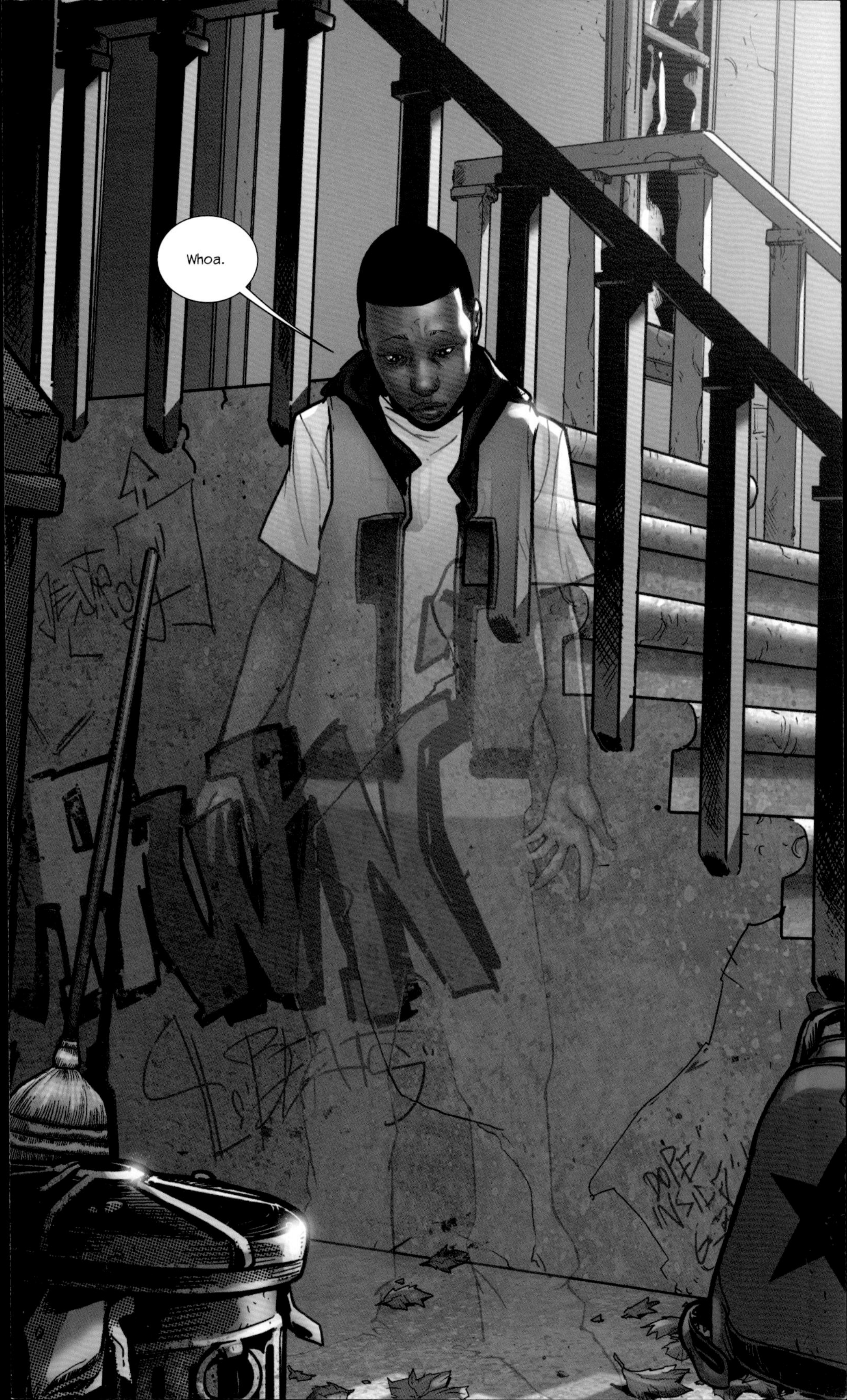
Whoa.

ULTIMATE COMICS SPIDER-MAN (2011) #2

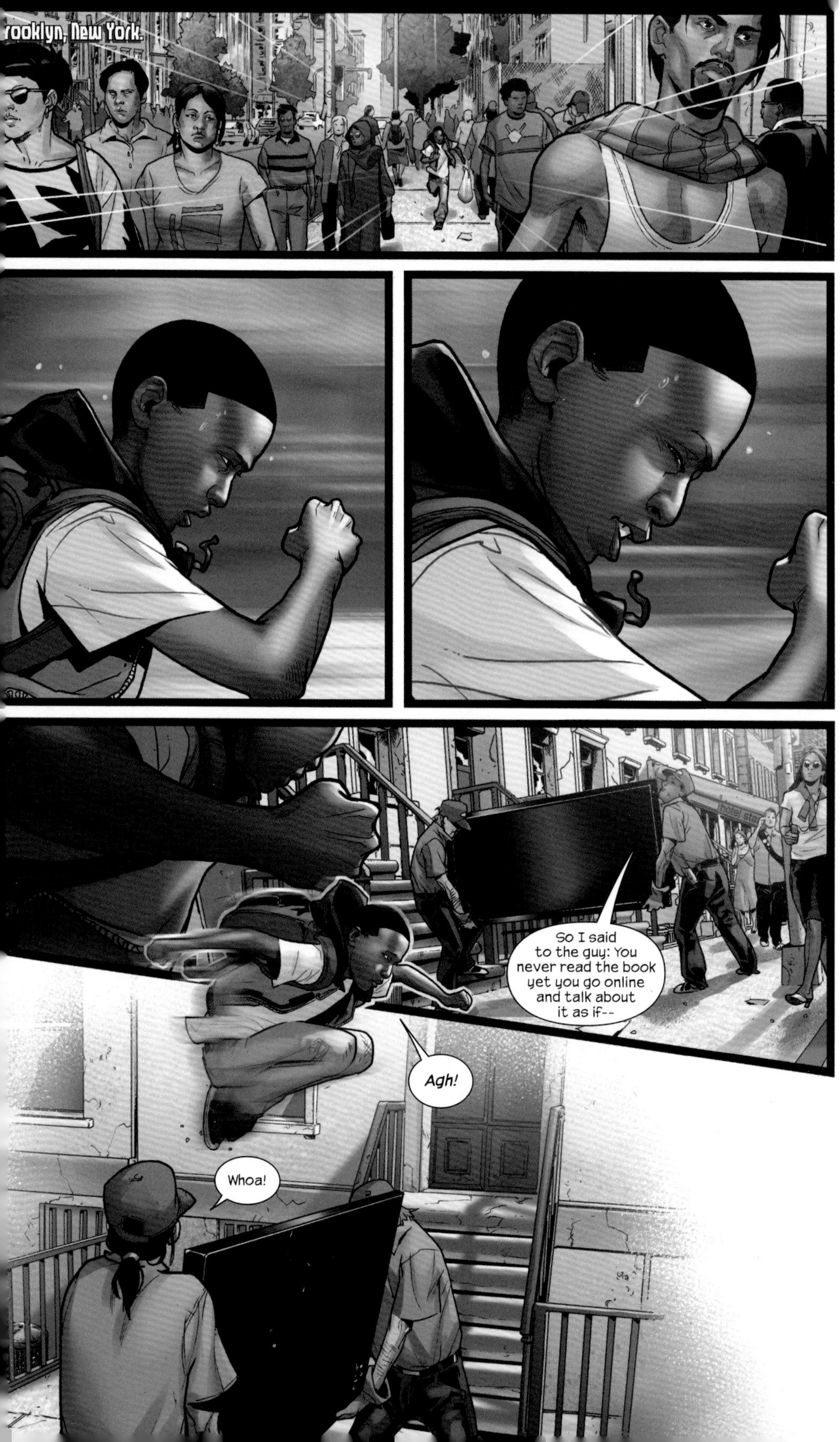
rooklyn, New York.
So I said to the guy: You never read the book yet you go online and talk about it as if--
Agh!
Whoa!

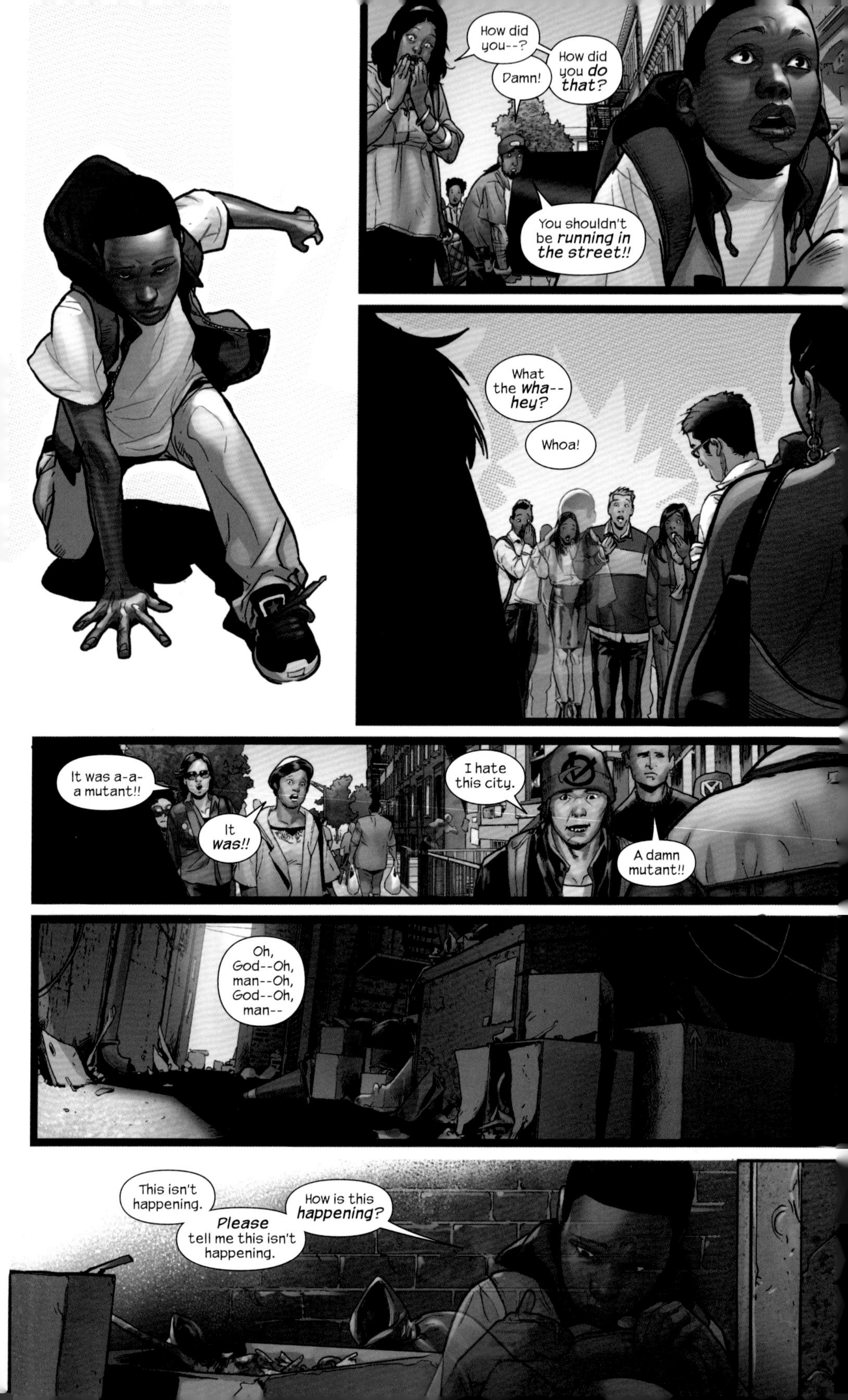
How did you--?
How did you do that?
Damn!
You shouldn't be running in the street!!
What the wha-- hey?
Whoa!
It was a-a-a mutant!!
It was!!
I hate this city.
A damn mutant!!
Oh, God--Oh, man--Oh, God--Oh, man--
This isn't happening.
Please tell me this isn't happening.
How is this happening?

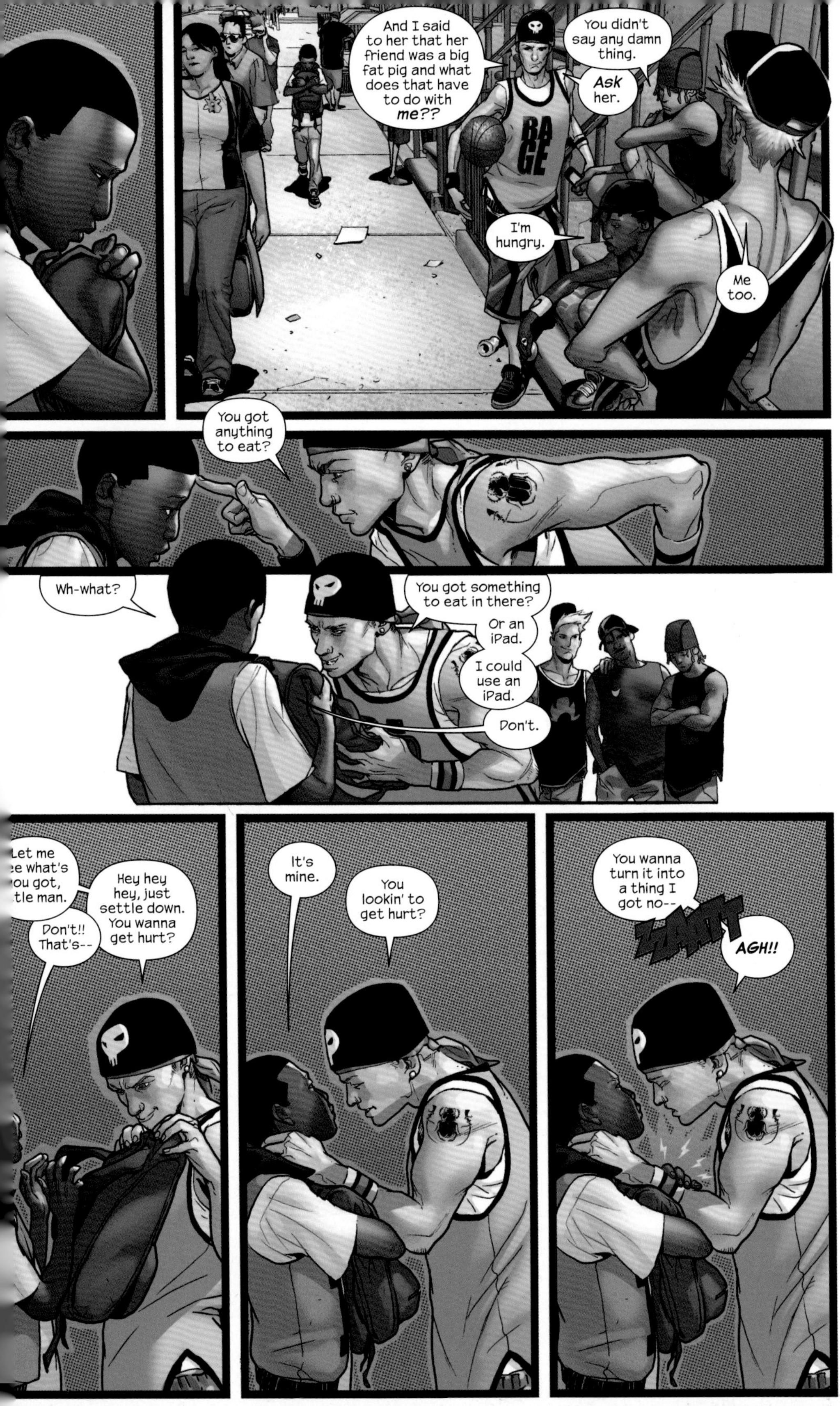
And I said to her that her friend was a big fat pig and what does that have to do with *me*??
You didn't say any damn thing.
Ask her.
I'm hungry.
Me too.
You got anything to eat?
Wh-what?
You got something to eat in there?
Or an iPad.
I could use an iPad.
Don't.
Let me ee what's ou got, tle man.
Hey hey hey, just settle down. You wanna get hurt?
Don't!! That's--
It's mine.
You lookin' to get hurt?
You wanna turn it into a thing I got no--
ZZAATT
AGH!!

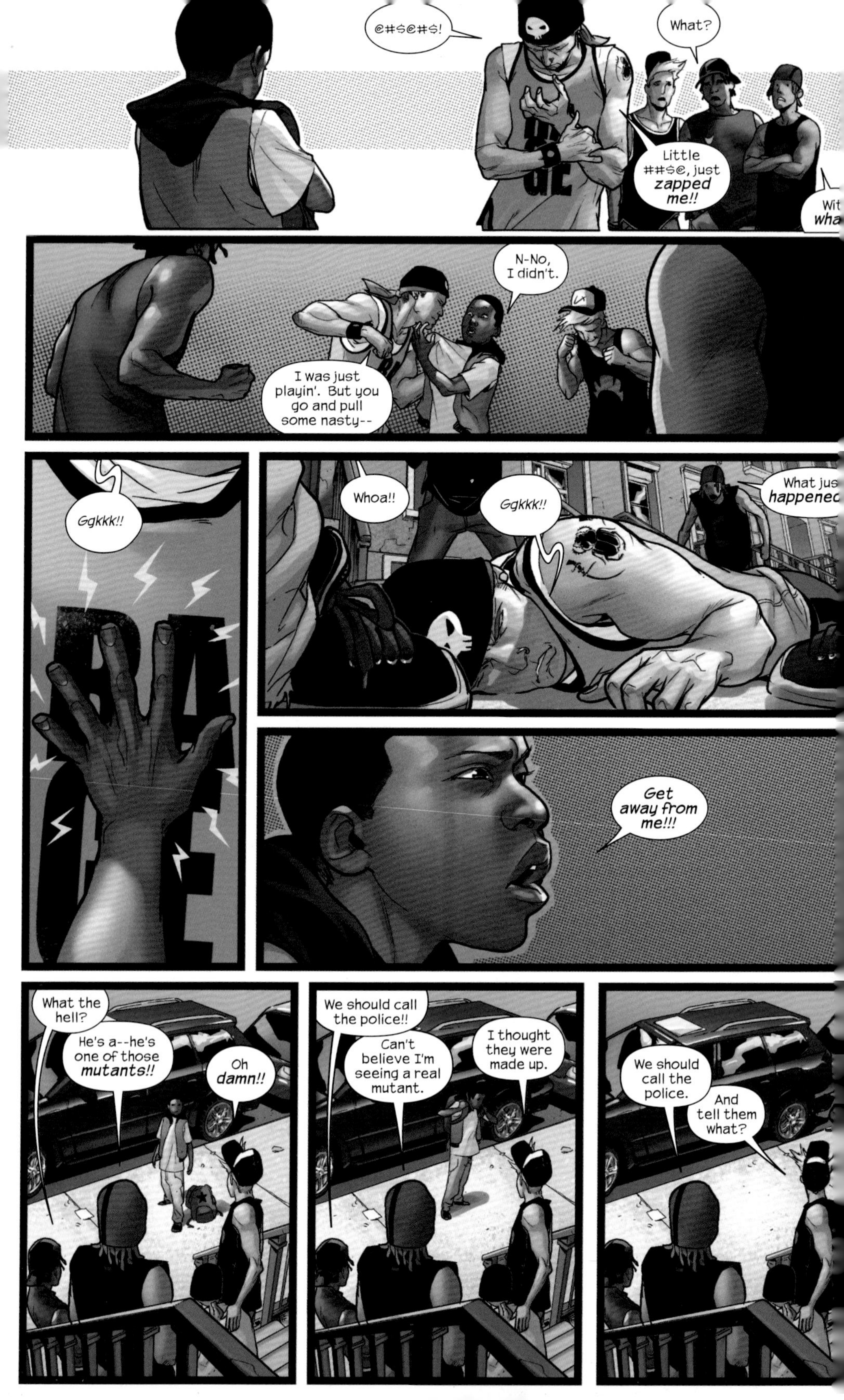

@#$@#$!
What?
Little ##$@, just *zapped* *me!!*
Wit *wha*
N-No, I didn't.
I was just playin'. But you go and pull some nasty--
Ggkkk!!
Whoa!!
Ggkkk!!
What jus *happened*
Get away from me!!!
What the hell?
He's a--he's one of those *mutants!!*
Oh *damn!!*
We should call the police!!
Can't believe I'm seeing a real mutant.
I thought they were made up.
We should call the police.
And tell them what?

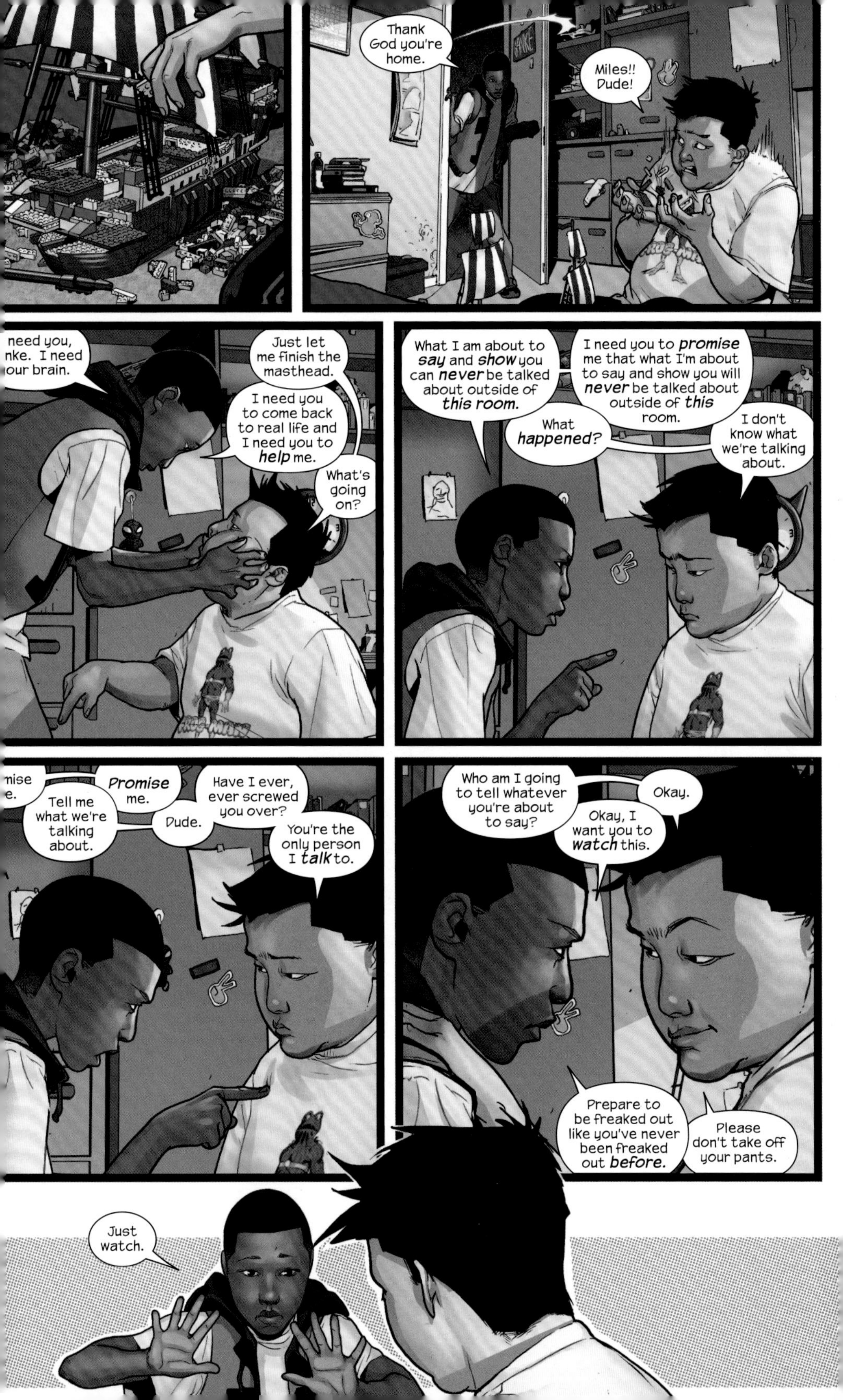

Thank God you're home.
Miles!! Dude!
need you, nke. I need our brain.
Just let me finish the masthead.
I need you to come back to real life and I need you to *help* me.
What's going on?
What I am about to *say* and *show* you can *never* be talked about outside of *this room.*
I need you to *promise* me that what I'm about to say and show you will *never* be talked about outside of *this* room.
What *happened?*
I don't know what we're talking about.
nise e.
Promise me.
Tell me what we're talking about.
Dude.
Have I ever, ever screwed you over?
You're the only person I *talk* to.
Who am I going to tell whatever you're about to say?
Okay.
Okay, I want you to *watch* this.
Prepare to be freaked out like you've never been freaked out *before.*
Please don't take off your pants.
Just watch.

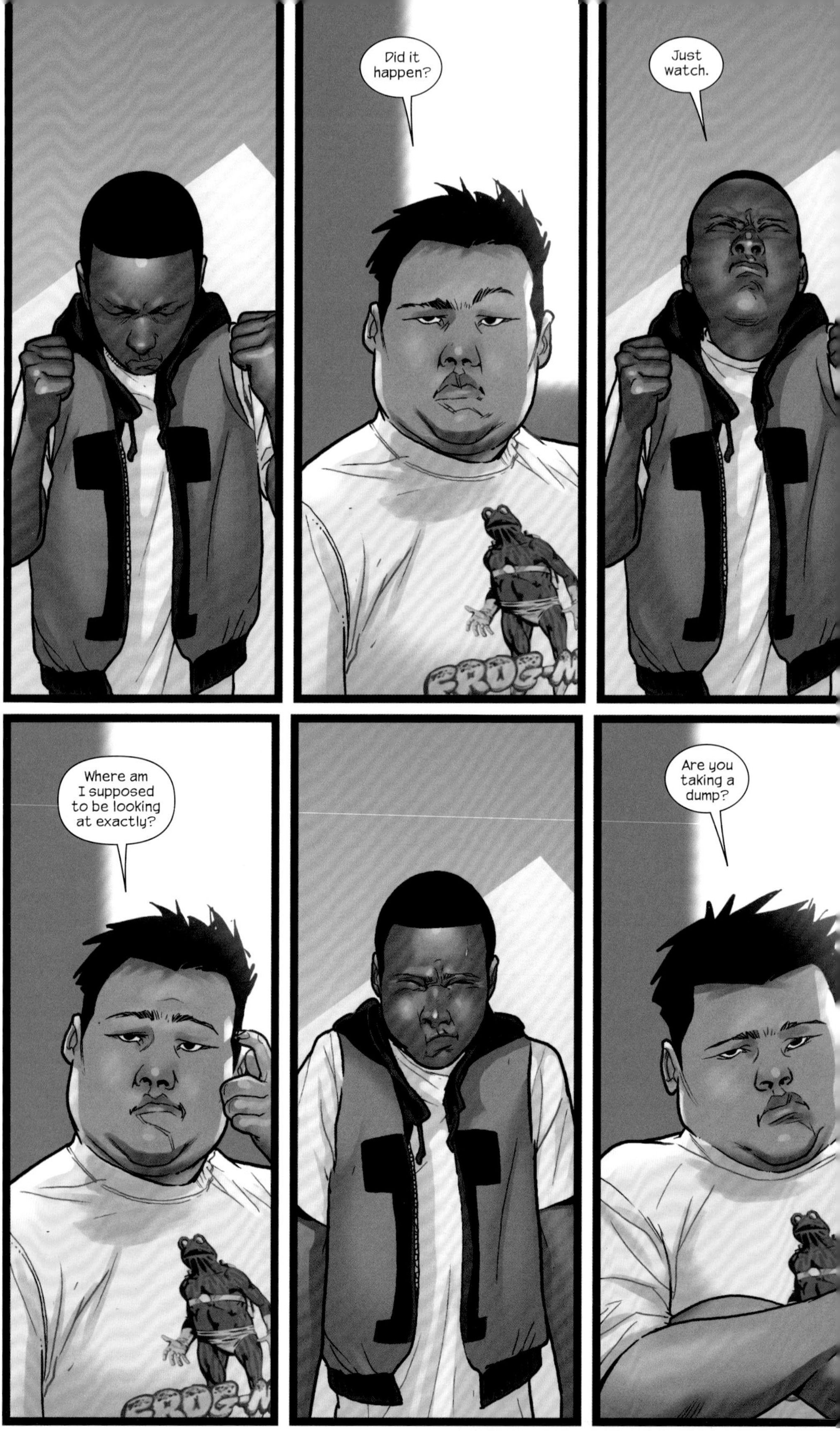
Did it happen?
Just watch.
Where am I supposed to be looking at exactly?
Are you taking a dump?

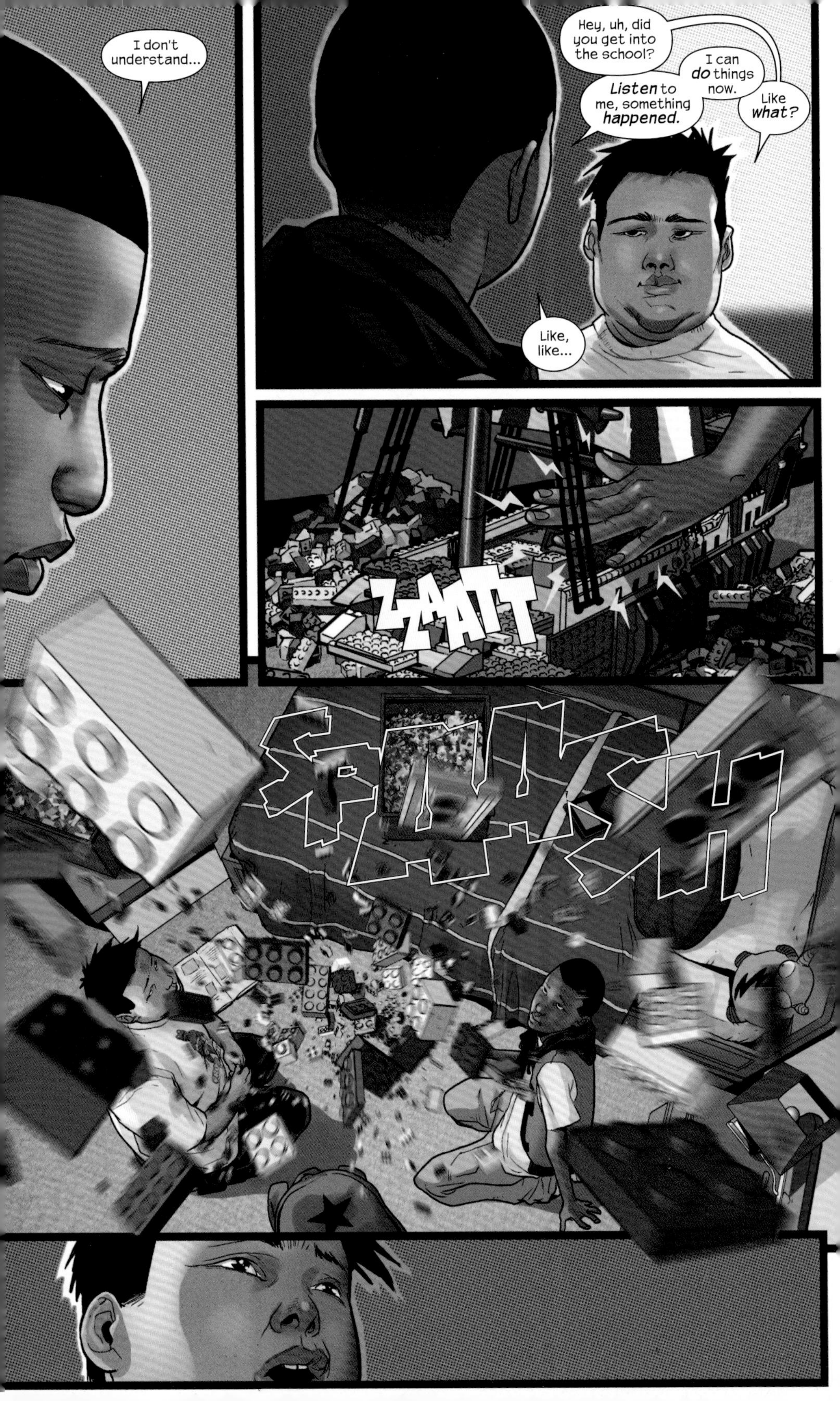
I don't understand...
Hey, uh, did you get into the school?
Listen to me, something happened.
I can do things now.
Like what?
Like, like...
ZZAATT
SPLAKSH

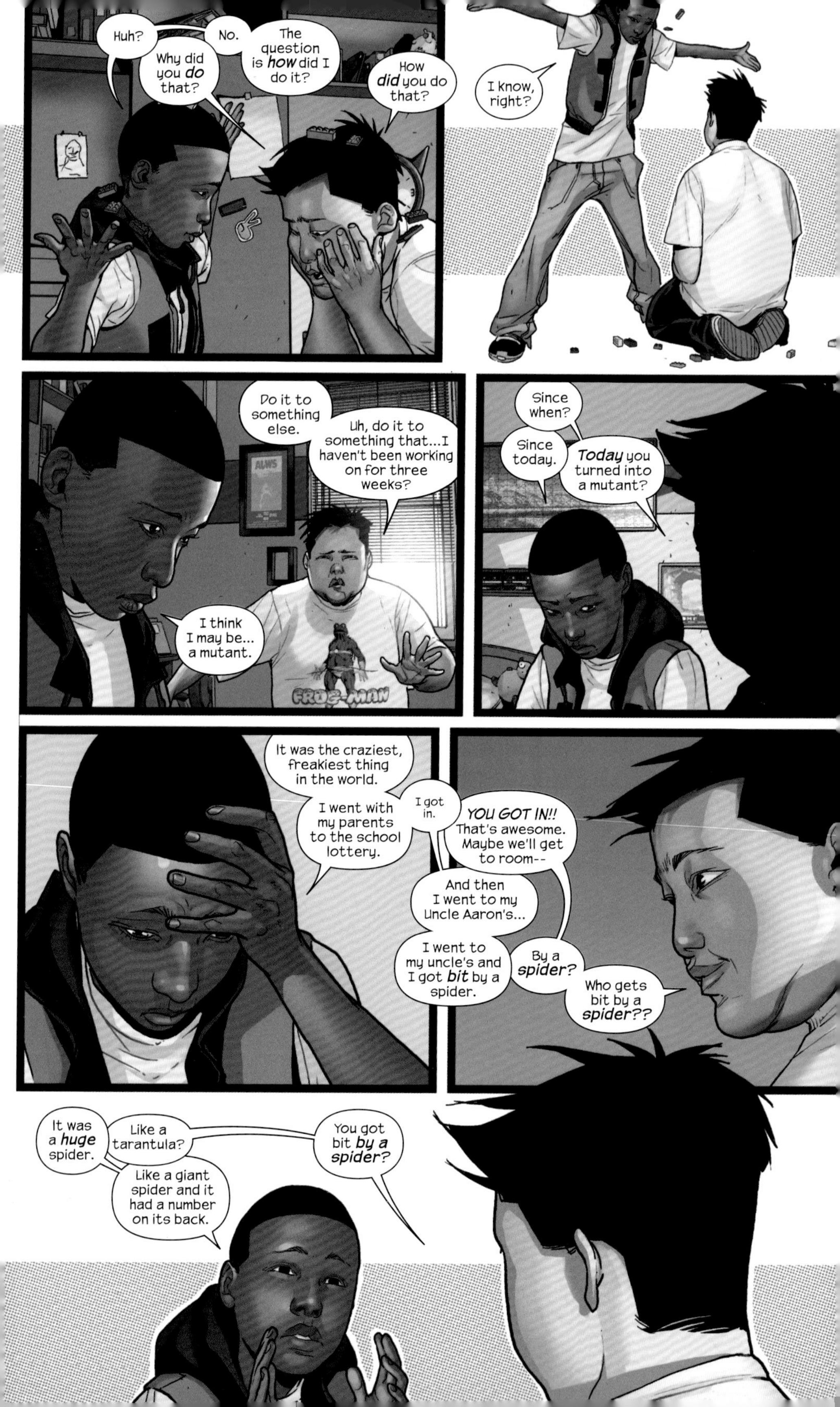
Huh?
Why did you *do* that?
No.
The question is *how* did I do it?
How *did* you do that?
I know, right?
Do it to something else.
Uh, do it to something that... I haven't been working on for three weeks?
I think I may be... a mutant.
Since when?
Since today.
Today you turned into a mutant?
It was the craziest, freakiest thing in the world.
I went with my parents to the school lottery.
I got in.
YOU GOT IN!! That's awesome. Maybe we'll get to room--
And then I went to my Uncle Aaron's...
I went to my uncle's and I got *bit* by a spider.
By a *spider?*
Who gets bit by a *spider??*
You got bit *by a spider?*
It was a *huge* spider.
Like a tarantula?
Like a giant spider and it had a number on its back.
FROG-MAN

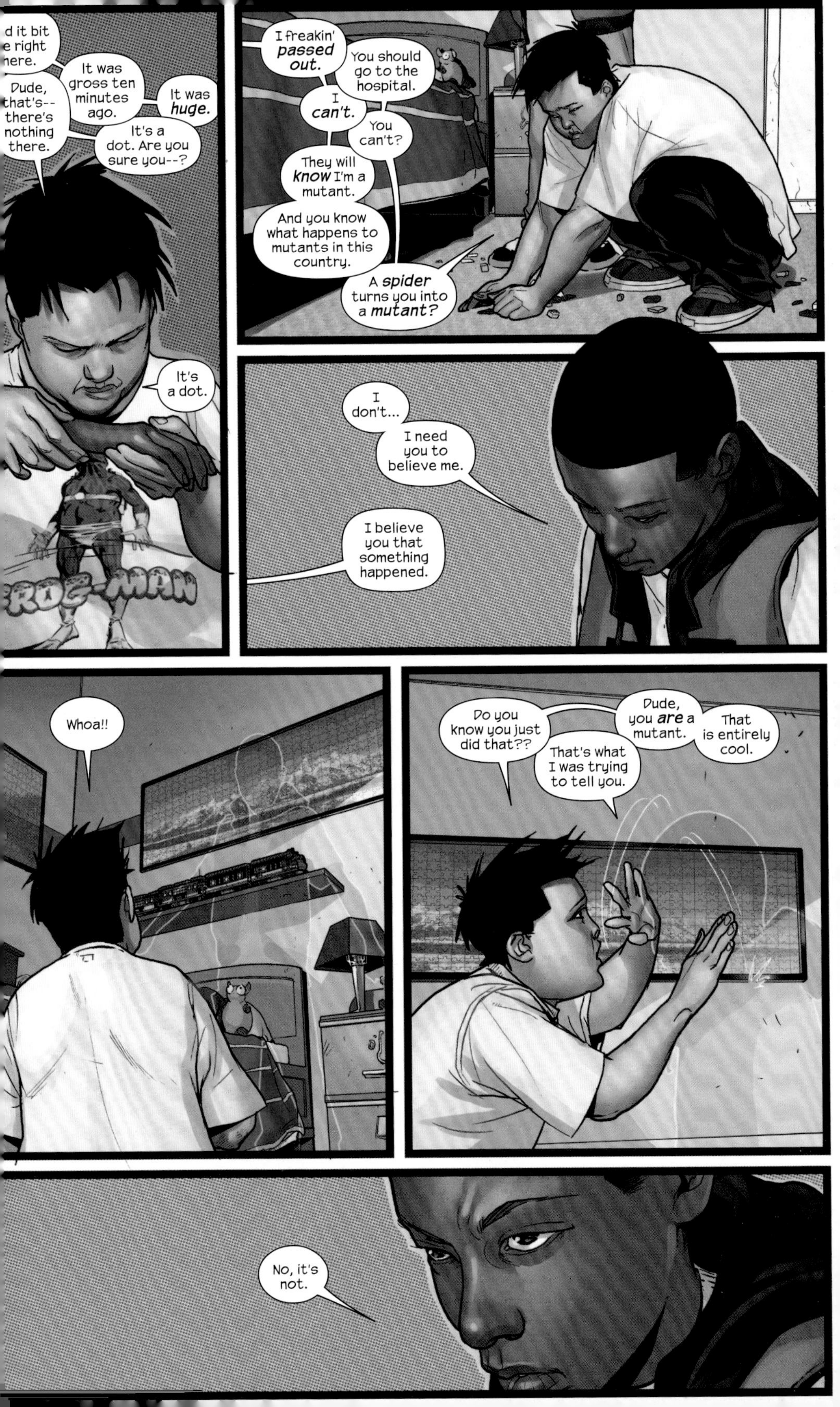
d it bit
e right
here.
It was gross ten minutes ago.
It was *huge.*
Dude, that's-- there's nothing there.
It's a dot. Are you sure you--?
It's a dot.
ROG-MAN
I freakin' ***passed out.***
You should go to the hospital.
I ***can't.***
You can't?
They will ***know*** I'm a mutant.
And you know what happens to mutants in this country.
A ***spider*** turns you into a ***mutant?***
I don't...
I need you to believe me.
I believe you that something happened.
Whoa!!
Do you know you just did that??
That's what I was trying to tell you.
Dude, you ***are*** a mutant.
That is entirely cool.
No, it's not.

It's not *cool* to give up any sense of a--A normal life.

You get to--

It's not *cool* to end up in a military *concentration camp* or something.

They don't put mutants in camps.

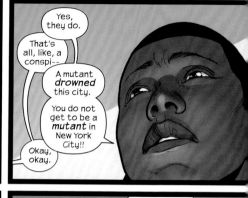

Yes, they do.

That's all, like, a conspi--

A mutant *drowned* this city.

You do not get to be a *mutant* in New York City!!

Okay, okay.

You can't tell anybody about this.

Hold on, roll back... a spider bit you? A spider with a *number*?

What number?

You can't tell anyone.

We have to figure out how your powers work.

I don't have *powers.*

Dude, *you* have powers.

And I don't care what you say: this is insanely cool.

I'm scared out of my mind.

Son. Let's go.

I didn't even know he was here in our house.

Let's *go!*

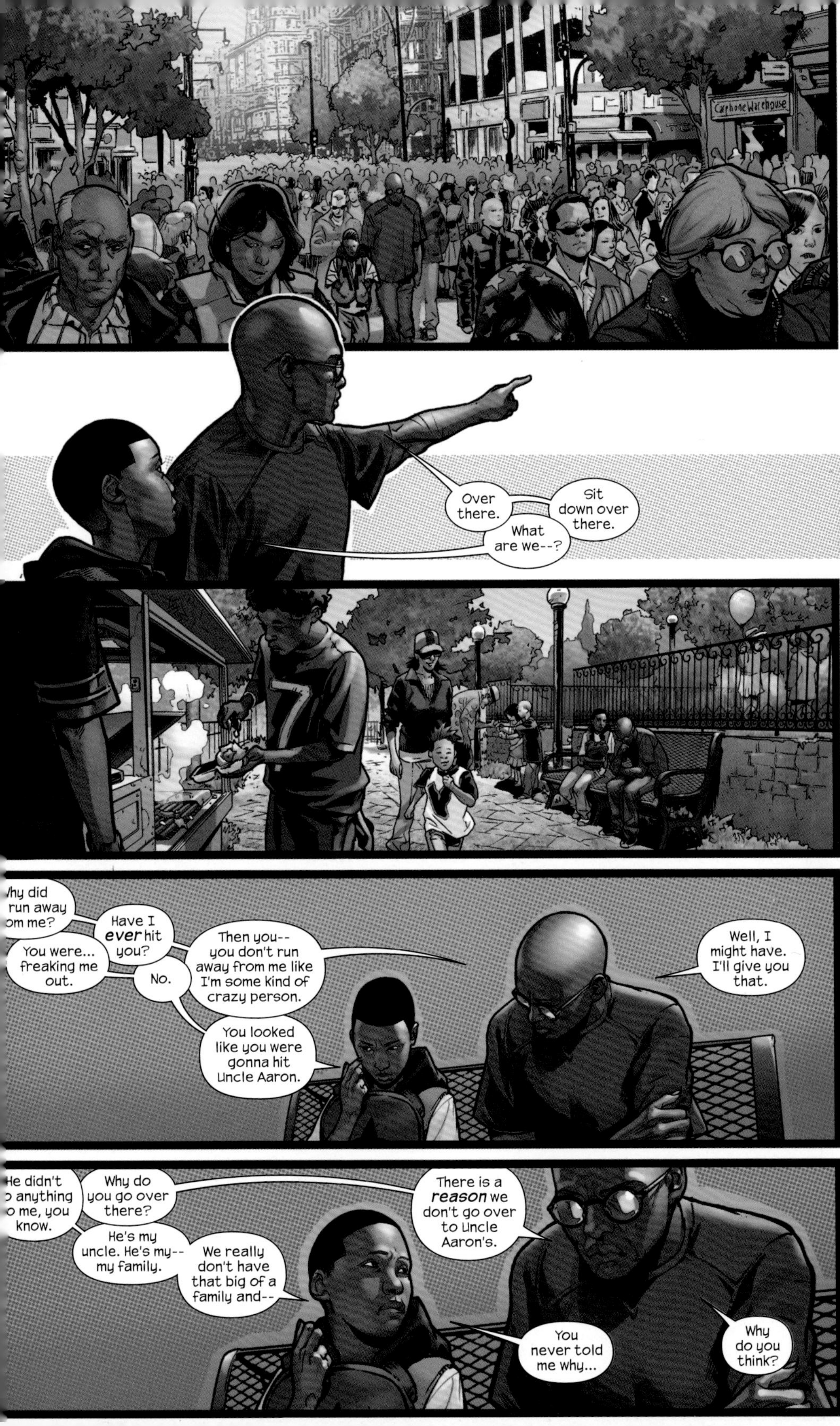

Carphone Warehouse
Over there.
What are we--?
Sit down over there.
hy did run away om me?
You were... freaking me out.
Have I *ever* hit you?
No.
Then you-- you don't run away from me like I'm some kind of crazy person.
You looked like you were gonna hit Uncle Aaron.
Well, I might have. I'll give you that.
He didn't o anything o me, you know.
Why do you go over there?
He's my uncle. He's my-- my family.
We really don't have that big of a family and--
There is a *reason* we don't go over to Uncle Aaron's.
You never told me why...
Why do you think?

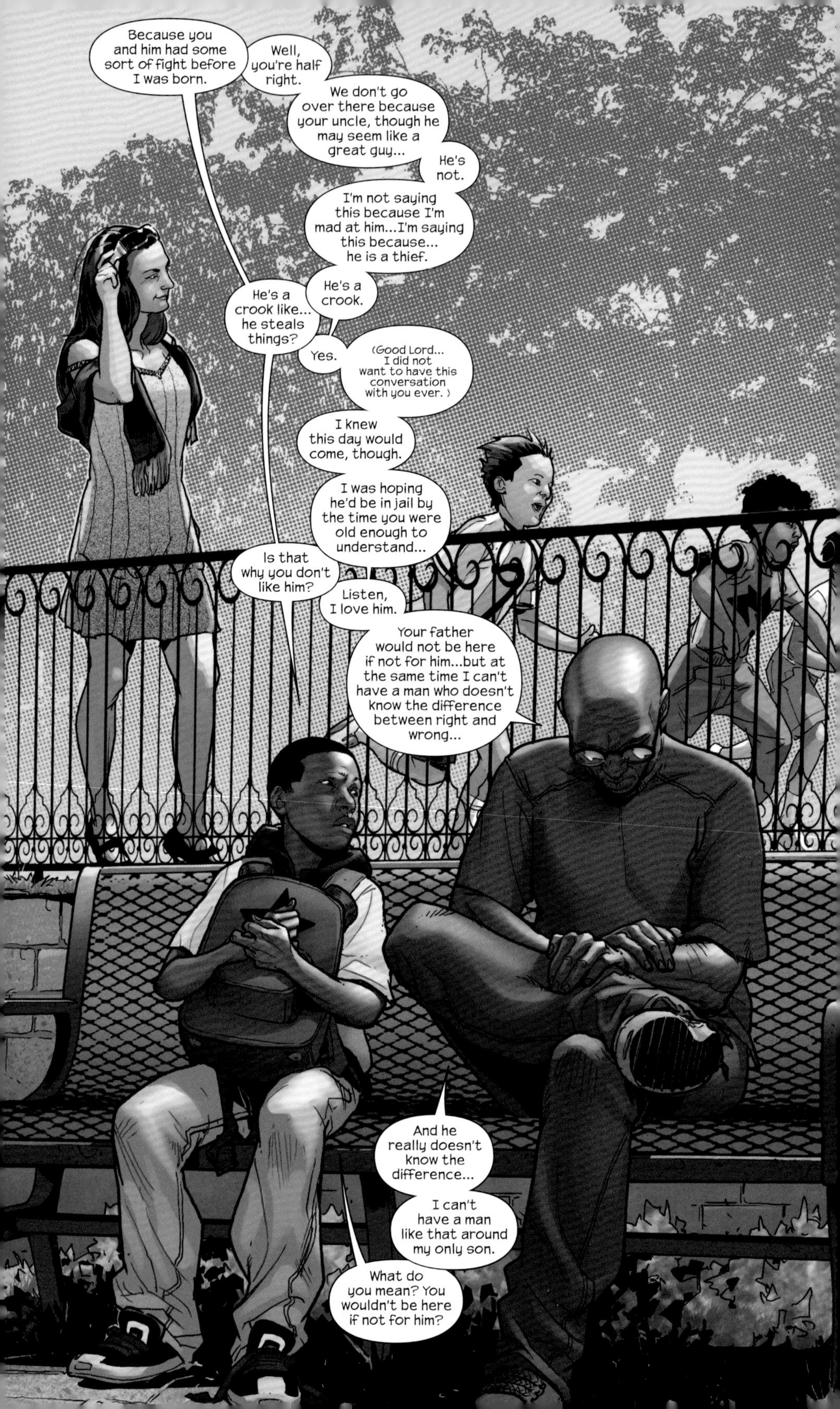
Because you and him had some sort of fight before I was born.
Well, you're half right.
We don't go over there because your uncle, though he may seem like a great guy...
He's not.
I'm not saying this because I'm mad at him...I'm saying this because... he is a thief.
He's a crook.
He's a crook like... he steals things?
Yes.
(Good Lord... I did not want to have this conversation with you ever.)
I knew this day would come, though.
I was hoping he'd be in jail by the time you were old enough to understand...
Is that why you don't like him?
Listen, I love him.
Your father would not be here if not for him...but at the same time I can't have a man who doesn't know the difference between right and wrong...
And he really doesn't know the difference...
I can't have a man like that around my only son.
What do you mean? You wouldn't be here if not for him?

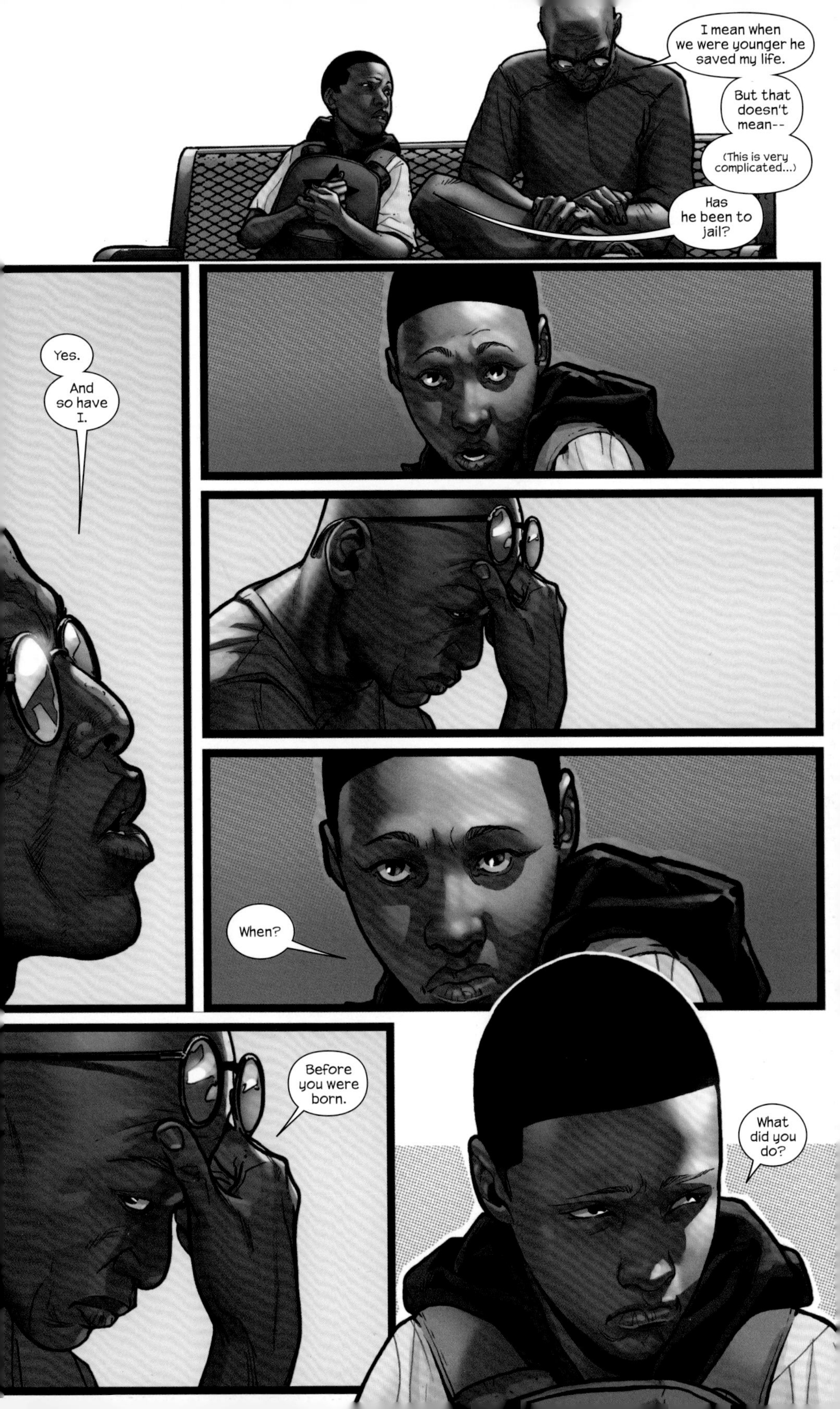
I mean when we were younger he saved my life.
But that doesn't mean--
(This is very complicated...)
Has he been to jail?
Yes.
And so have I.
When?
Before you were born.
What did you do?

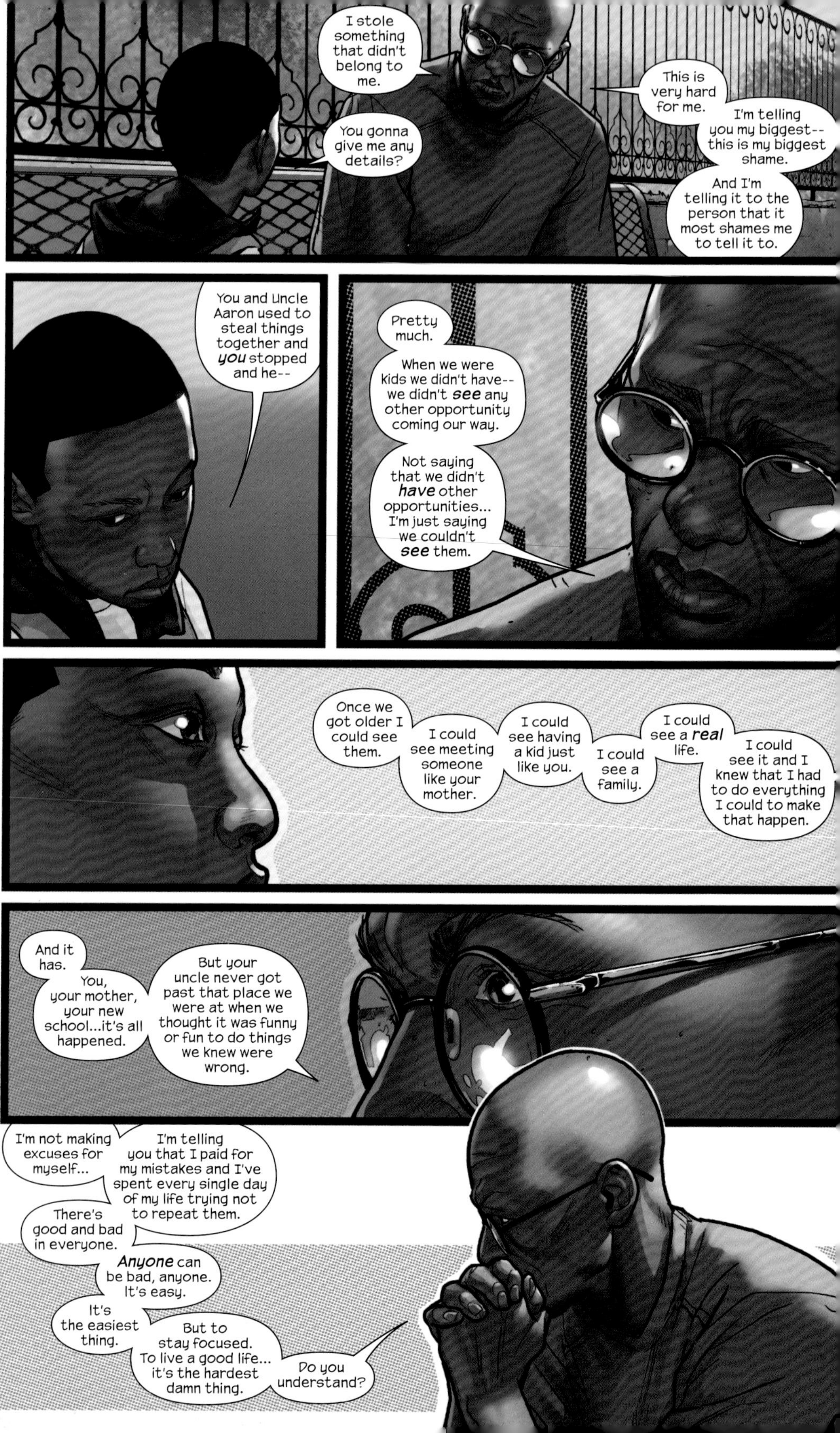

I stole something that didn't belong to me.
You gonna give me any details?
This is very hard for me.
I'm telling you my biggest-- this is my biggest shame.
And I'm telling it to the person that it most shames me to tell it to.
You and Uncle Aaron used to steal things together and *you* stopped and he--
Pretty much.
When we were kids we didn't have-- we didn't *see* any other opportunity coming our way.
Not saying that we didn't *have* other opportunities... I'm just saying we couldn't *see* them.
Once we got older I could see them.
I could see meeting someone like your mother.
I could see having a kid just like you.
I could see a family.
I could see a *real* life.
I could see it and I knew that I had to do everything I could to make that happen.
And it has.
You, your mother, your new school...it's all happened.
But your uncle never got past that place we were at when we thought it was funny or fun to do things we knew were wrong.
I'm not making excuses for myself...
I'm telling you that I paid for my mistakes and I've spent every single day of my life trying not to repeat them.
There's good and bad in everyone.
Anyone can be bad, anyone. It's easy.
It's the easiest thing.
But to stay focused. To live a good life... it's the hardest damn thing.
Do you understand?

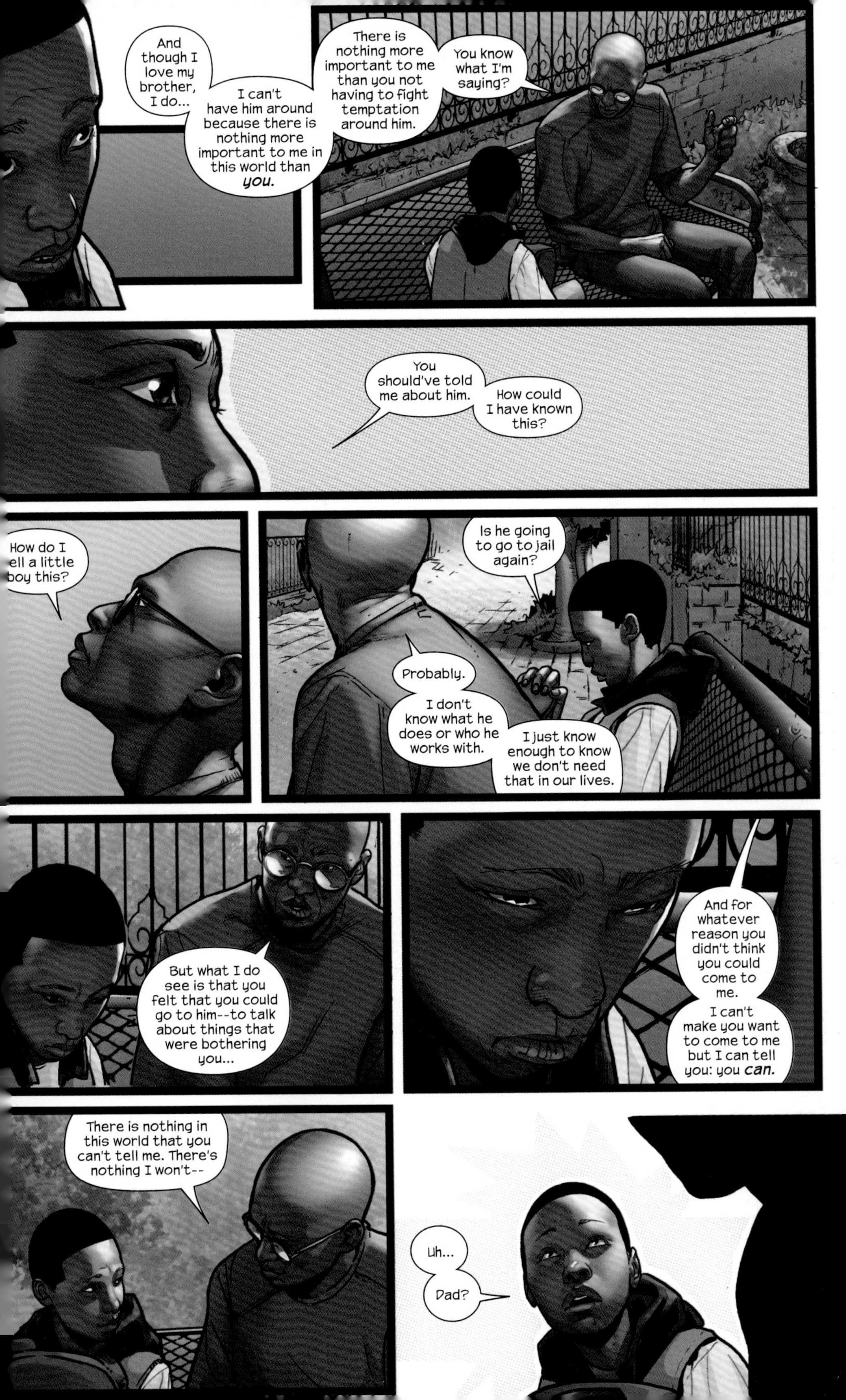
And though I love my brother, I do...
I can't have him around because there is nothing more important to me in this world than *you.*
There is nothing more important to me than you not having to fight temptation around him.
You know what I'm saying?
You should've told me about him.
How could I have known this?
How do I
ell a little
boy this?
Is he going to go to jail again?
Probably.
I don't know what he does or who he works with.
I just know enough to know we don't need that in our lives.
But what I do see is that you felt that you could go to him--to talk about things that were bothering you...
And for whatever reason you didn't think you could come to me.
I can't make you want to come to me but I can tell you: you *can.*
There is nothing in this world that you can't tell me. There's nothing I won't--
Uh...
Dad?

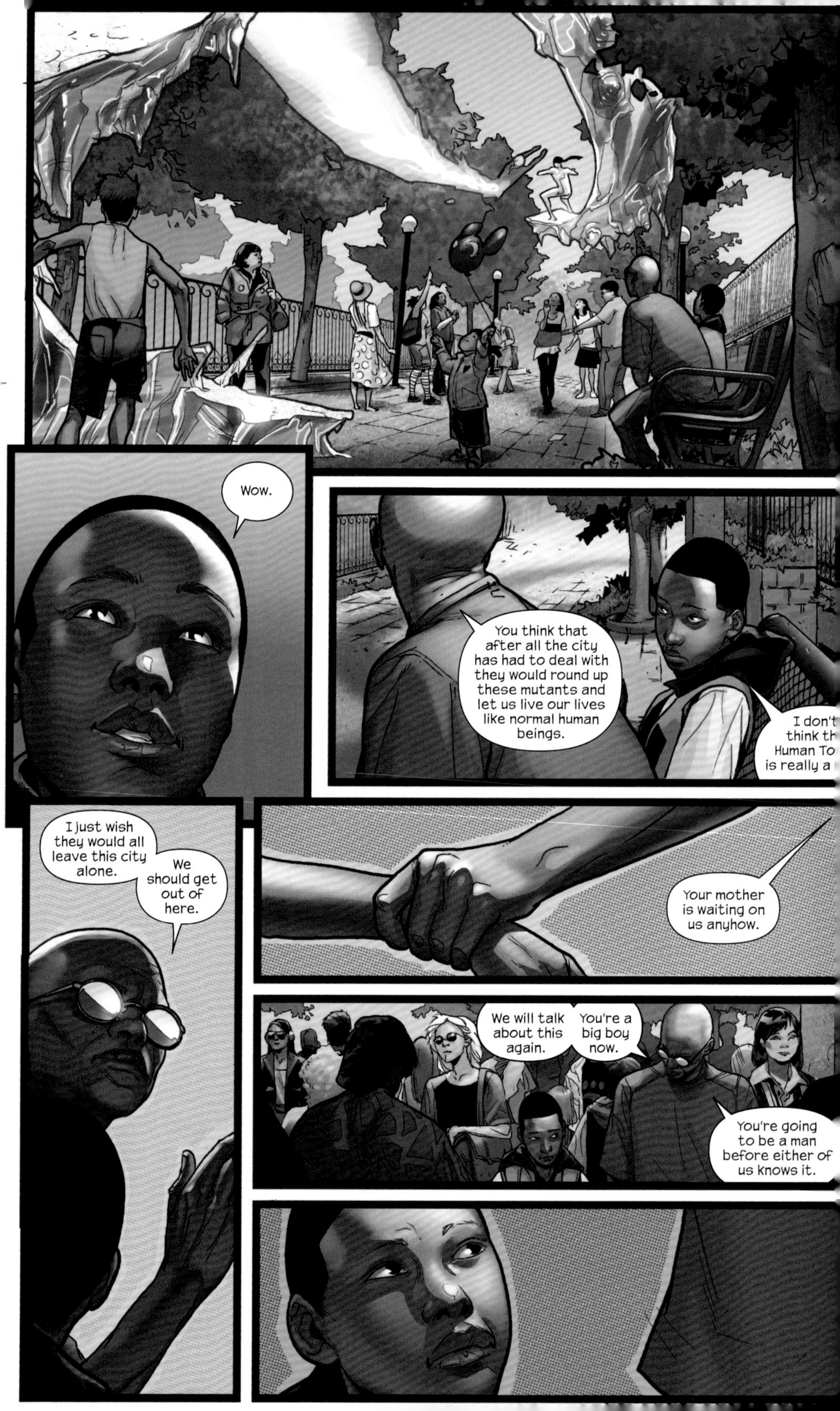

Wow.
You think that after all the city has had to deal with they would round up these mutants and let us live our lives like normal human beings.
I don't think th Human To is really a
I just wish they would all leave this city alone.
We should get out of here.
Your mother is waiting on us anyhow.
We will talk about this again.
You're a big boy now.
You're going to be a man before either of us knows it.

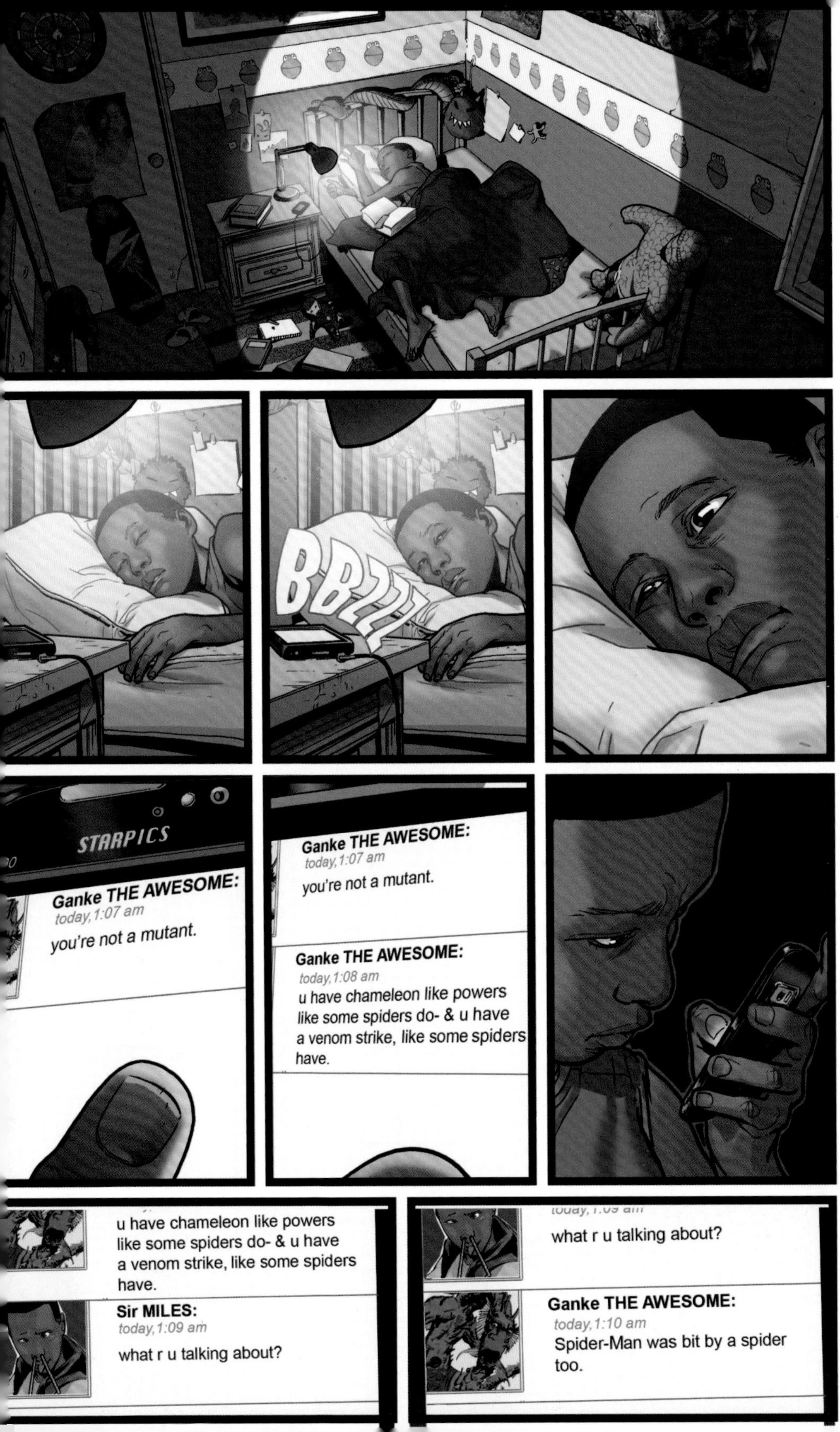

BBZZZT
STARPICS
Ganke THE AWESOME:
today, 1:07 am
you're not a mutant.
Ganke THE AWESOME:
today, 1:07 am
you're not a mutant.
Ganke THE AWESOME:
today, 1:08 am
u have chameleon like powers like some spiders do- & u have a venom strike, like some spiders have.
u have chameleon like powers like some spiders do- & u have a venom strike, like some spiders have.
Sir MILES:
today, 1:09 am
what r u talking about?
what r u talking about?
Ganke THE AWESOME:
today, 1:10 am
Spider-Man was bit by a spider too.

STARPICS
Z100

Spider-man was bit by a spi...
too.

Ganke THE AWESOME:
today,1:12 am
Spider-Man myth busted By
Ben Urich

Ganke THE AWESOME:
today,1:12 am
Sp____n myth busted By

HOW SPIDER-MAN BECAME SPIDER-MAN

By BEN URICH
Last Updated: 3:37 PM, July 13, 2011
Posted: 5:54 AM, July 13, 2011

Like | Send | 7,042 people like this. Be the first of your friends.

+1 | 35 | 586 | More Print

picture by Peter Parker

The dismembered body of a missing 6-year old Hasidic boy was found early today at two locations in Brooklyn — with police arresting a suspect in the grisly slaying who had the child's severed feet in his freezer, authorities said.

Police made the gruesome discovery after raiding a Kensington home and arresting 35-year-old Levi Aron, who led them to parts of missing boy Leiby Kletzky's body, stuffed in a red suitcase

though said with levity, Spider-Man told police officers
that he was bit by a spider that gave him
spider-powers.

STARPICS
Z100

Ganke THE AWESOME:
today,1:10 am
sorry u'r not a mutant but...
R U Spider-Man?!!

Ganke THE AWES
today,1:10 am
sorry u'r not a mu
R U Spider-Man?

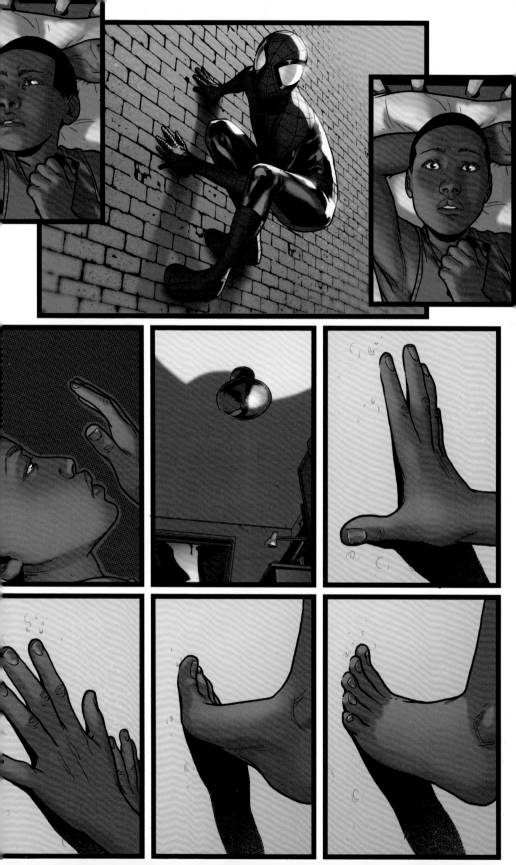

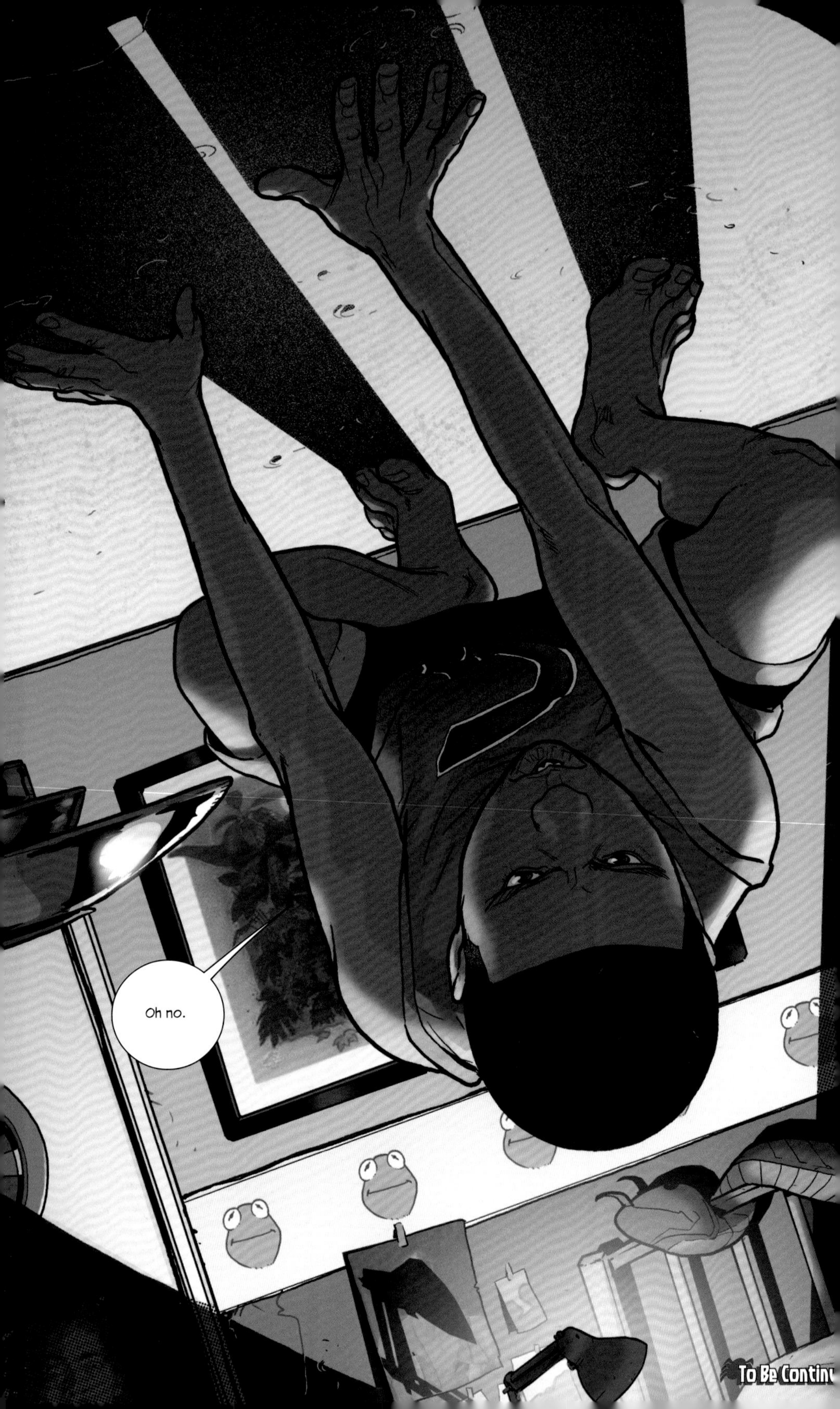
Oh no.
To Be Contin

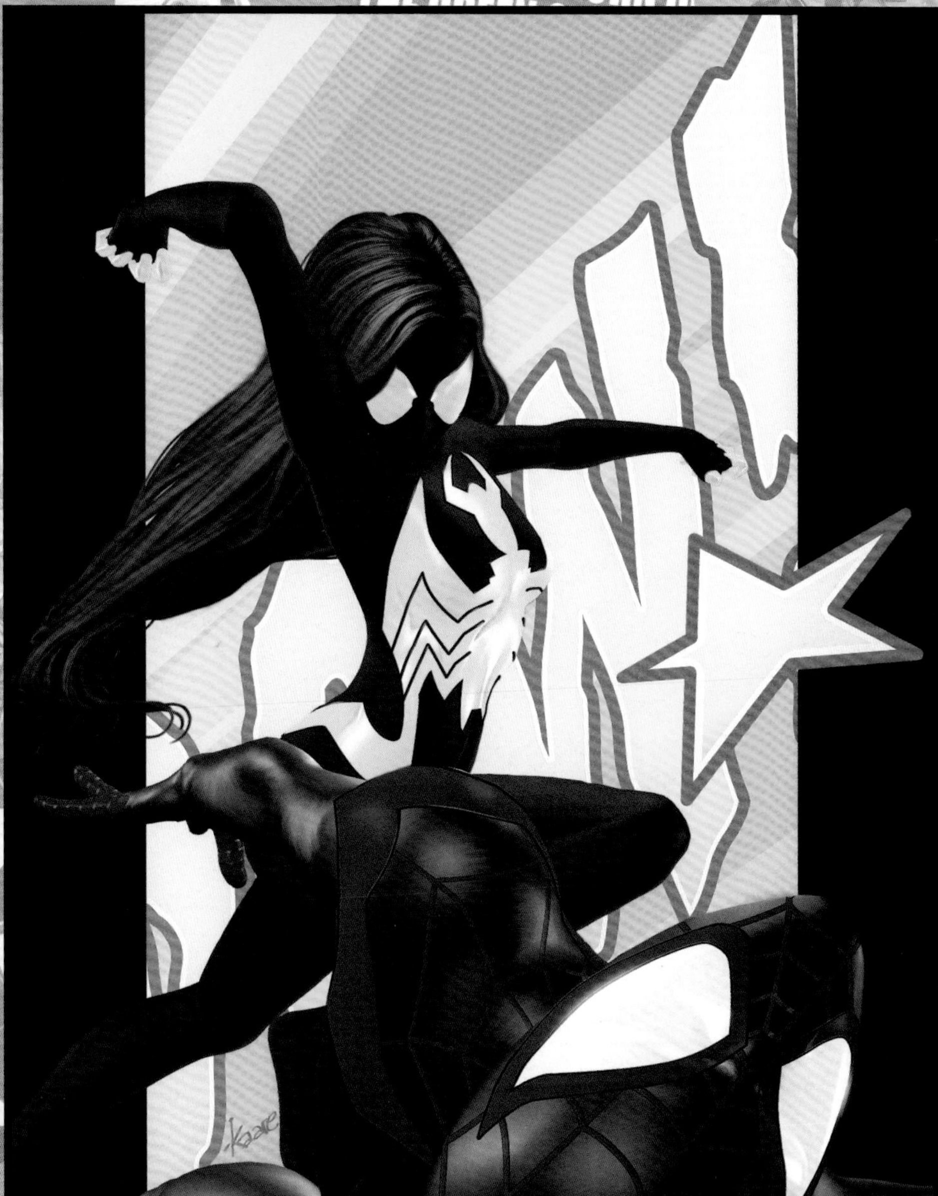

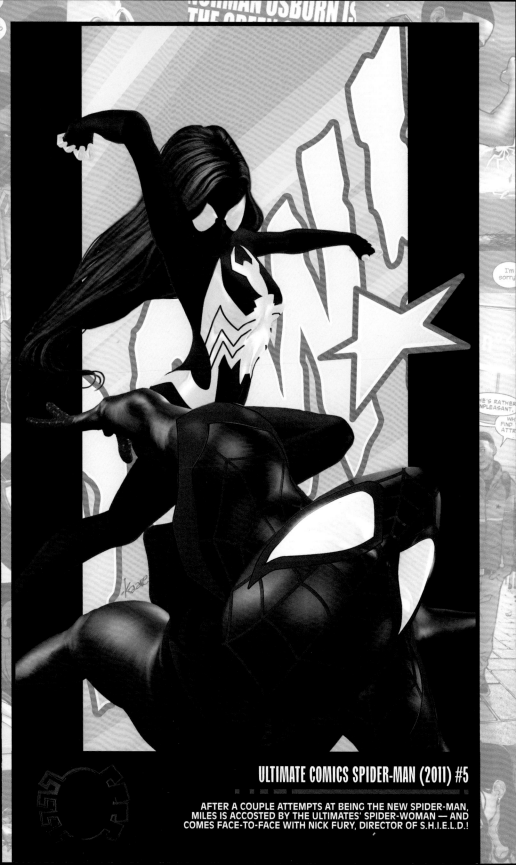

ULTIMATE COMICS SPIDER-MAN (2011) #5

AFTER A COUPLE ATTEMPTS AT BEING THE NEW SPIDER-MAN, MILES IS ACCOSTED BY THE ULTIMATES' SPIDER-WOMAN — AND COMES FACE-TO-FACE WITH NICK FURY, DIRECTOR OF S.H.I.E.L.D.!

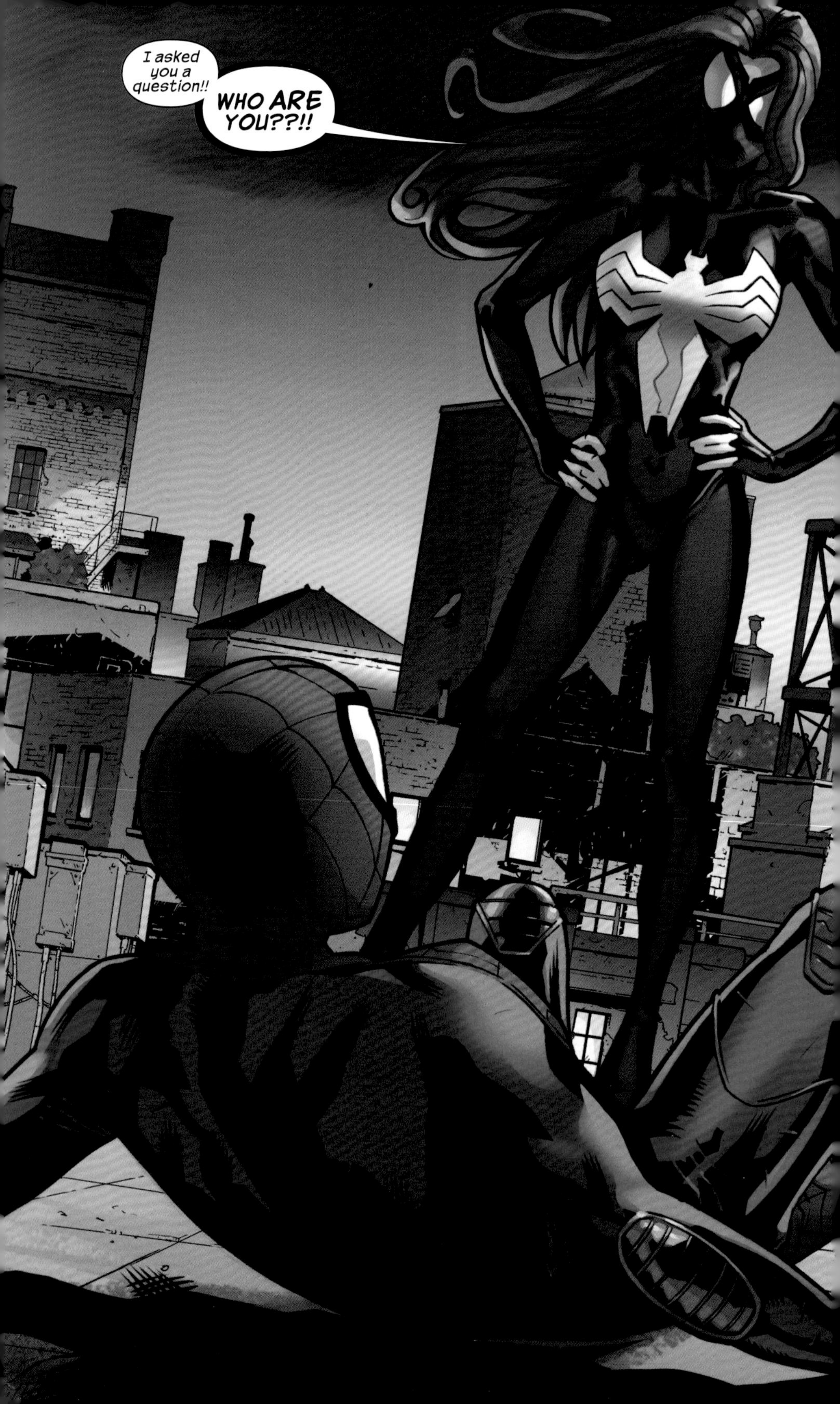
I asked you a question!!
WHO ARE YOU??!!

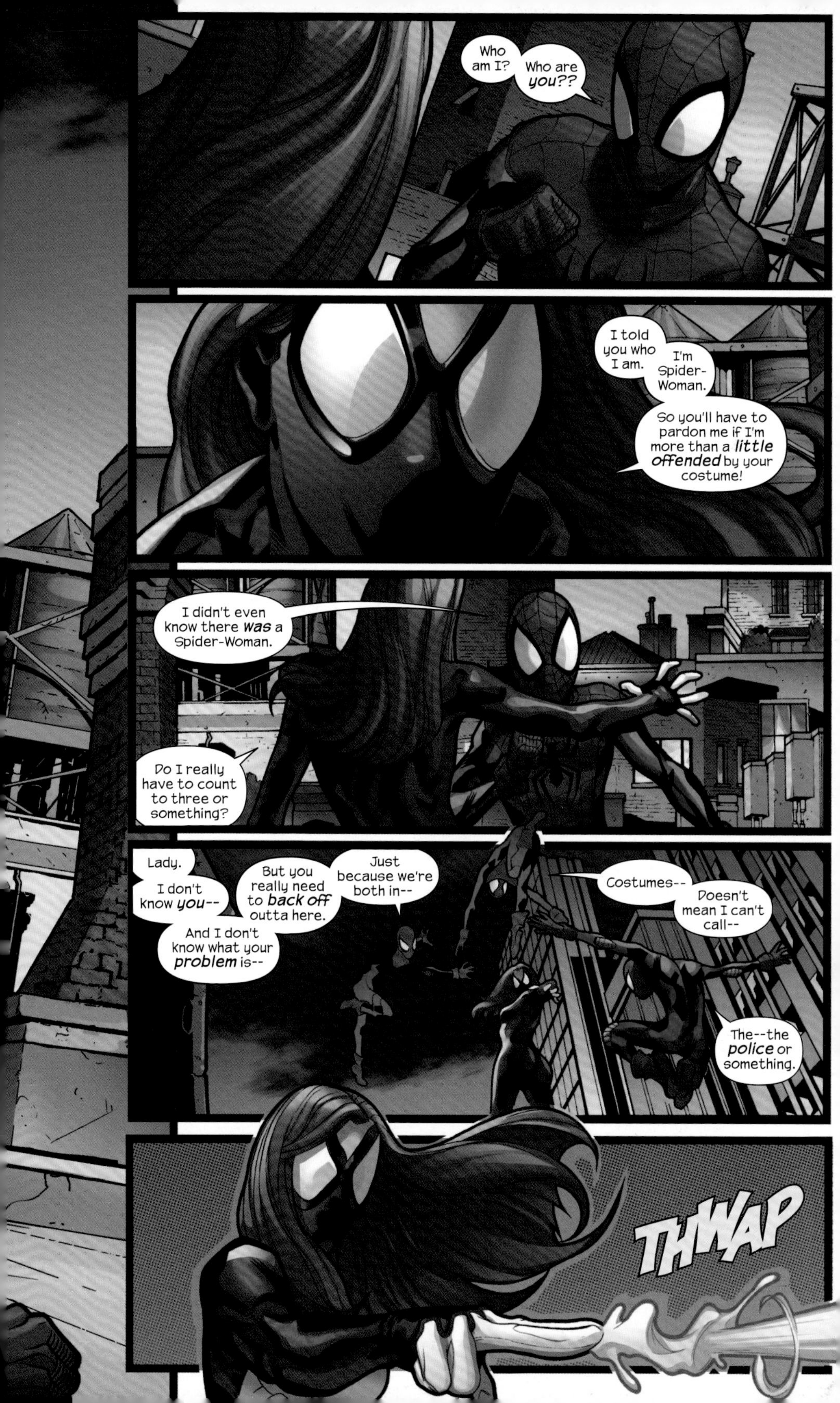
Who am I?
Who are you??
I told you who I am.
I'm Spider-Woman.
So you'll have to pardon me if I'm more than a little offended by your costume!
I didn't even know there was a Spider-Woman.
Do I really have to count to three or something?
Lady.
I don't know you--
And I don't know what your problem is--
But you really need to back off outta here.
Just because we're both in--
Costumes--
Doesn't mean I can't call--
The--the police or something.
THWAP

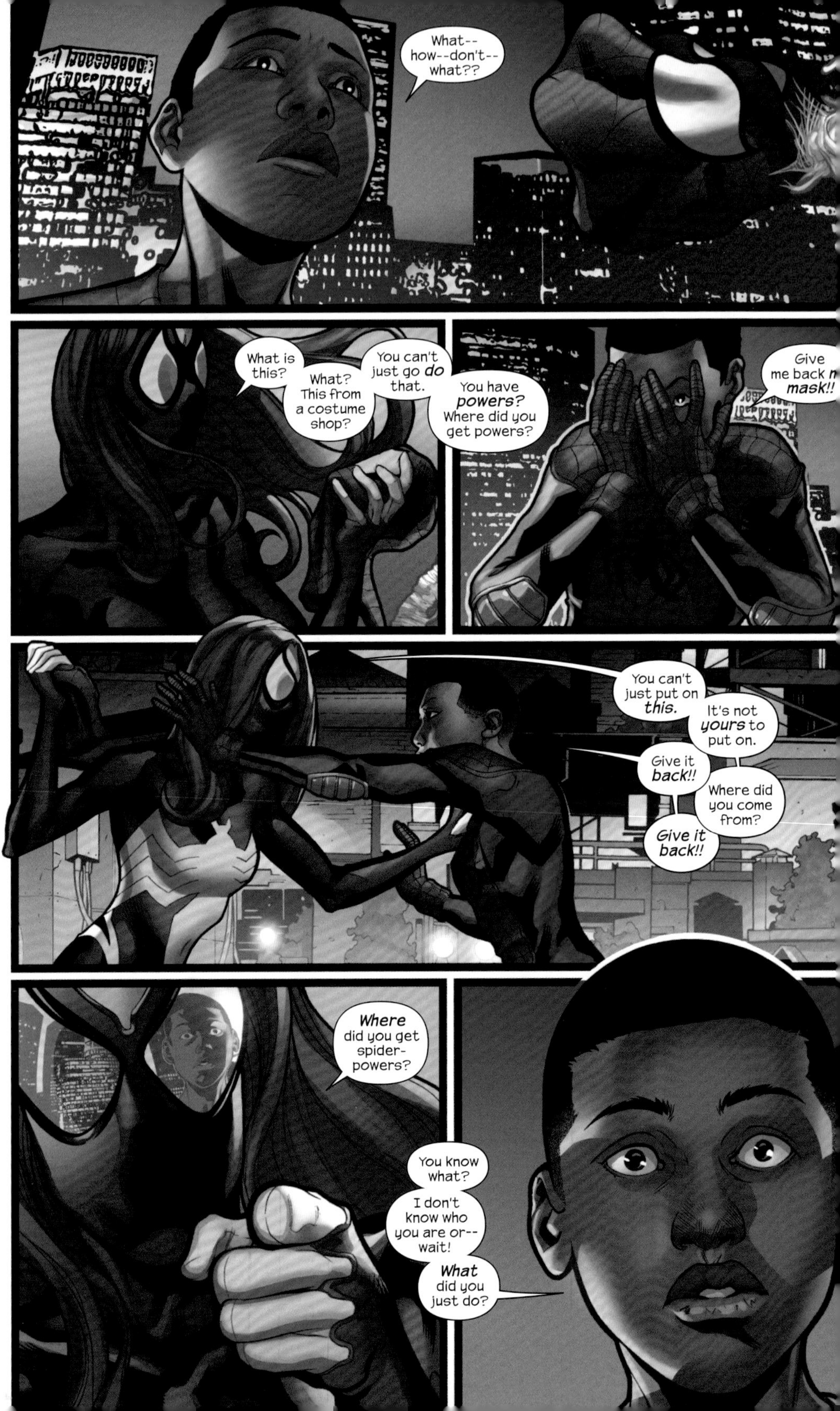

What--
how--don't--
what??
What is this?
What? This from a costume shop?
You can't just go *do* that.
You have *powers?* Where did you get powers?
Give me back m *mask!!*
You can't just put on *this.*
It's not *yours* to put on.
Give it *back!!*
Where did you come from?
Give it back!!
Where did you get spider-powers?
You know what?
I don't know who you are or--
wait!
What did you just do?

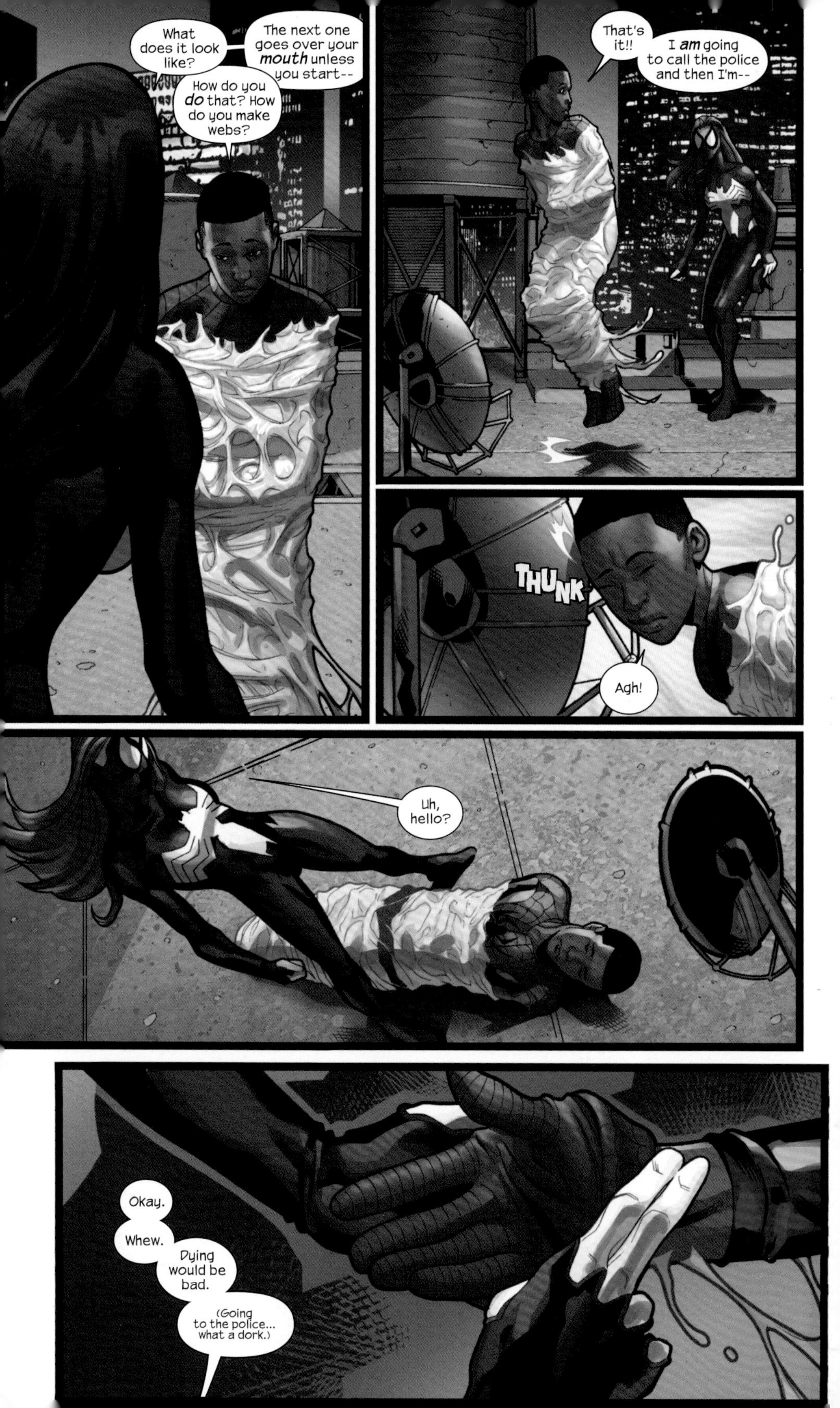
What does it look like?
The next one goes over your *mouth* unless you start--
How do you *do* that? How do you make webs?
That's it!!
I *am* going to call the police and then I'm--
THUNK
Agh!
Uh, hello?
Okay.
Whew.
Dying would be bad.
(Going to the police... what a dork.)

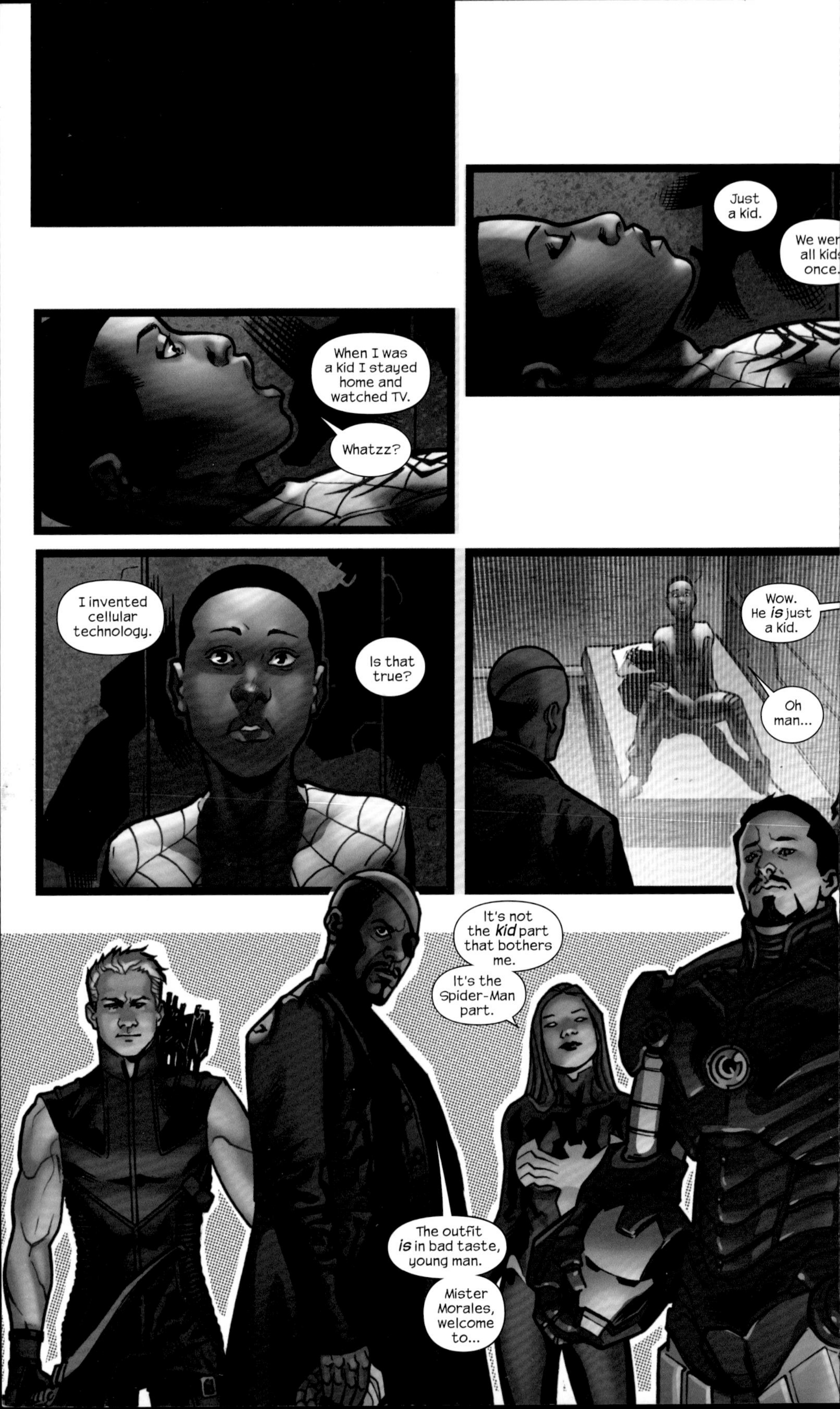
Just a kid.
We wer all kid once.
When I was a kid I stayed home and watched TV.
Whatzz?
I invented cellular technology.
Is that true?
Wow. He *is* just a kid.
Oh man...
It's not the *kid* part that bothers me.
It's the Spider-Man part.
The outfit *is* in bad taste, young man.
Mister Morales, welcome to...

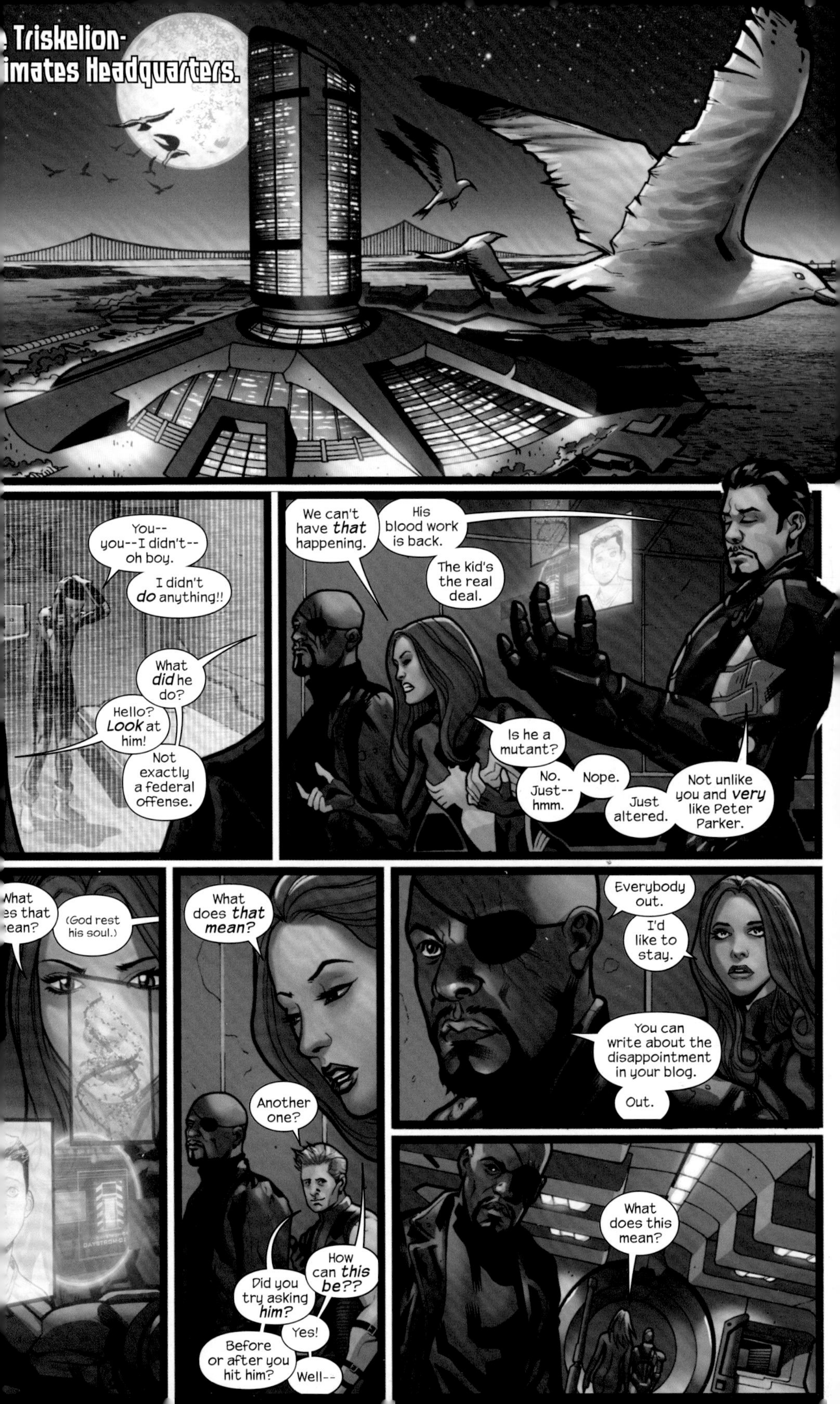

Triskelion-
imates Headquarters.
You--
you--I didn't--
oh boy.
I didn't *do* anything!!
What *did* he do?
Hello? *Look* at him!
Not exactly a federal offense.
We can't have *that* happening.
His blood work is back.
The kid's the real deal.
Is he a mutant?
No. Just--hmm.
Nope.
Just altered.
Not unlike you and *very* like Peter Parker.
What es that ean?
(God rest his soul.)
What does *that mean?*
Another one?
How can *this be??*
Did you try asking *him?*
Yes!
Before or after you hit him?
Well--
Everybody out.
I'd like to stay.
You can write about the disappointment in your blog.
Out.
What does this mean?

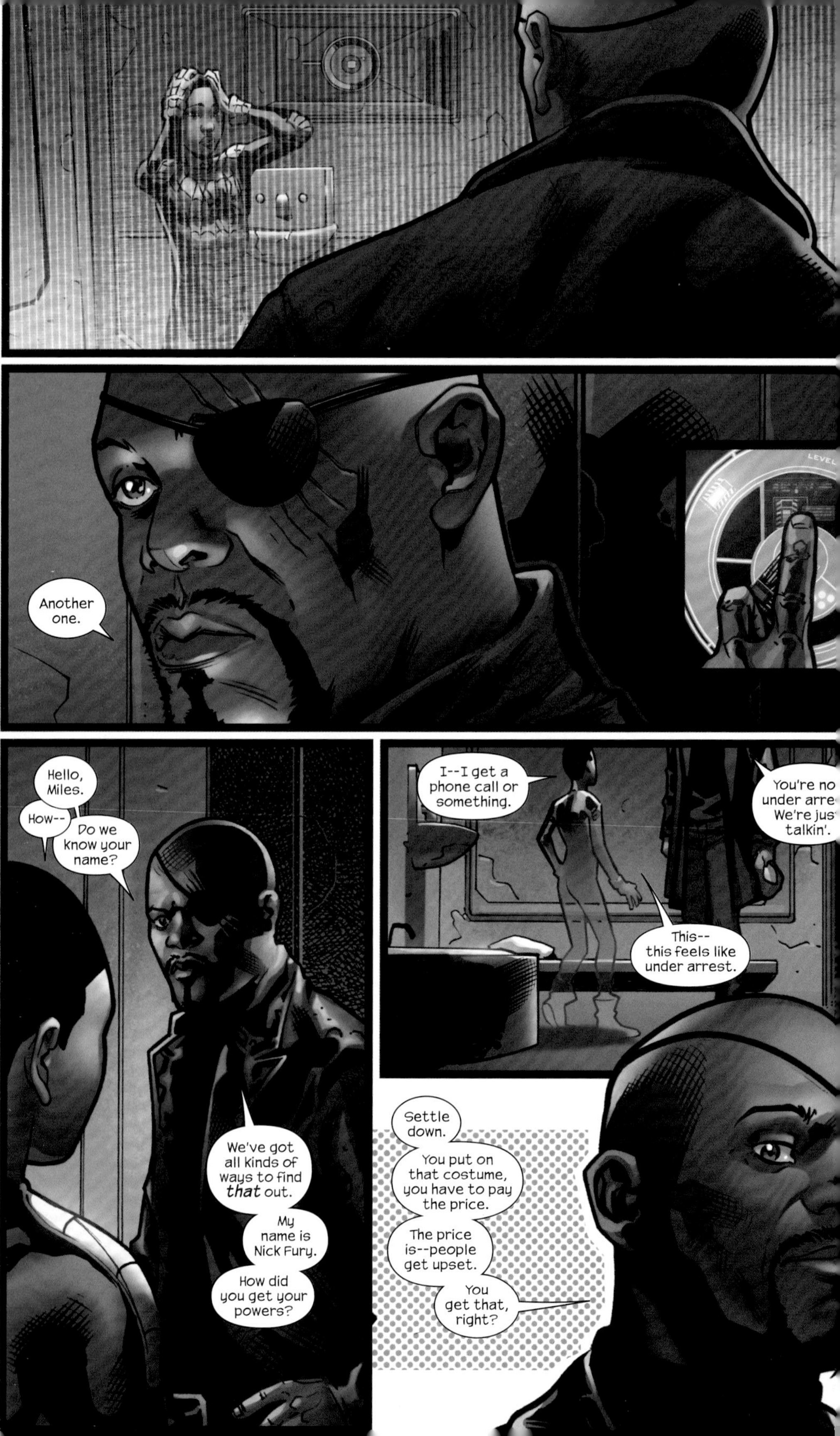

Another one.
Hello, Miles.
How--
Do we know your name?
We've got all kinds of ways to find *that* out.
My name is Nick Fury.
How did you get your powers?
I--I get a phone call or something.
You're no under arre We're jus talkin'.
This-- this feels like under arrest.
Settle down.
You put on that costume, you have to pay the price.
The price is--people get upset.
You get that, right?

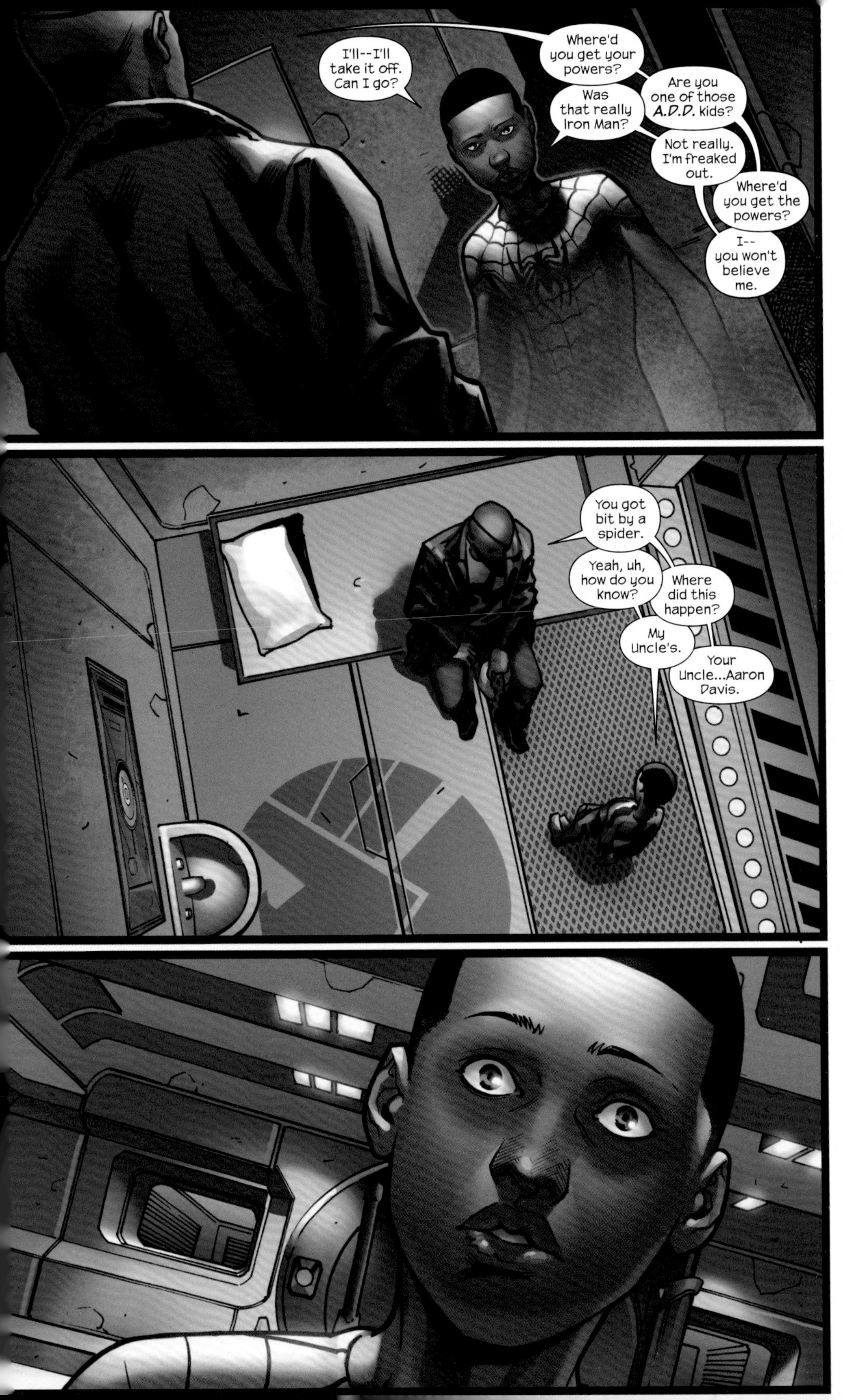

Where'd you get your powers?
I'll--I'll take it off. Can I go?
Are you one of those A.D.D. kids?
Was that really Iron Man?
Not really. I'm freaked out.
Where'd you get the powers?
I-- you won't believe me.
You got bit by a spider.
Yeah, uh, how do you know?
Where did this happen?
My Uncle's.
Your Uncle...Aaron Davis.

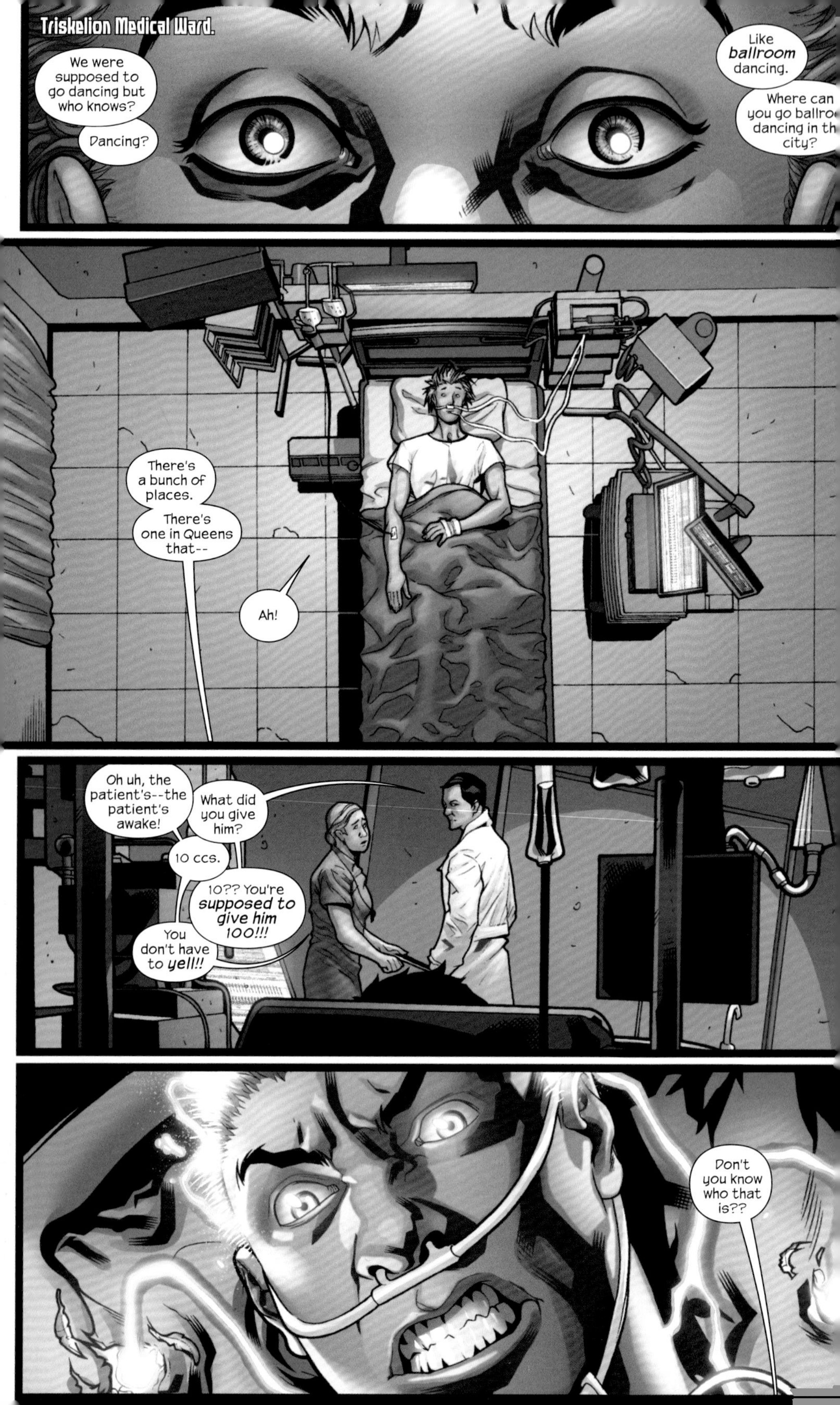
Triskelion Medical Ward.
We were supposed to go dancing but who knows?
Dancing?
Like ballroom dancing.
Where can you go ballro dancing in th city?
There's a bunch of places.
There's one in Queens that--
Ah!
Oh uh, the patient's--the patient's awake!
What did you give him?
10 ccs.
10?? You're supposed to give him 100!!!
You don't have to yell!!
Don't you know who that is??

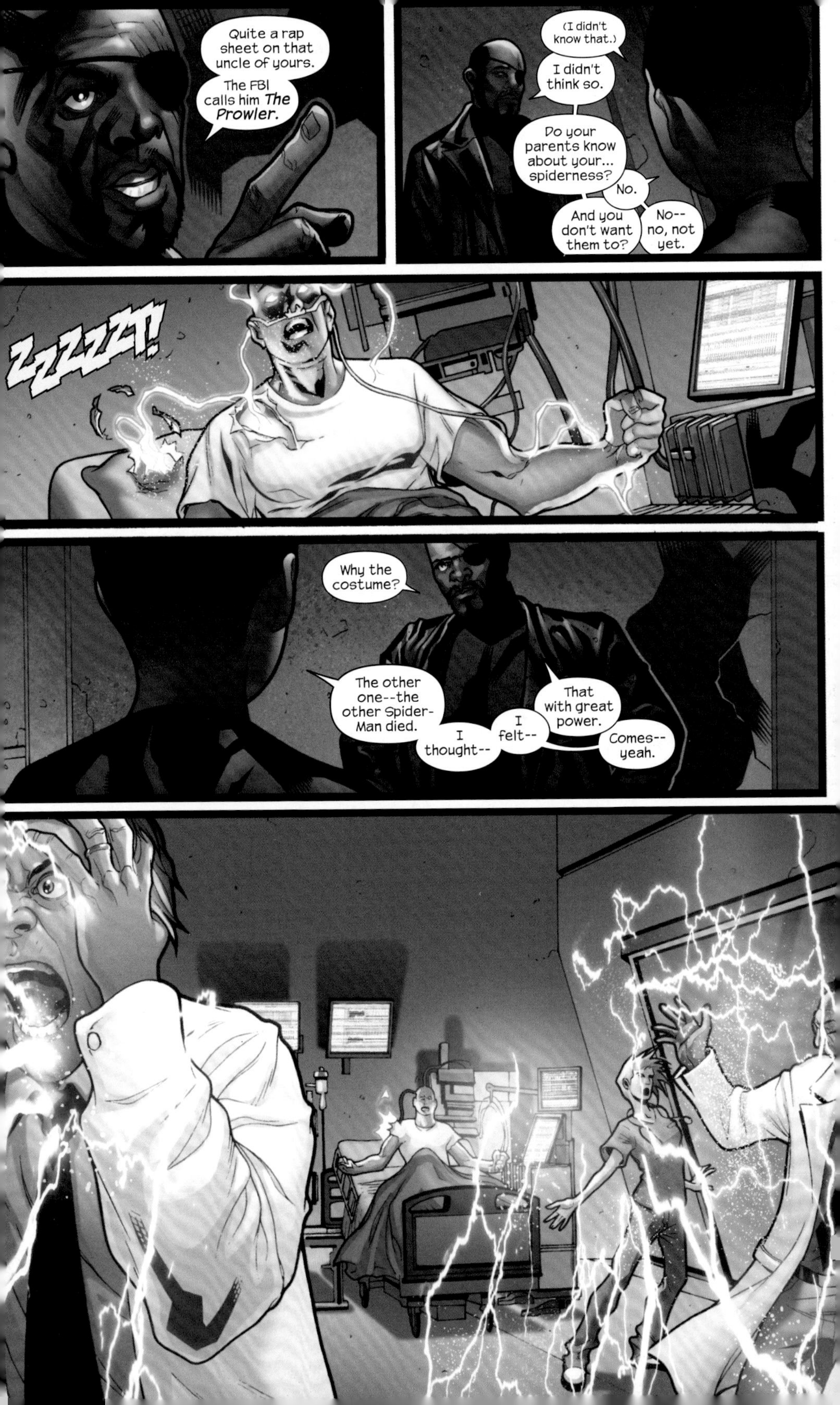
Quite a rap sheet on that uncle of yours.
The FBI calls him *The Prowler.*
(I didn't know that.)
I didn't think so.
Do your parents know about your... spiderness?
No.
And you don't want them to?
No-- no, not yet.
ZZZZZT!
Why the costume?
The other one--the other Spider-Man died.
I thought--
I felt--
That with great power.
Comes-- yeah.

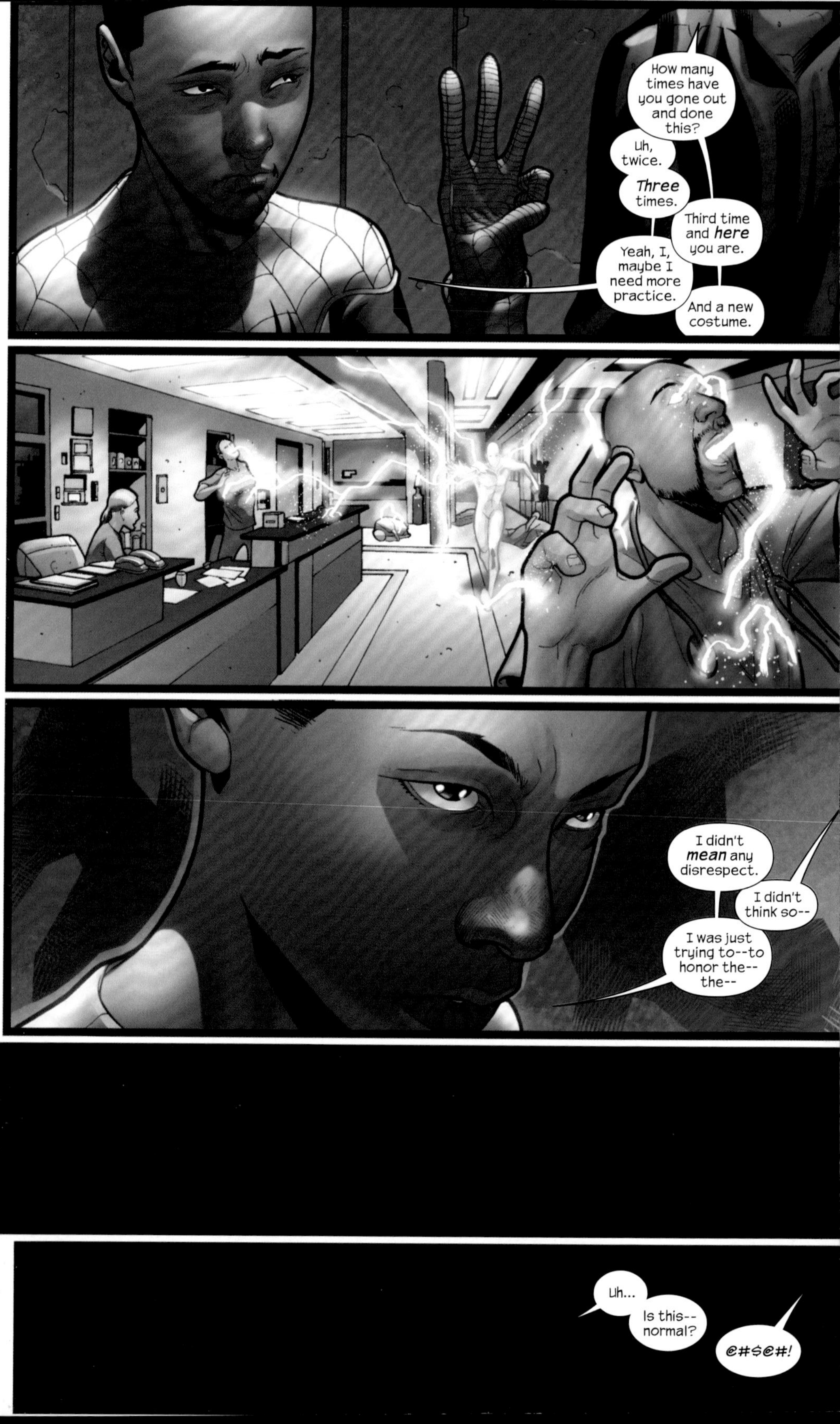
How many times have you gone out and done this?
Uh, twice.
Three times.
Third time and here you are.
Yeah, I, maybe I need more practice.
And a new costume.
I didn't mean any disrespect.
I didn't think so--
I was just trying to--to honor the-- the--
Uh...
Is this-- normal?
@#$@#!

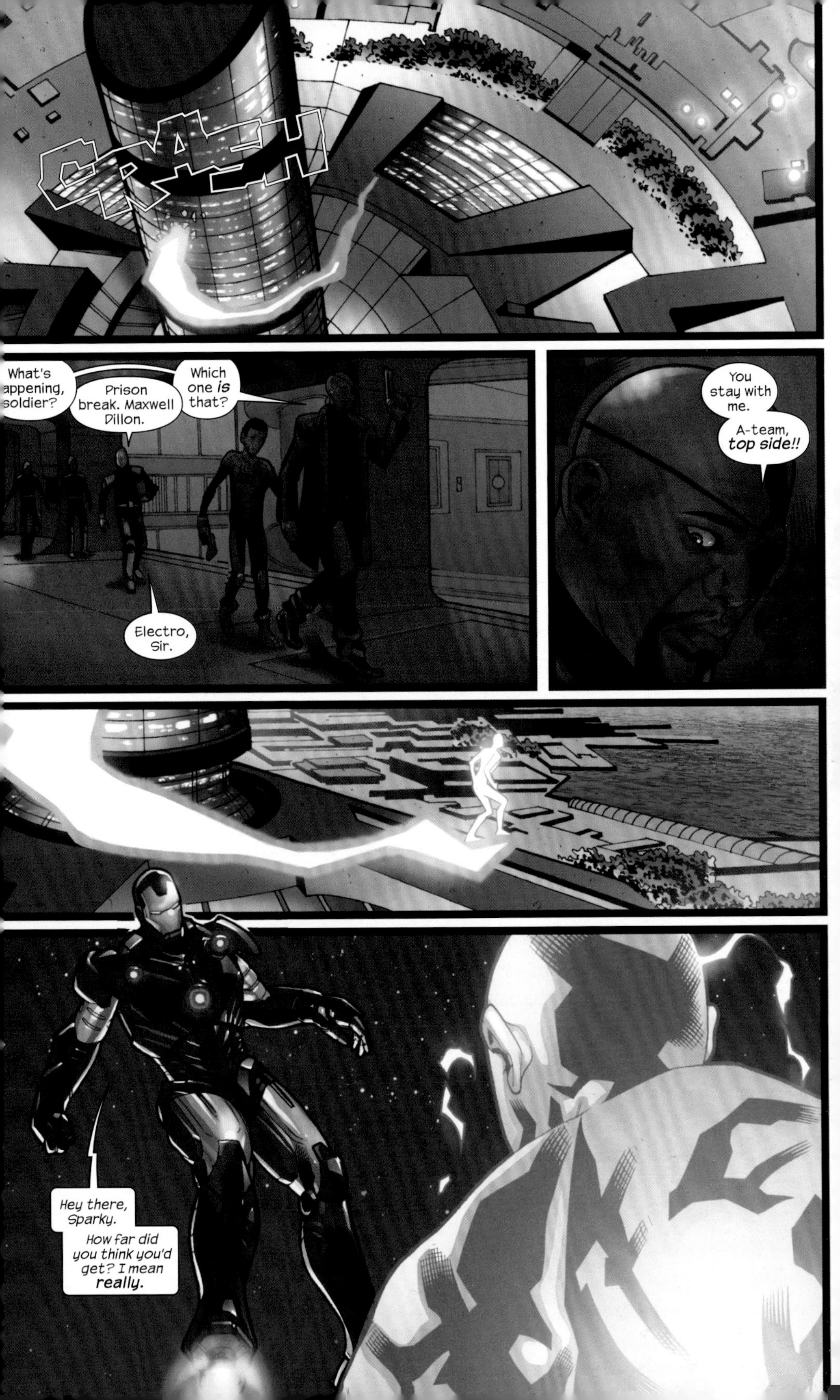
CRASH
What's appening, soldier?
Prison break. Maxwell Dillon.
Which one *is* that?
Electro, Sir.
You stay with me.
A-team, ***top side!!***
Hey there, Sparky.
How far did you think you'd get? I mean **really.**

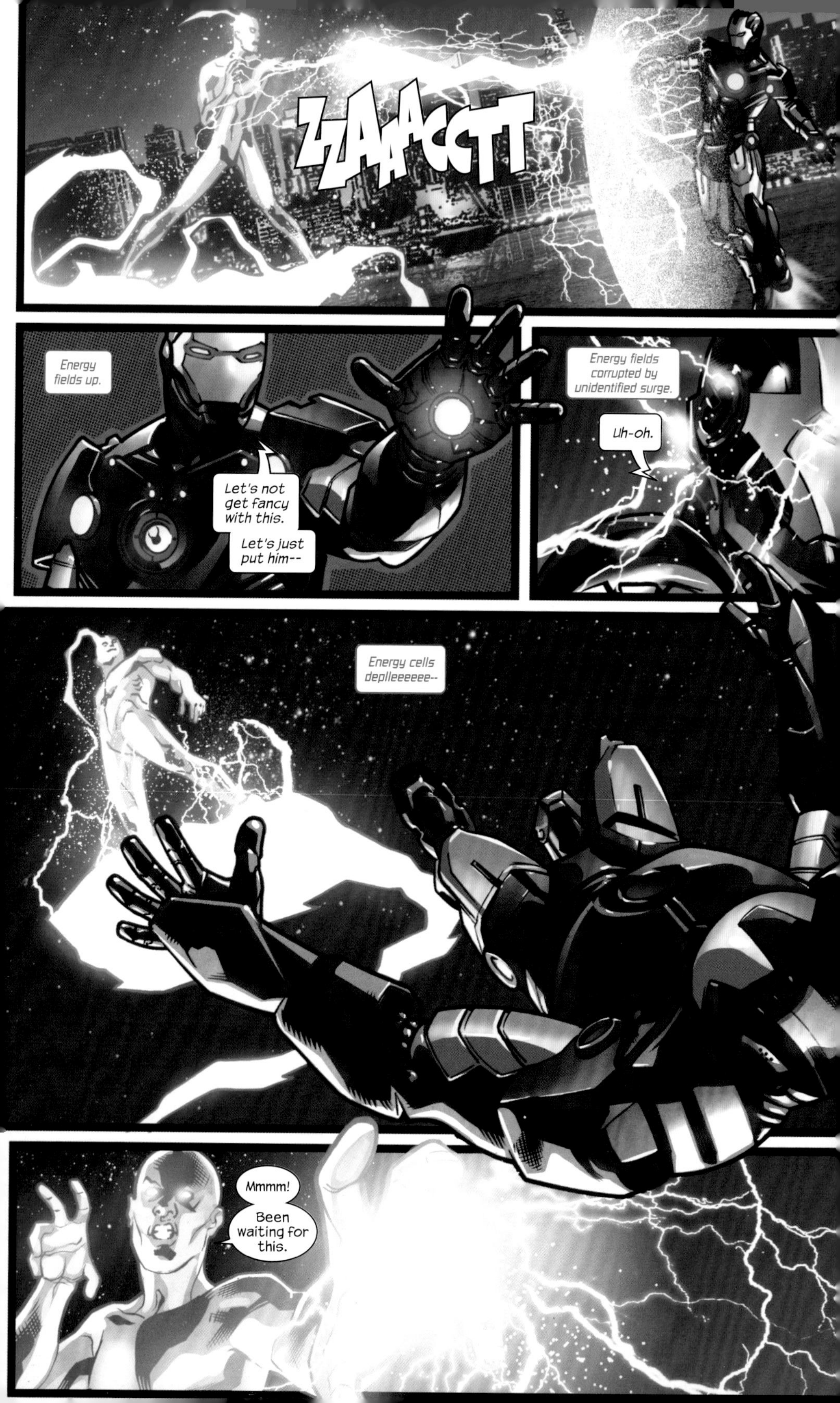
ZZAAACCTT
Energy fields up.
Let's not get fancy with this.
Let's just put him--
Energy fields corrupted by unidentified surge.
Uh-oh.
Energy cells deplleeeeee--
Mmmm!
Been waiting for this.

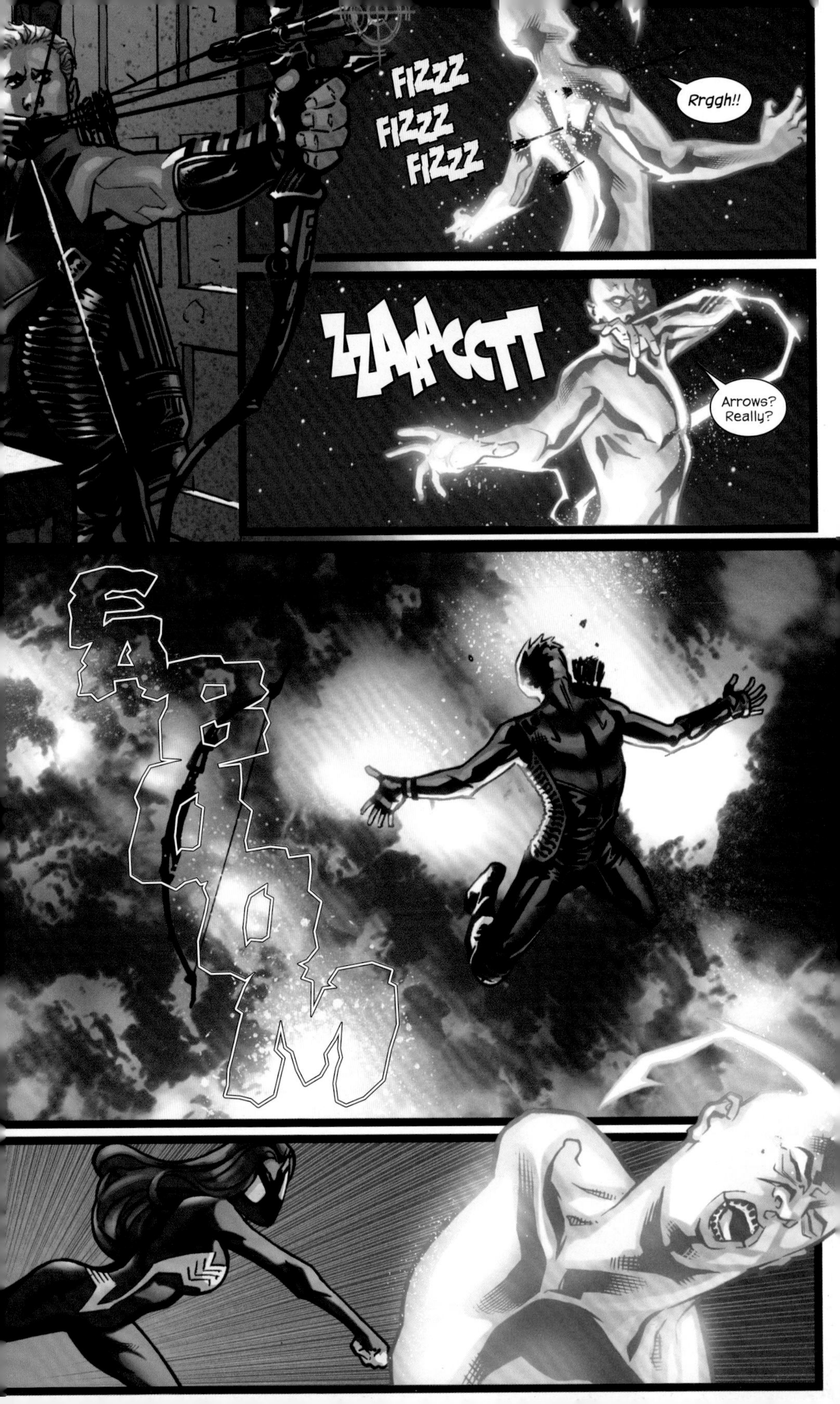
FIZZZ
FIZZZ
FIZZZ
Rrggh!!
ZZZAAACCTT
Arrows? Really?
FABOOM

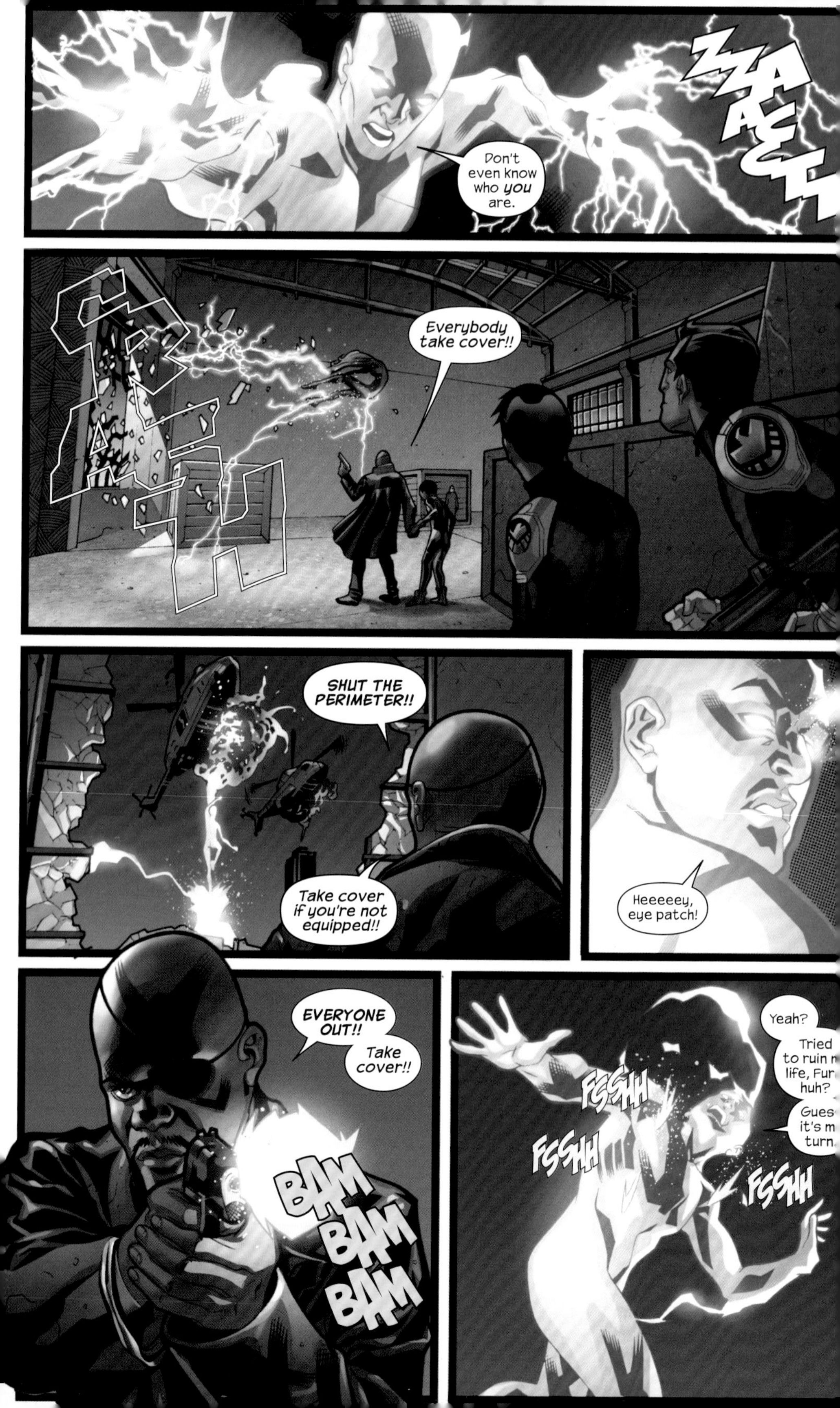

Don't even know who you are.
ZZAAAKT
CRAASH
Everybody take cover!!
SHUT THE PERIMETER!!
Take cover if you're not equipped!!
Heeeeey, eye patch!
EVERYONE OUT!!
Take cover!!
BAM BAM BAM
FSSHH
FSSHH
FSSHH
Yeah?
Tried to ruin m life, Fur huh?
Gues it's m turn.

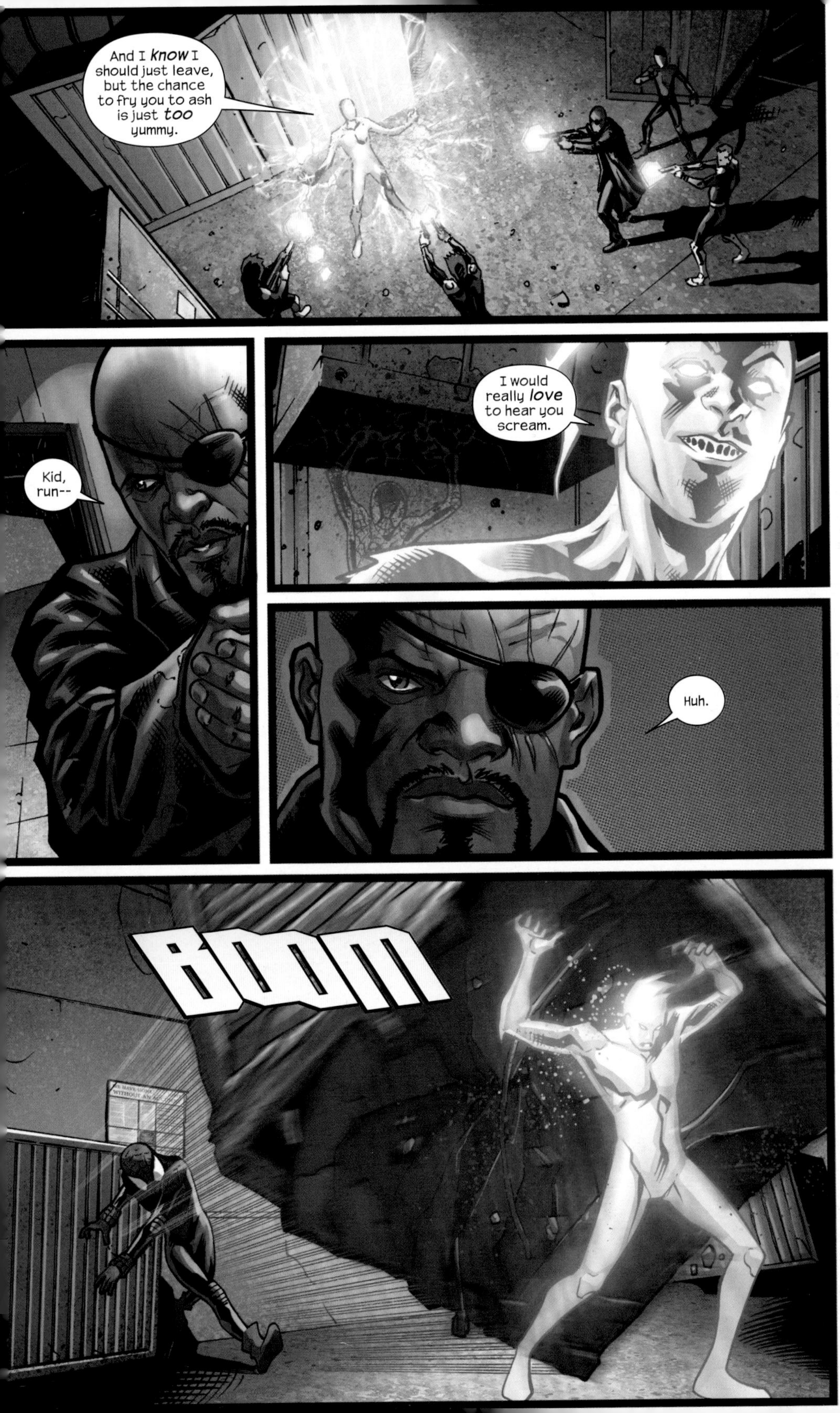

And I *know* I should just leave, but the chance to fry you to ash is just *too* yummy.
Kid, run--
I would really *love* to hear you scream.
Huh.
BOOM

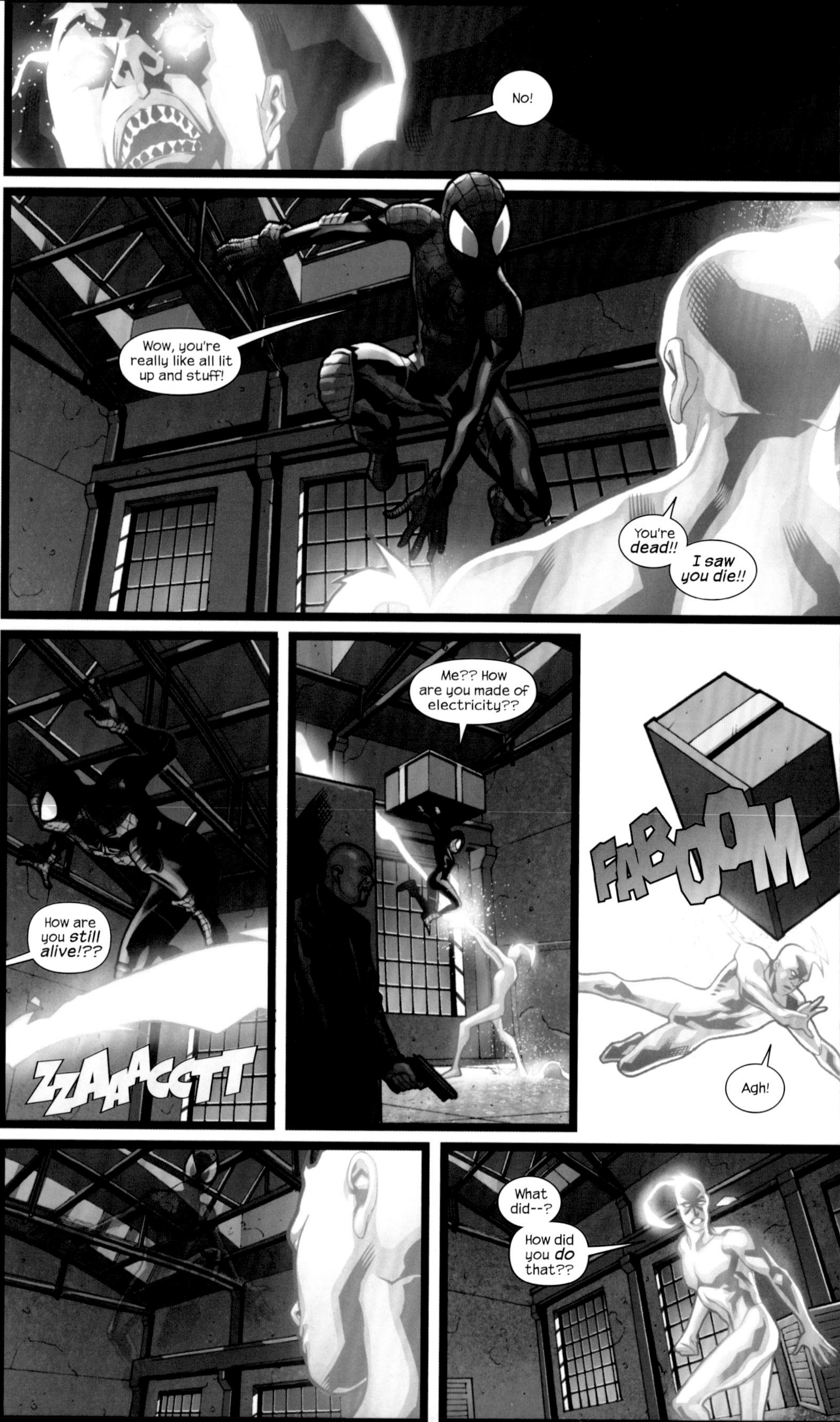
No!
Wow, you're really like all lit up and stuff!
You're *dead*!!
I saw you die!!
How are you *still alive*!??
ZZAAACCTT
Me?? How are you made of electricity??
FABOOM
Agh!
What did--?
How did you *do* that??

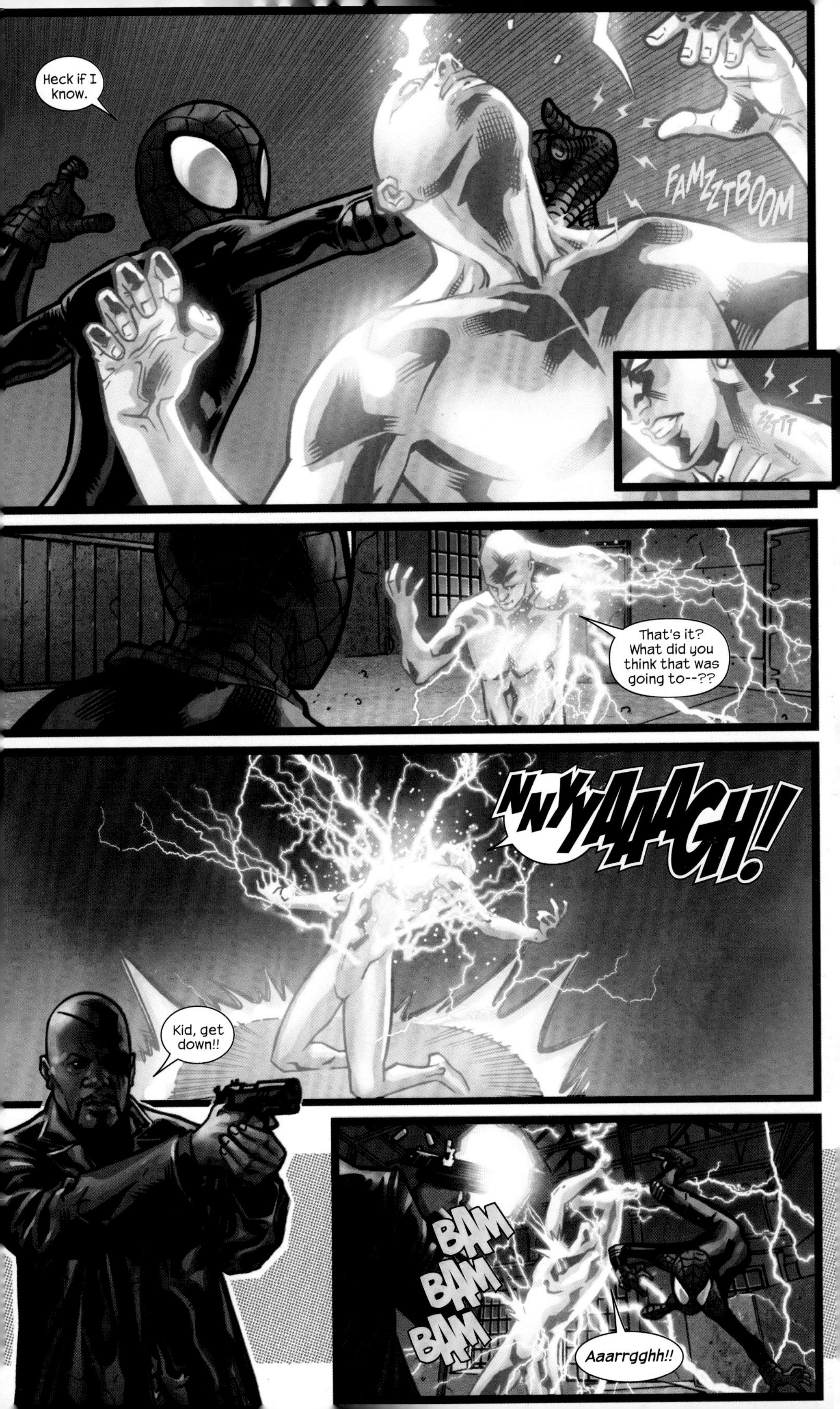
Heck if I know.
FAMZZTBOOM
ZZTTT
That's it? What did you think that was going to--??
NNYYAAAAGH!
Kid, get down!!
BAM
BAM
BAM
Aaarrgghh!!

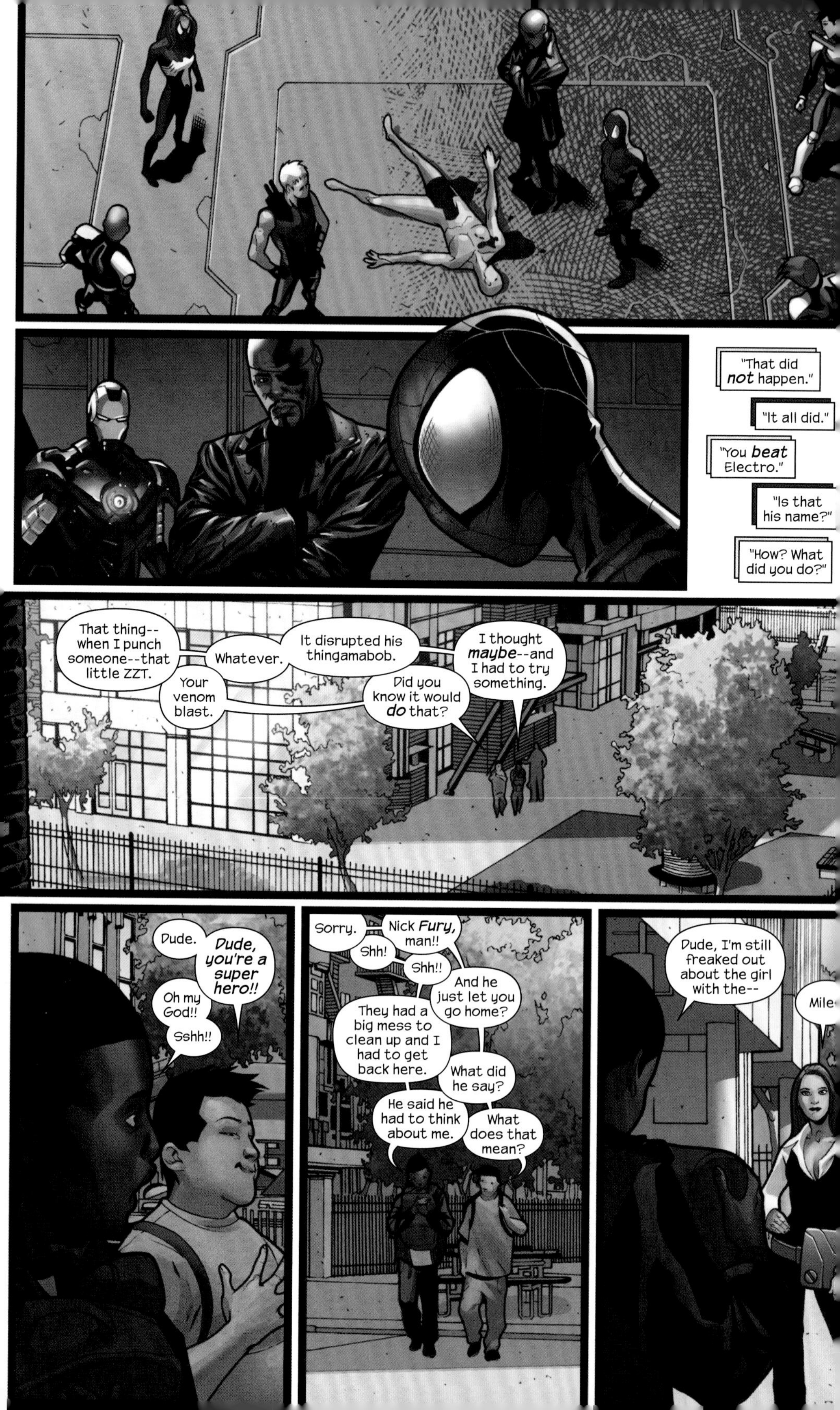
"That did not happen."
"It all did."
"You beat Electro."
"Is that his name?"
"How? What did you do?"
That thing--when I punch someone--that little ZZT.
Whatever.
It disrupted his thingamabob.
I thought maybe--and I had to try something.
Your venom blast.
Did you know it would do that?
Dude.
Dude, you're a super hero!!
Oh my God!!
Sshh!!
Sorry.
Nick Fury, man!!
Shh!
Shh!!
And he just let you go home?
They had a big mess to clean up and I had to get back here.
What did he say?
He said he had to think about me.
What does that mean?
Dude, I'm still freaked out about the girl with the--
Mile

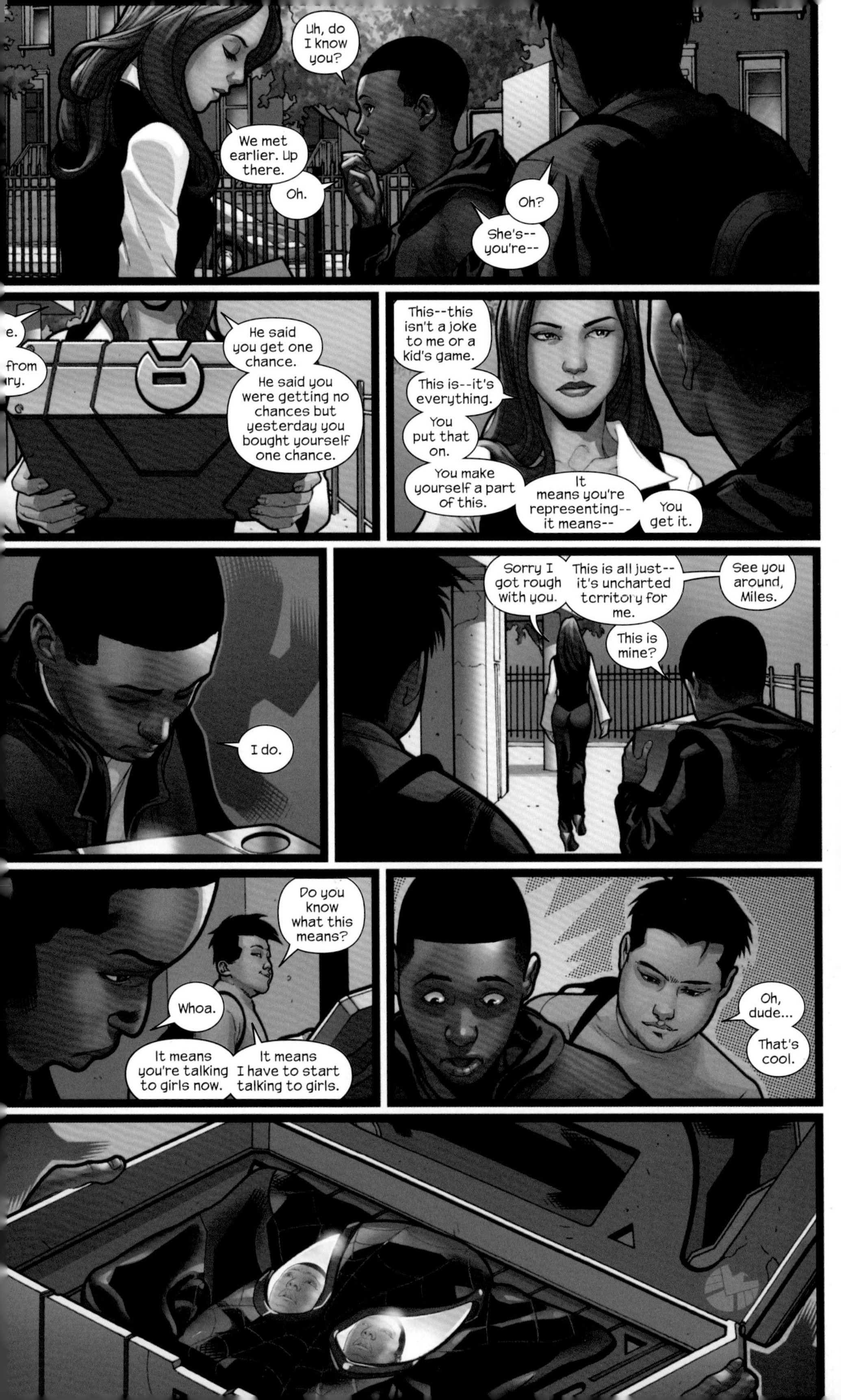

Uh, do I know you?
We met earlier. Up there.
Oh.
Oh?
She's-- you're--
e.
from
ry.
He said you get one chance.
He said you were getting no chances but yesterday you bought yourself one chance.
This--this isn't a joke to me or a kid's game.
This is--it's everything.
You put that on.
You make yourself a part of this.
It means you're representing-- it means--
You get it.
I do.
Sorry I got rough with you.
This is all just-- it's uncharted territory for me.
See you around, Miles.
This is mine?
Do you know what this means?
Whoa.
It means you're talking to girls now.
It means I have to start talking to girls.
Oh, dude...
That's cool.

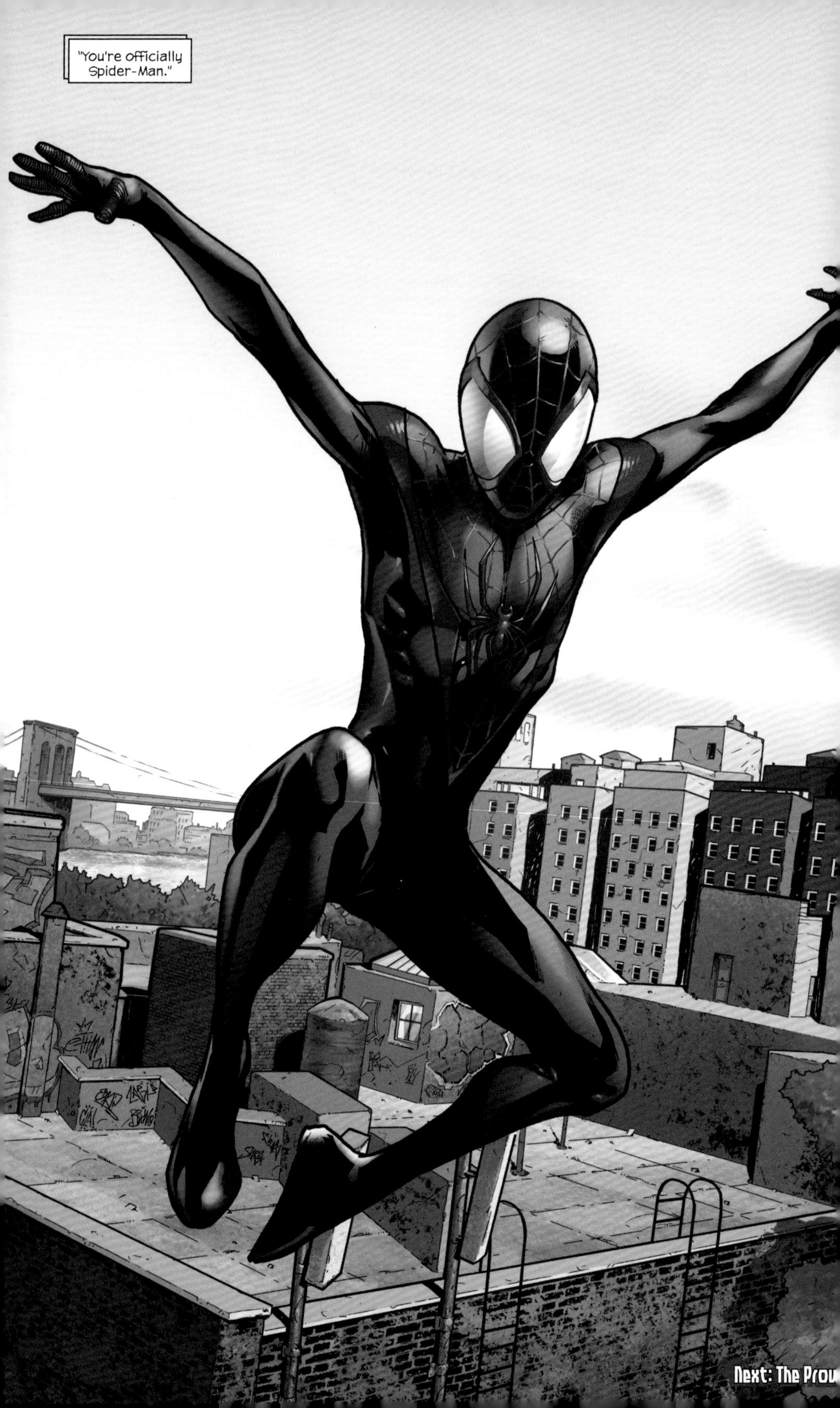
"You're officially Spider-Man."
Next: The Prov

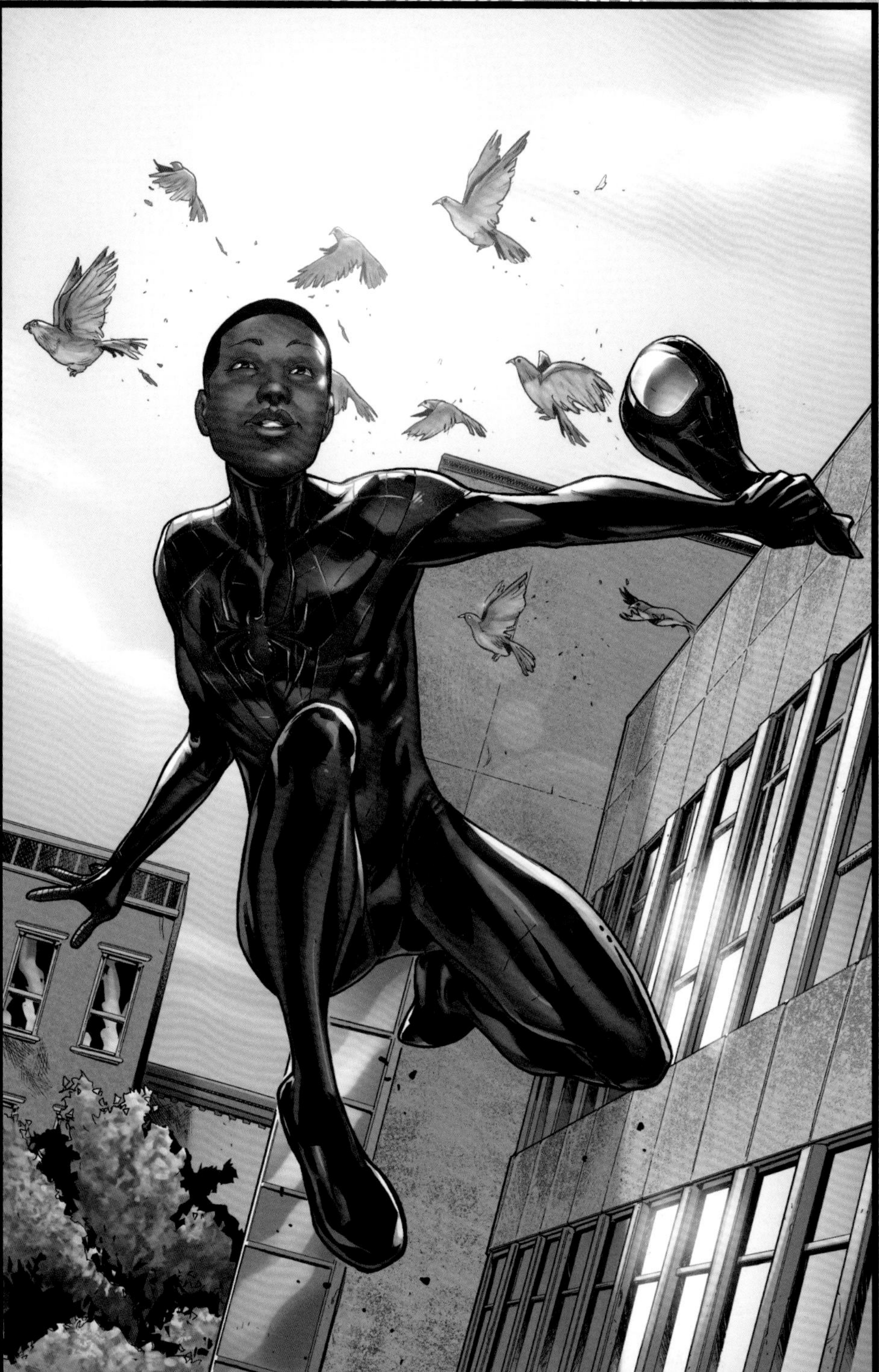

ULTIMATE SPIDER-MAN (2011) #1 VARIANT

BY SARA PICHELLI & JUSTIN PONSOR

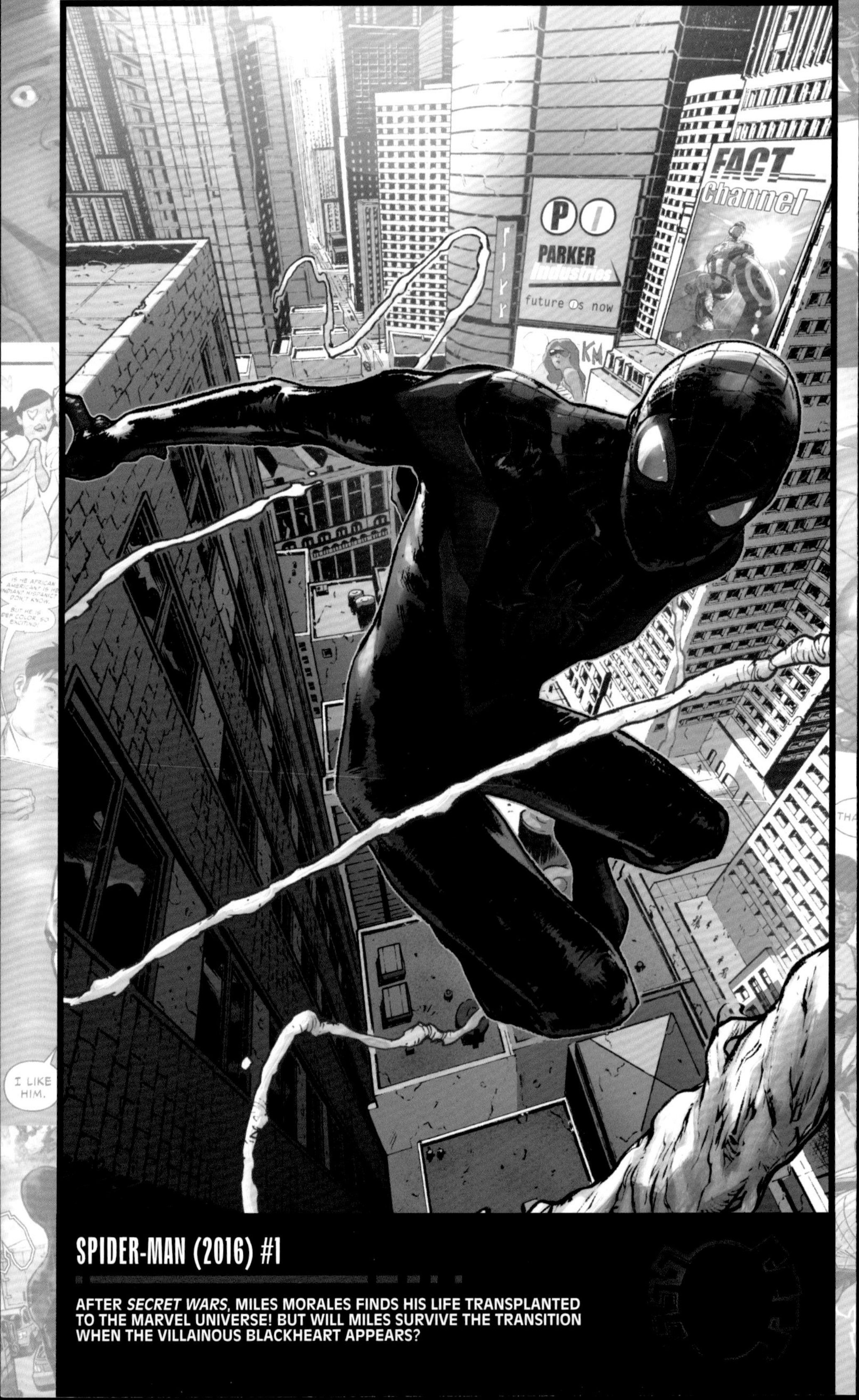
FACT
Channel
PARKER
Industries
future is now

SPIDER-MAN (2016) #1

AFTER *SECRET WARS*, MILES MORALES FINDS HIS LIFE TRANSPLANTED TO THE MARVEL UNIVERSE! BUT WILL MILES SURVIVE THE TRANSITION WHEN THE VILLAINOUS BLACKHEART APPEARS?

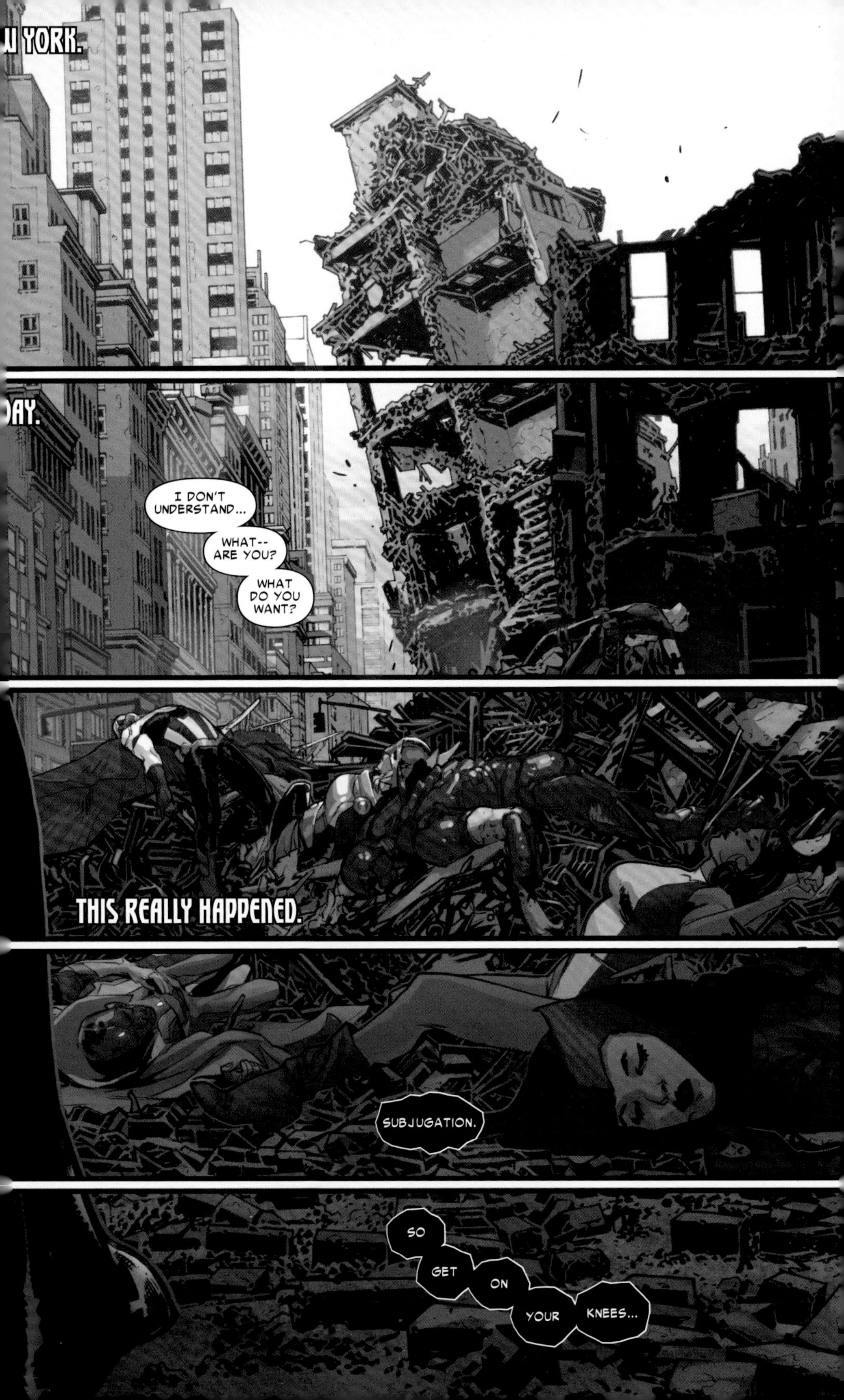

...W YORK.
...DAY.
I DON'T UNDERSTAND...
WHAT-- ARE YOU?
WHAT DO YOU WANT?
THIS REALLY HAPPENED.
SUBJUGATION.
SO
GET
ON
YOUR
KNEES...

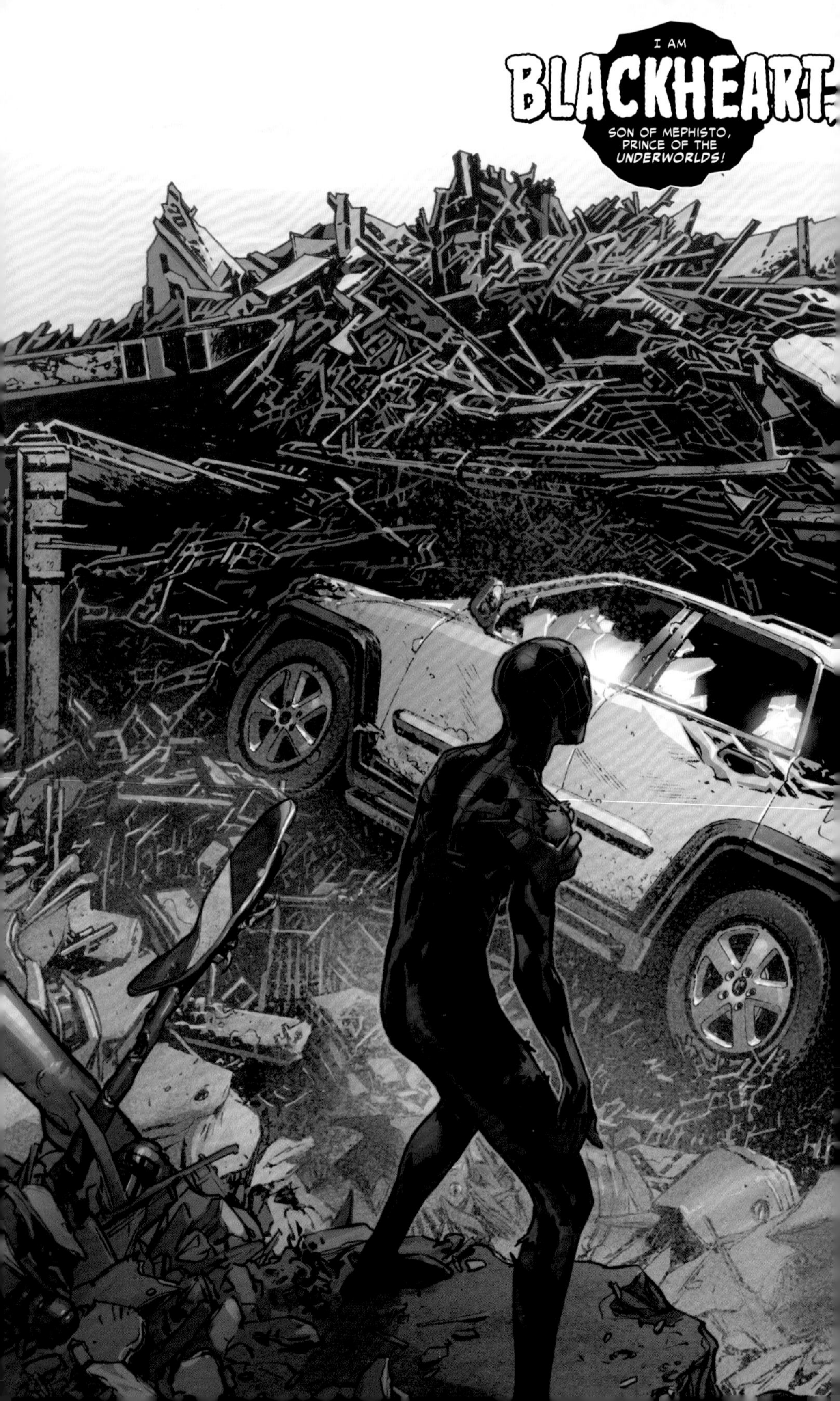
I AM
BLACKHEART,
SON OF MEPHISTO, PRINCE OF THE UNDERWORLDS!

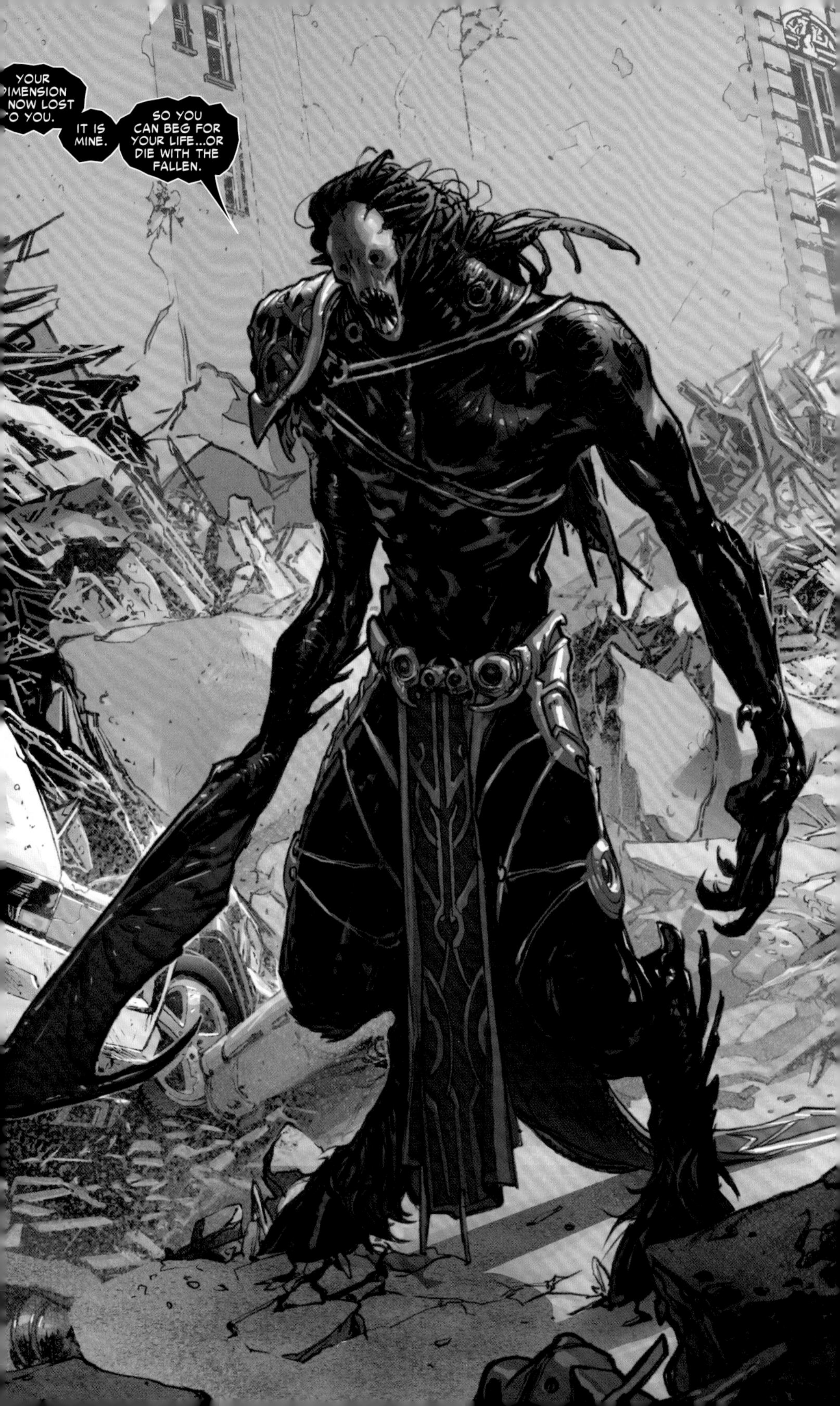
YOUR DIMENSION NOW LOST TO YOU.
IT IS MINE.
SO YOU CAN BEG FOR YOUR LIFE...OR DIE WITH THE FALLEN.

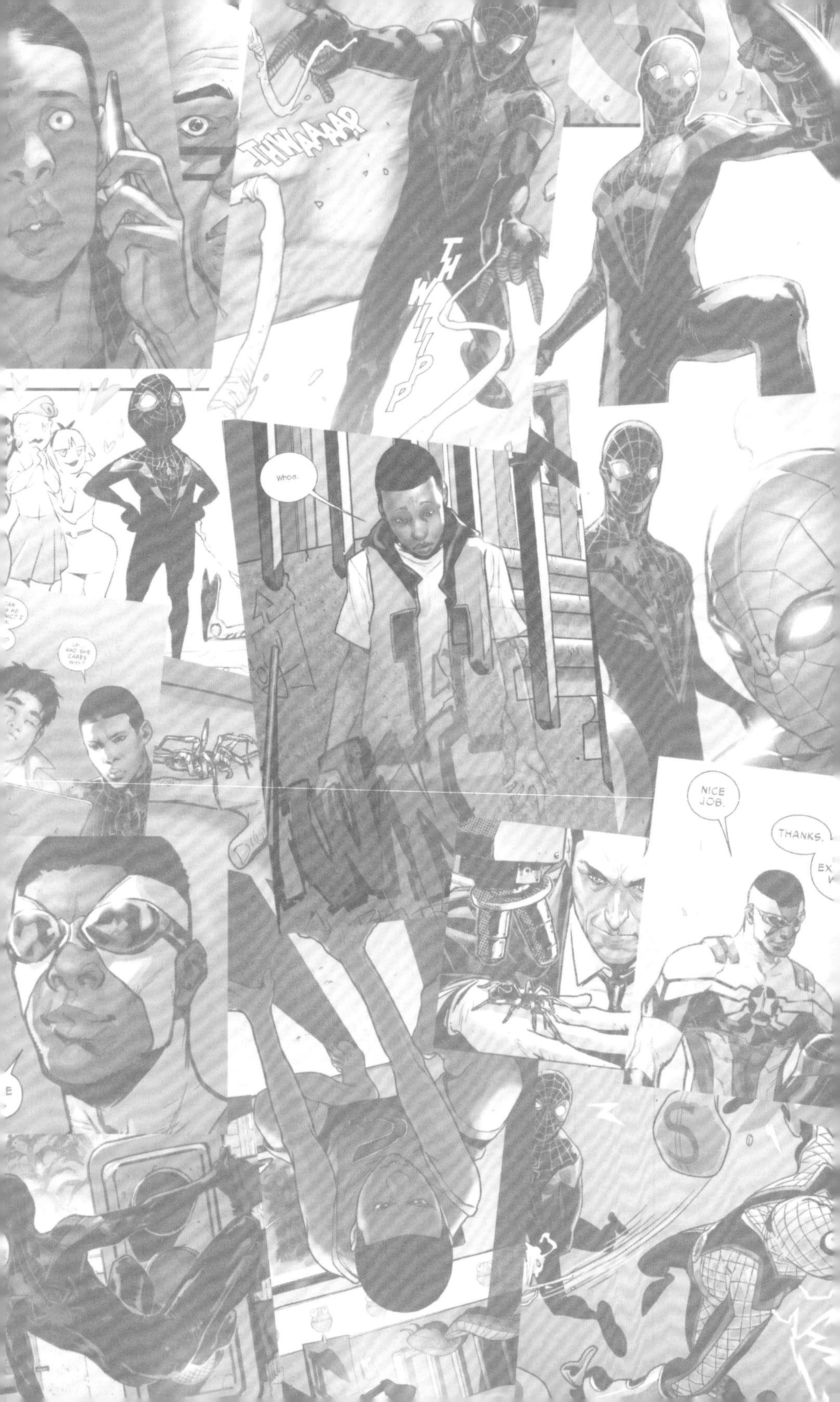
THWAAAP
THWIIPP
Whoa.
UH... AND SHE CARES WHY?
NICE JOB.
THANKS.

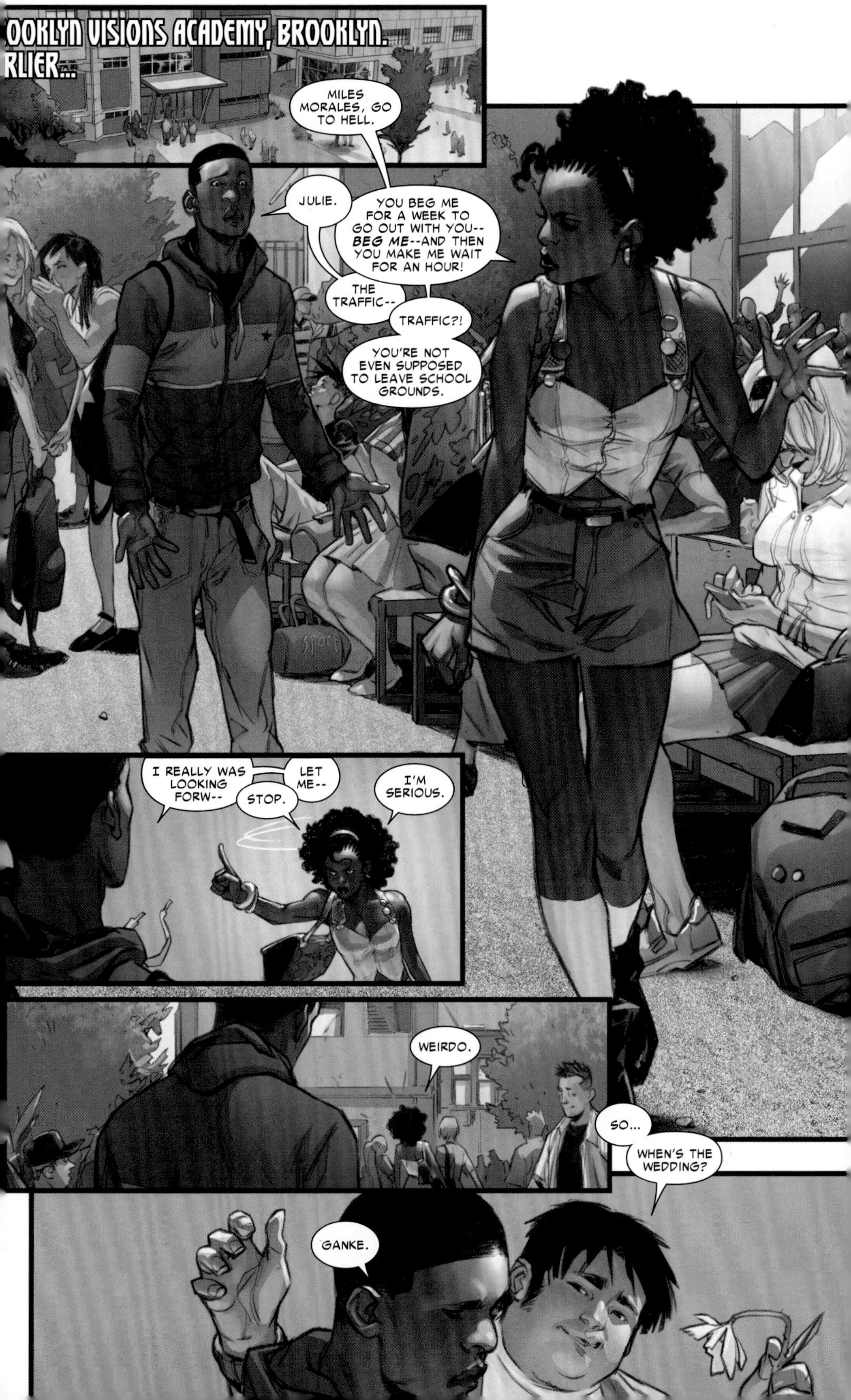
OOKLYN VISIONS ACADEMY, BROOKLYN.
RLIER...
MILES MORALES, GO TO HELL.
JULIE.
YOU BEG ME FOR A WEEK TO GO OUT WITH YOU-- BEG ME--AND THEN YOU MAKE ME WAIT FOR AN HOUR!
THE TRAFFIC--
TRAFFIC?!
YOU'RE NOT EVEN SUPPOSED TO LEAVE SCHOOL GROUNDS.
I REALLY WAS LOOKING FORW--
LET ME--
STOP.
I'M SERIOUS.
WEIRDO.
SO...
WHEN'S THE WEDDING?
GANKE.

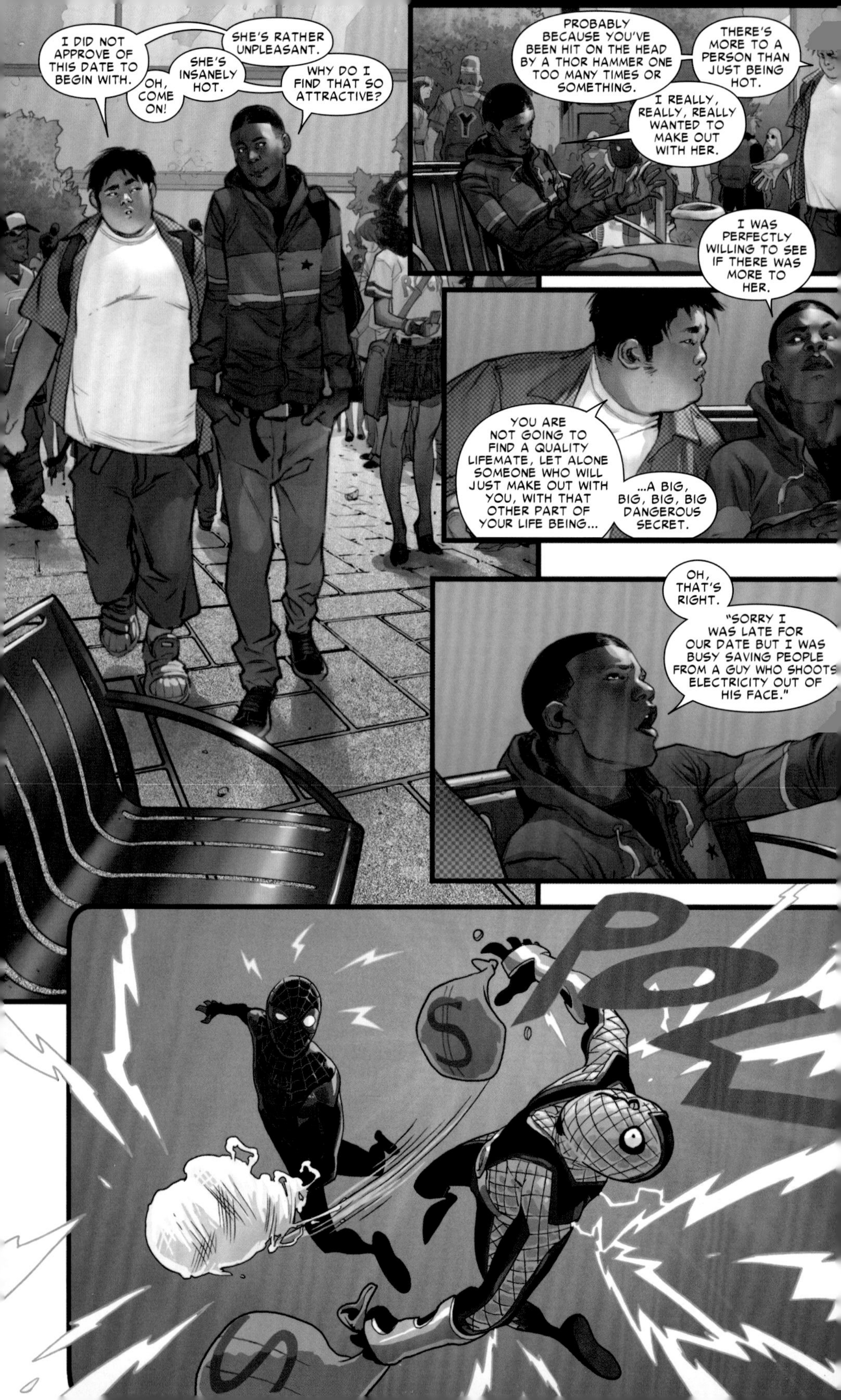
I DID NOT APPROVE OF THIS DATE TO BEGIN WITH.
SHE'S RATHER UNPLEASANT.
OH, COME ON!
SHE'S INSANELY HOT.
WHY DO I FIND THAT SO ATTRACTIVE?
PROBABLY BECAUSE YOU'VE BEEN HIT ON THE HEAD BY A THOR HAMMER ONE TOO MANY TIMES OR SOMETHING.
THERE'S MORE TO A PERSON THAN JUST BEING HOT.
I REALLY, REALLY, REALLY WANTED TO MAKE OUT WITH HER.
I WAS PERFECTLY WILLING TO SEE IF THERE WAS MORE TO HER.
YOU ARE NOT GOING TO FIND A QUALITY LIFEMATE, LET ALONE SOMEONE WHO WILL JUST MAKE OUT WITH YOU, WITH THAT OTHER PART OF YOUR LIFE BEING...
...A BIG, BIG, BIG, BIG DANGEROUS SECRET.
OH, THAT'S RIGHT.
"SORRY I WAS LATE FOR OUR DATE BUT I WAS BUSY SAVING PEOPLE FROM A GUY WHO SHOOTS ELECTRICITY OUT OF HIS FACE."
POW

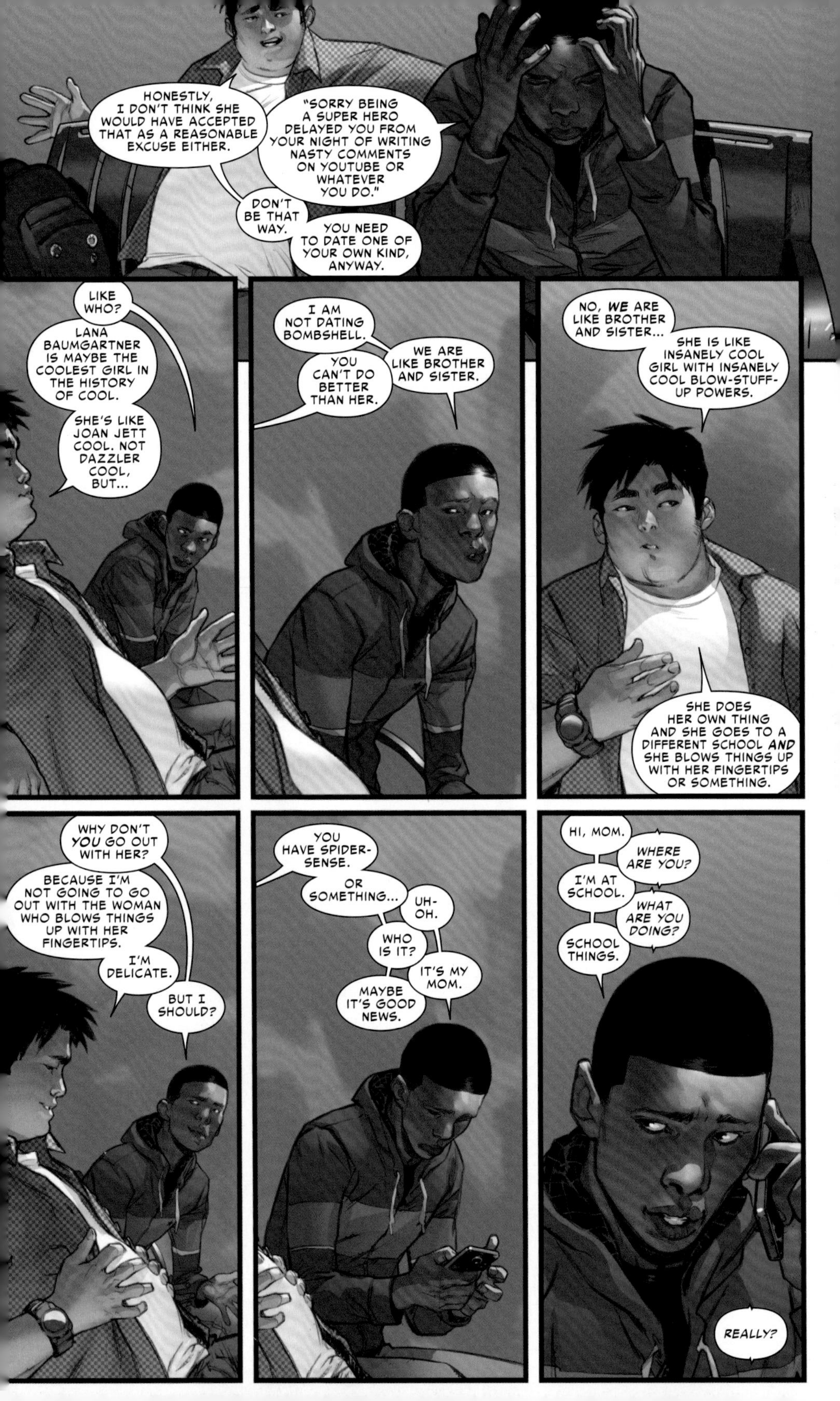
HONESTLY, I DON'T THINK SHE WOULD HAVE ACCEPTED THAT AS A REASONABLE EXCUSE EITHER.
"SORRY BEING A SUPER HERO DELAYED YOU FROM YOUR NIGHT OF WRITING NASTY COMMENTS ON YOUTUBE OR WHATEVER YOU DO."
DON'T BE THAT WAY.
YOU NEED TO DATE ONE OF YOUR OWN KIND, ANYWAY.
LIKE WHO?
LANA BAUMGARTNER IS MAYBE THE COOLEST GIRL IN THE HISTORY OF COOL.
SHE'S LIKE JOAN JETT COOL. NOT DAZZLER COOL, BUT...
I AM NOT DATING BOMBSHELL.
WE ARE LIKE BROTHER AND SISTER.
YOU CAN'T DO BETTER THAN HER.
NO, WE ARE LIKE BROTHER AND SISTER...
SHE IS LIKE INSANELY COOL GIRL WITH INSANELY COOL BLOW-STUFF-UP POWERS.
SHE DOES HER OWN THING AND SHE GOES TO A DIFFERENT SCHOOL AND SHE BLOWS THINGS UP WITH HER FINGERTIPS OR SOMETHING.
WHY DON'T YOU GO OUT WITH HER?
BECAUSE I'M NOT GOING TO GO OUT WITH THE WOMAN WHO BLOWS THINGS UP WITH HER FINGERTIPS.
I'M DELICATE.
BUT I SHOULD?
YOU HAVE SPIDER-SENSE.
OR SOMETHING...
UH-OH.
WHO IS IT?
IT'S MY MOM.
MAYBE IT'S GOOD NEWS.
HI, MOM.
WHERE ARE YOU?
I'M AT SCHOOL.
WHAT ARE YOU DOING?
SCHOOL THINGS.
REALLY?

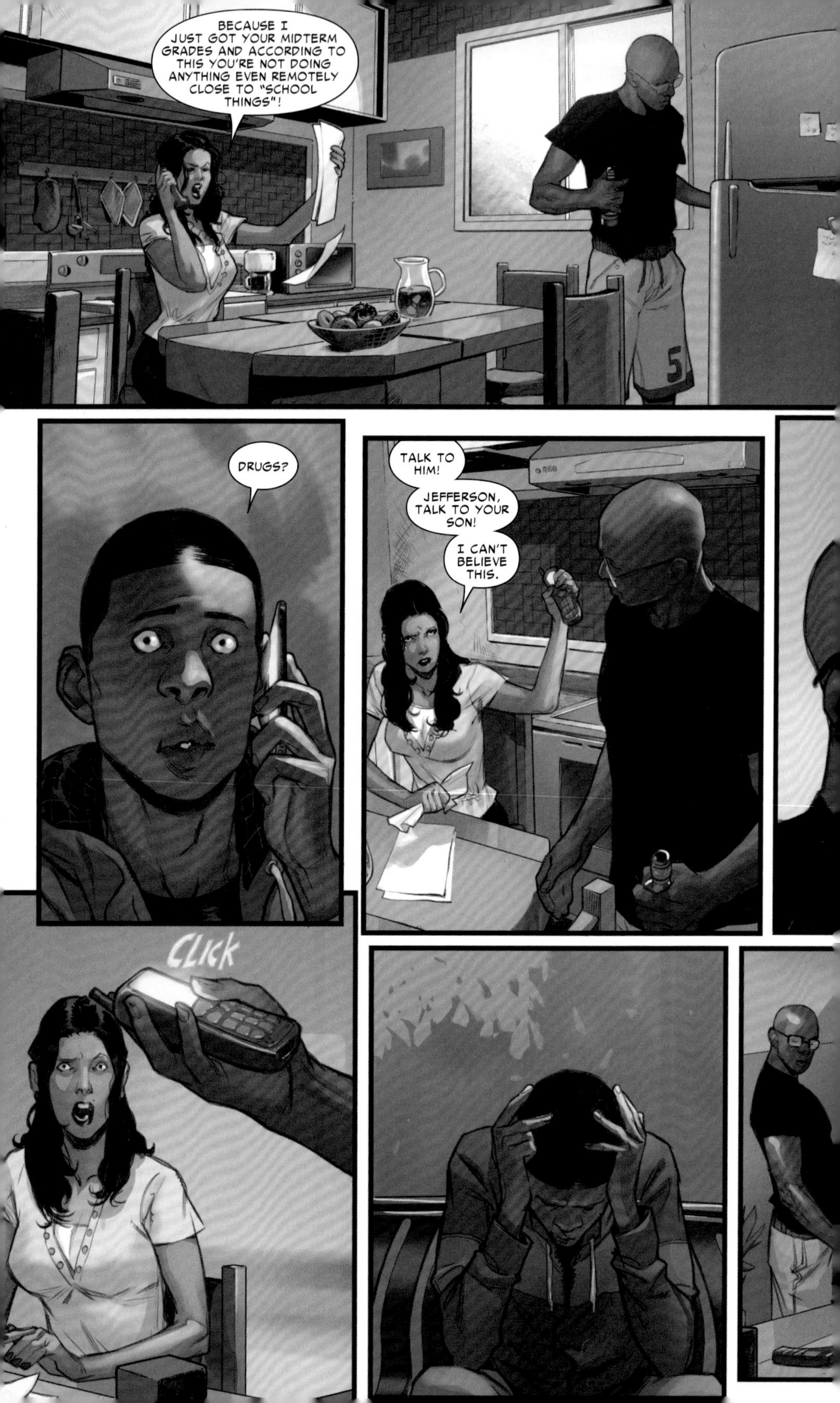
BECAUSE I JUST GOT YOUR MIDTERM GRADES AND ACCORDING TO THIS YOU'RE NOT DOING ANYTHING EVEN REMOTELY CLOSE TO "SCHOOL THINGS"!
DRUGS?
TALK TO HIM!
JEFFERSON, TALK TO YOUR SON!
I CAN'T BELIEVE THIS.
CLICK

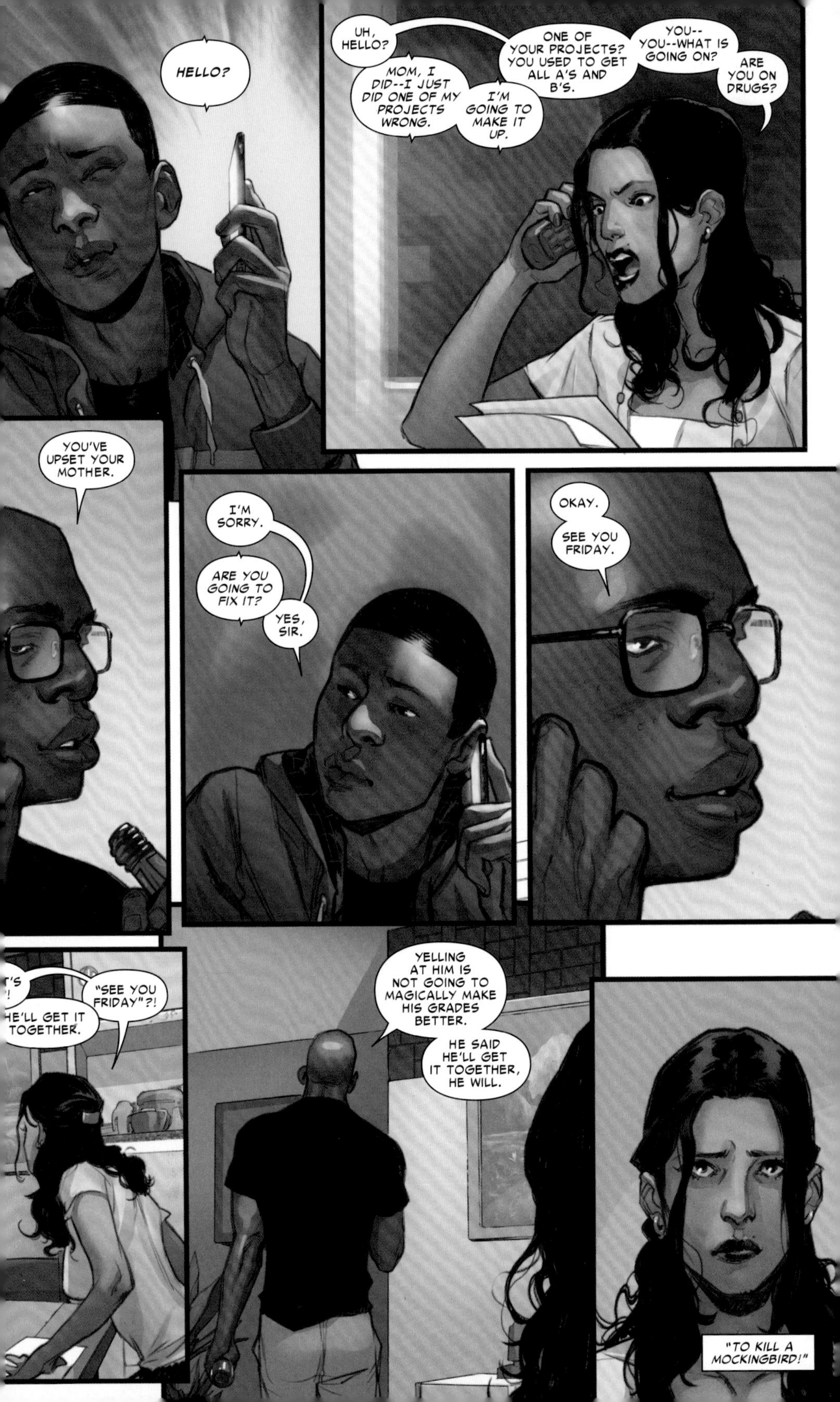
HELLO?
UH, HELLO?
MOM, I DID--I JUST DID ONE OF MY PROJECTS WRONG.
ONE OF YOUR PROJECTS? YOU USED TO GET ALL A'S AND B'S.
I'M GOING TO MAKE IT UP.
YOU-- YOU--WHAT IS GOING ON?
ARE YOU ON DRUGS?
YOU'VE UPSET YOUR MOTHER.
I'M SORRY.
ARE YOU GOING TO FIX IT?
YES, SIR.
OKAY.
SEE YOU FRIDAY.
HE'LL GET IT TOGETHER.
"SEE YOU FRIDAY"?!
YELLING AT HIM IS NOT GOING TO MAGICALLY MAKE HIS GRADES BETTER.
HE SAID HE'LL GET IT TOGETHER, HE WILL.
"TO KILL A MOCKINGBIRD!"

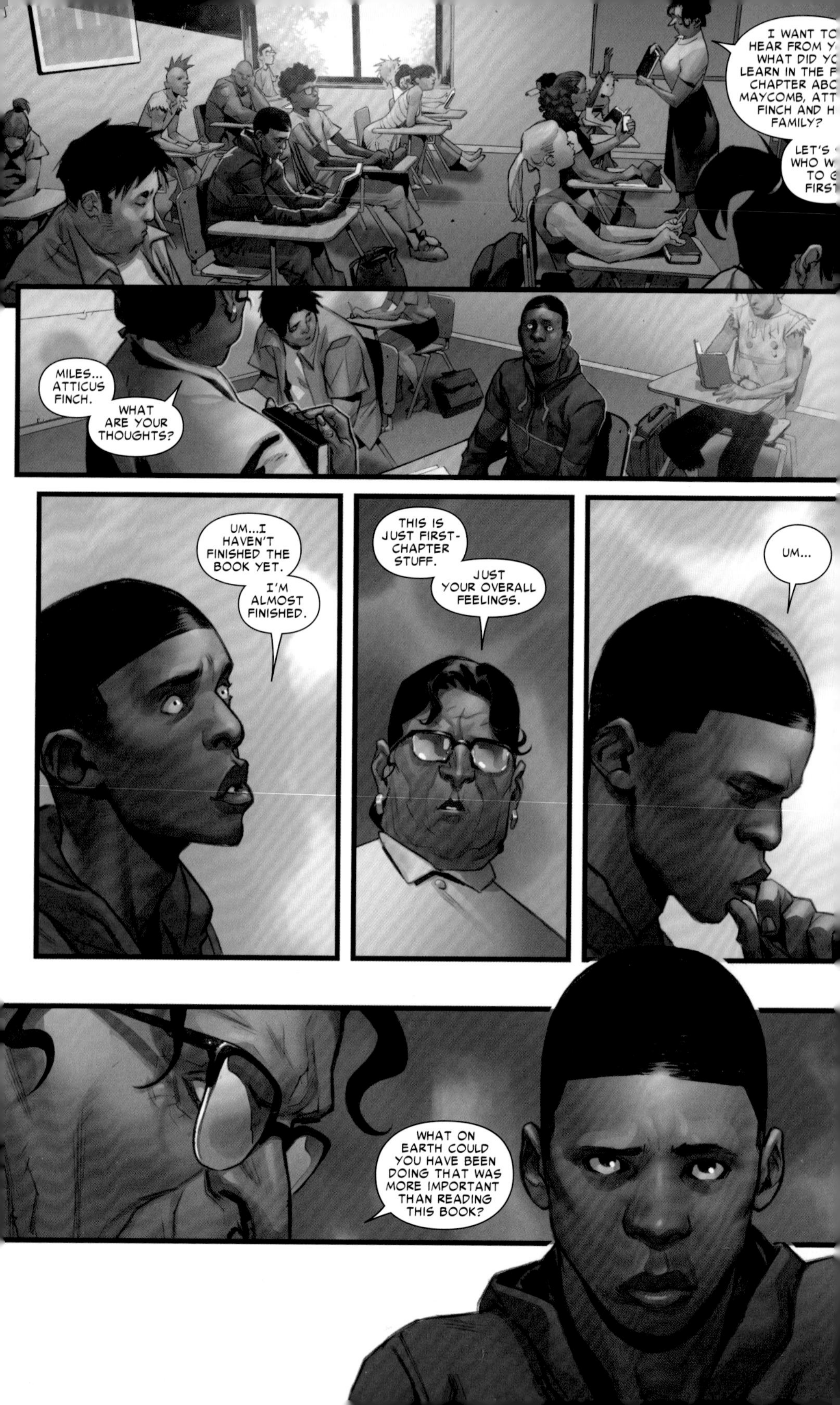
I WANT TO HEAR FROM Y WHAT DID YO LEARN IN THE F CHAPTER ABO MAYCOMB, ATT FINCH AND H FAMILY?
LET'S WHO W TO G FIRST
MILES... ATTICUS FINCH.
WHAT ARE YOUR THOUGHTS?
UM...I HAVEN'T FINISHED THE BOOK YET.
I'M ALMOST FINISHED.
THIS IS JUST FIRST-CHAPTER STUFF.
JUST YOUR OVERALL FEELINGS.
UM...
WHAT ON EARTH COULD YOU HAVE BEEN DOING THAT WAS MORE IMPORTANT THAN READING THIS BOOK?

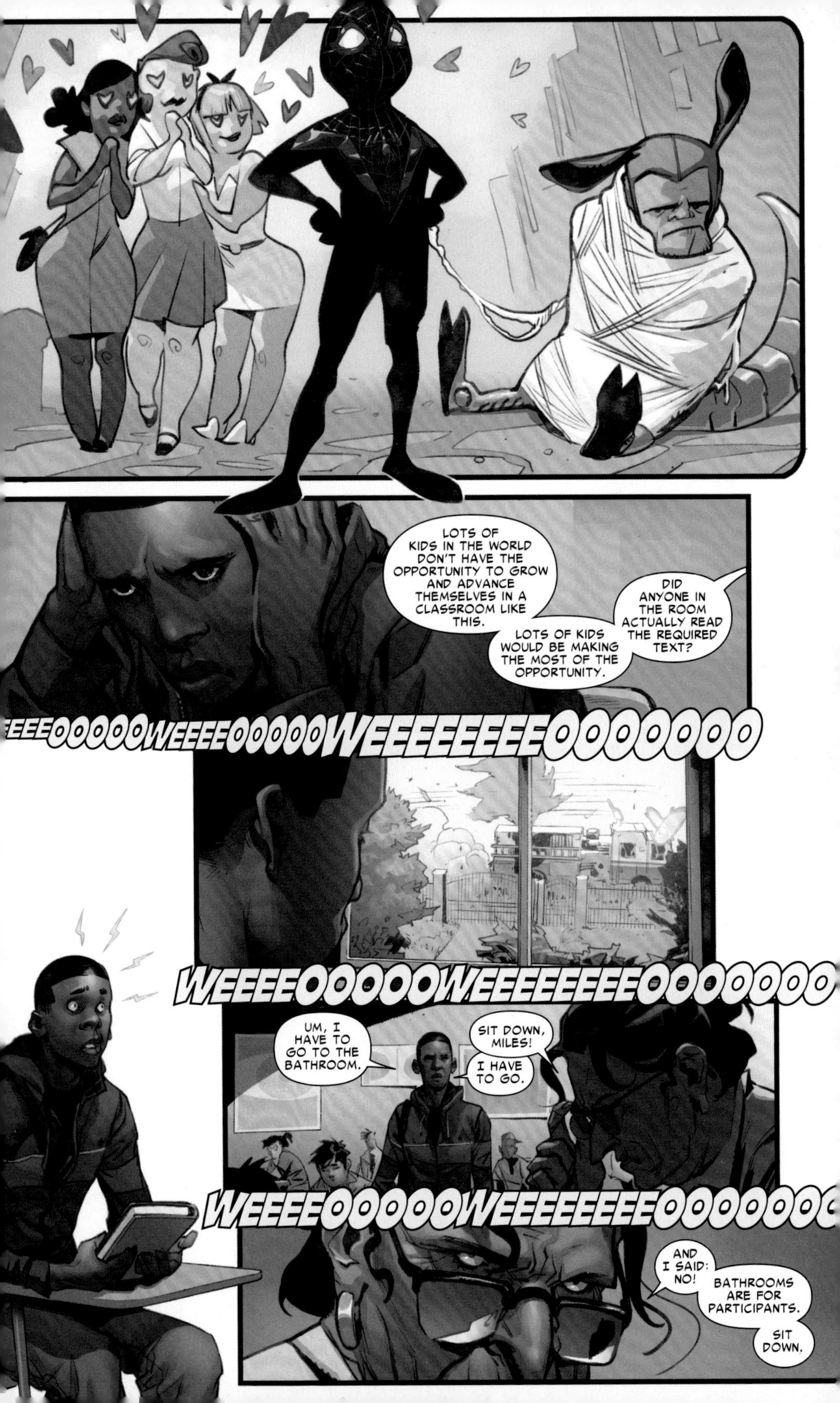
LOTS OF KIDS IN THE WORLD DON'T HAVE THE OPPORTUNITY TO GROW AND ADVANCE THEMSELVES IN A CLASSROOM LIKE THIS.
LOTS OF KIDS WOULD BE MAKING THE MOST OF THE OPPORTUNITY.
DID ANYONE IN THE ROOM ACTUALLY READ THE REQUIRED TEXT?
EEEOOOOOWEEEEOOOOOWEEEEEEEEEOOOOOOO
WEEEEOOOOOWEEEEEEEEEOOOOOOO
UM, I HAVE TO GO TO THE BATHROOM.
SIT DOWN, MILES!
I HAVE TO GO.
WEEEEOOOOOWEEEEEEEEEOOOOOO
AND I SAID: NO!
BATHROOMS ARE FOR PARTICIPANTS.
SIT DOWN.

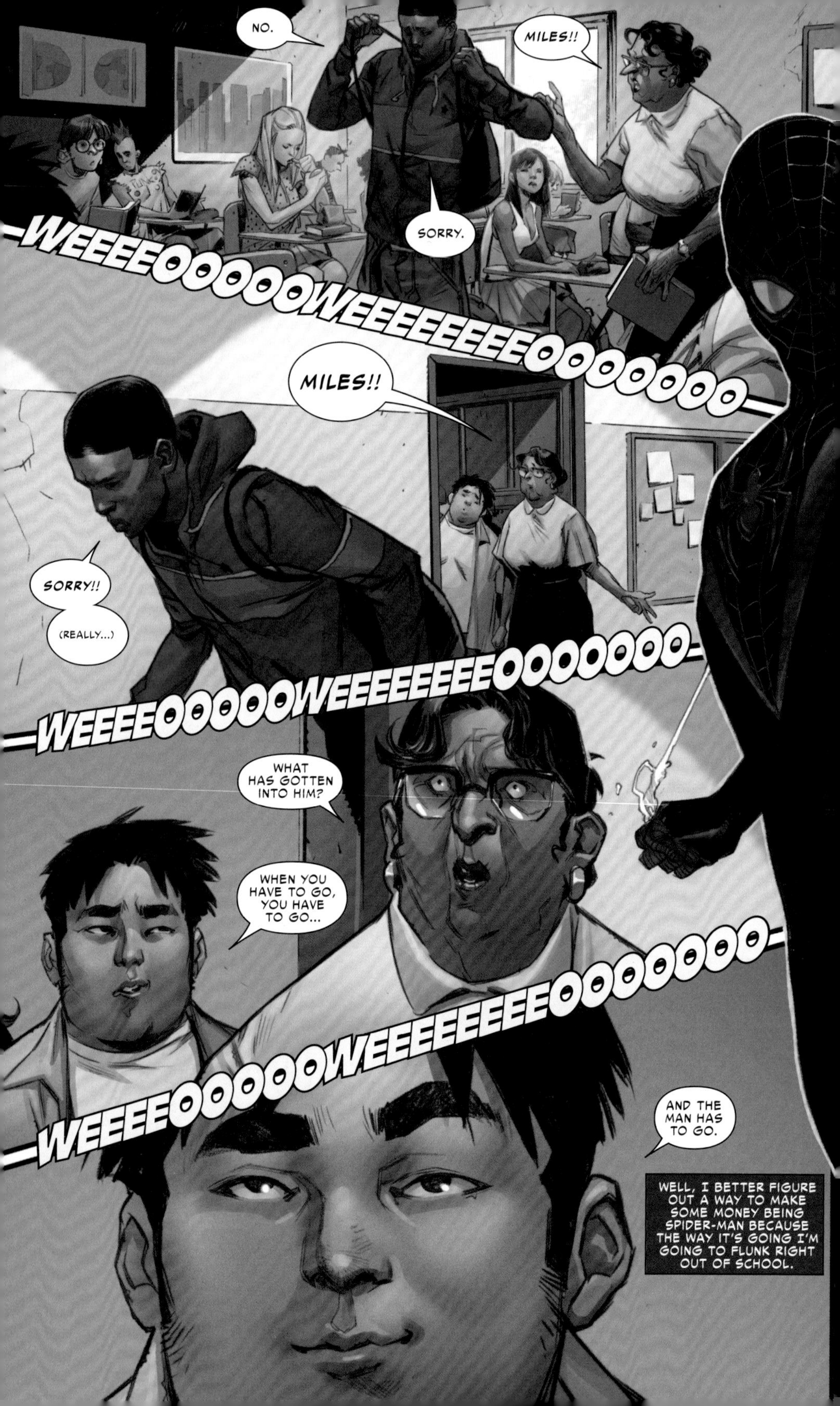
NO.
MILES!!
SORRY.
WEEEEOOOOOWEEEEEEEEEOOOOOOO
MILES!!
SORRY!!
(REALLY...)
WEEEEOOOOOWEEEEEEEEEOOOOOOO
WHAT HAS GOTTEN INTO HIM?
WHEN YOU HAVE TO GO, YOU HAVE TO GO...
WEEEEOOOOOWEEEEEEEEEOOOOOOO
AND THE MAN HAS TO GO.
WELL, I BETTER FIGURE OUT A WAY TO MAKE SOME MONEY BEING SPIDER-MAN BECAUSE THE WAY IT'S GOING I'M GOING TO FLUNK RIGHT OUT OF SCHOOL.

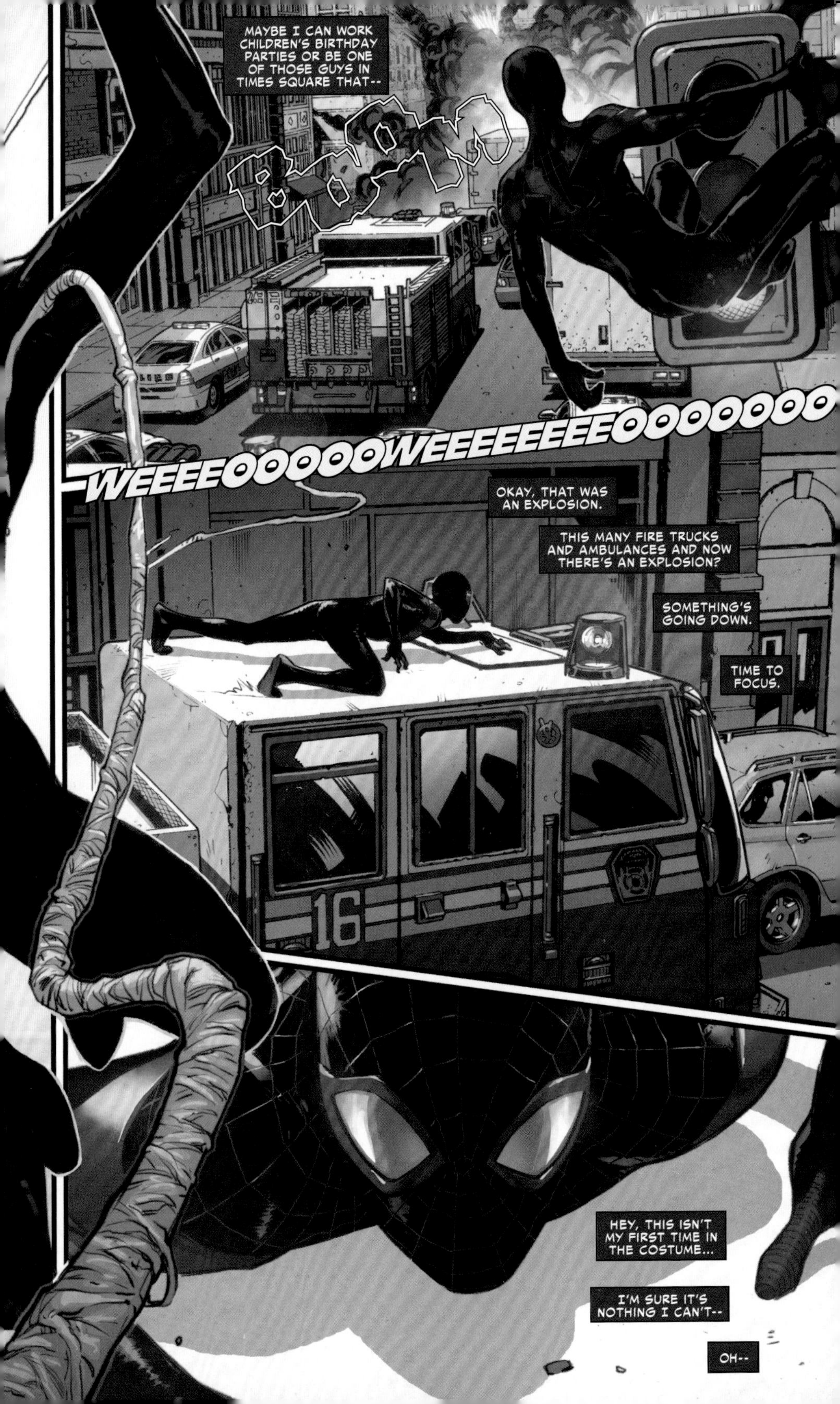
MAYBE I CAN WORK CHILDREN'S BIRTHDAY PARTIES OR BE ONE OF THOSE GUYS IN TIMES SQUARE THAT--
BOOM
WEEEEOOOOOWEEEEEEEEOOOOOOOO
OKAY, THAT WAS AN EXPLOSION.
THIS MANY FIRE TRUCKS AND AMBULANCES AND NOW THERE'S AN EXPLOSION?
SOMETHING'S GOING DOWN.
TIME TO FOCUS.
16
HEY, THIS ISN'T MY FIRST TIME IN THE COSTUME...
I'M SURE IT'S NOTHING I CAN'T--
OH--

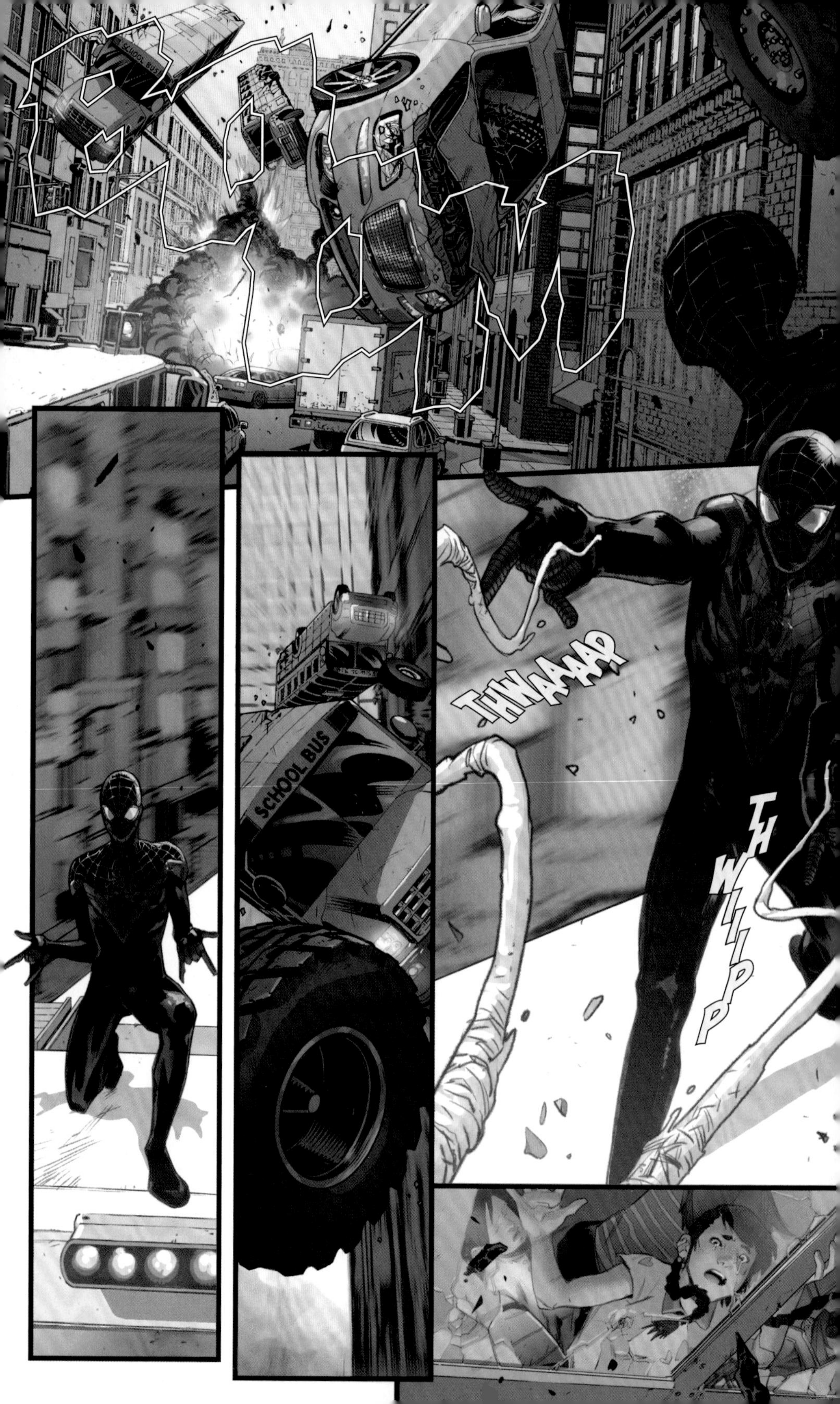
SCHOOL BUS
BOOM
SCHOOL BUS
THWAAAP
THWIIIPP

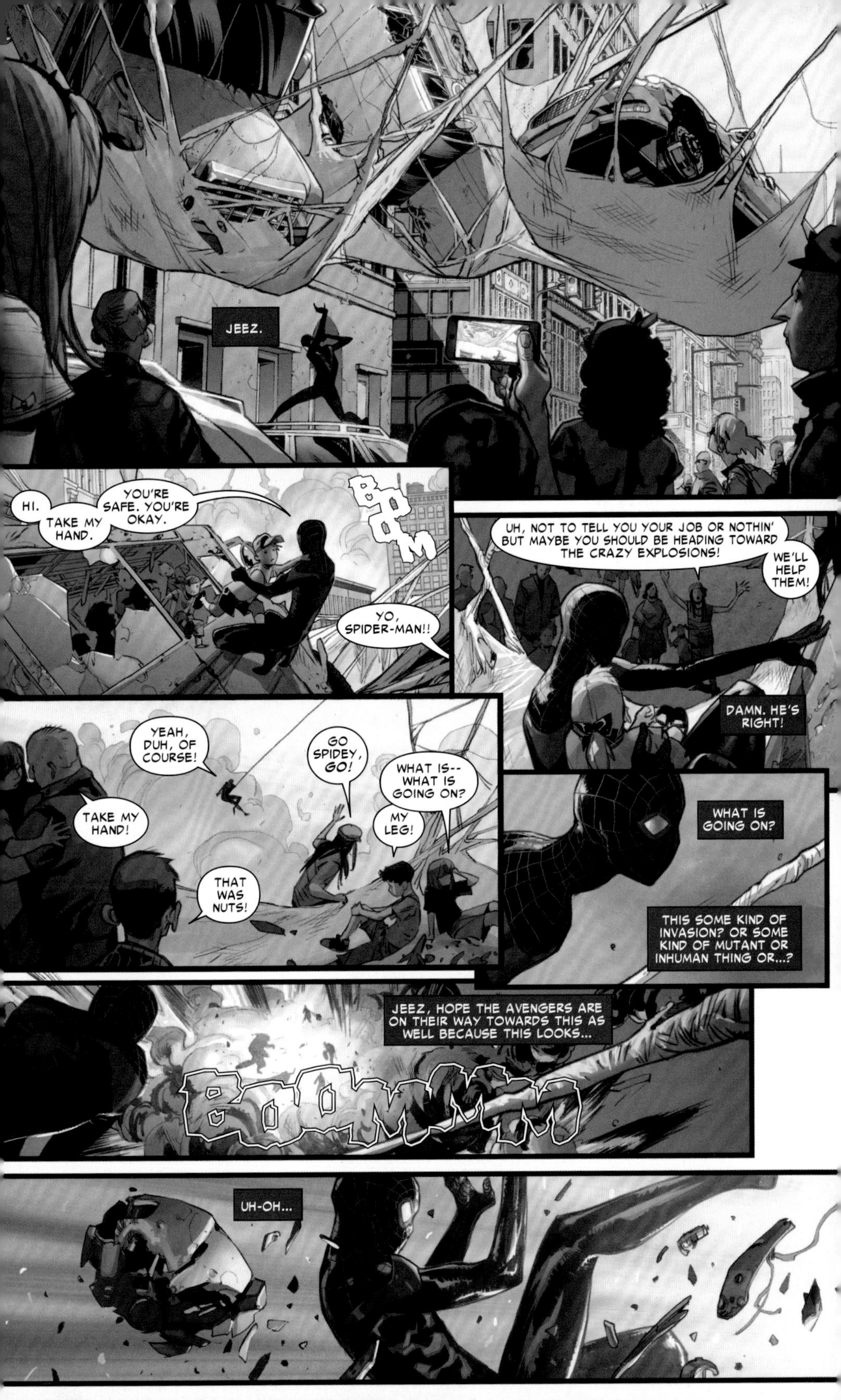
JEEZ.
HI.
TAKE MY HAND.
YOU'RE SAFE. YOU'RE OKAY.
BOOM
YO, SPIDER-MAN!!
UH, NOT TO TELL YOU YOUR JOB OR NOTHIN' BUT MAYBE YOU SHOULD BE HEADING TOWARD THE CRAZY EXPLOSIONS!
WE'LL HELP THEM!
DAMN. HE'S RIGHT!
YEAH, DUH, OF COURSE!
TAKE MY HAND!
GO SPIDEY, GO!
WHAT IS-- WHAT IS GOING ON?
MY LEG!
THAT WAS NUTS!
WHAT IS GOING ON?
THIS SOME KIND OF INVASION? OR SOME KIND OF MUTANT OR INHUMAN THING OR...?
JEEZ, HOPE THE AVENGERS ARE ON THEIR WAY TOWARDS THIS AS WELL BECAUSE THIS LOOKS...
BOOMMMM
UH-OH...

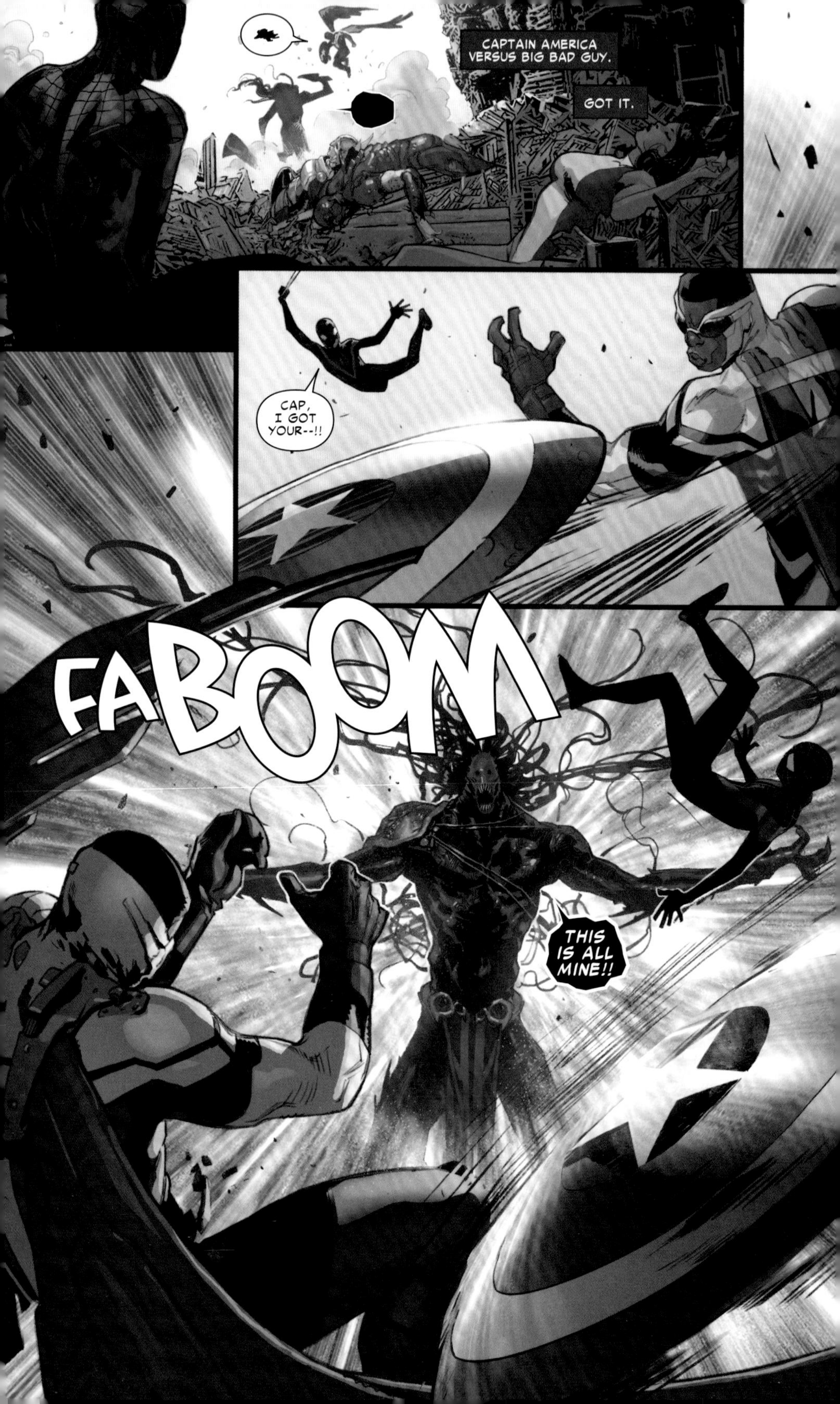
CAPTAIN AMERICA VERSUS BIG BAD GUY.
GOT IT.
CAP, I GOT YOUR--!!
FABOOM
THIS IS ALL MINE!!

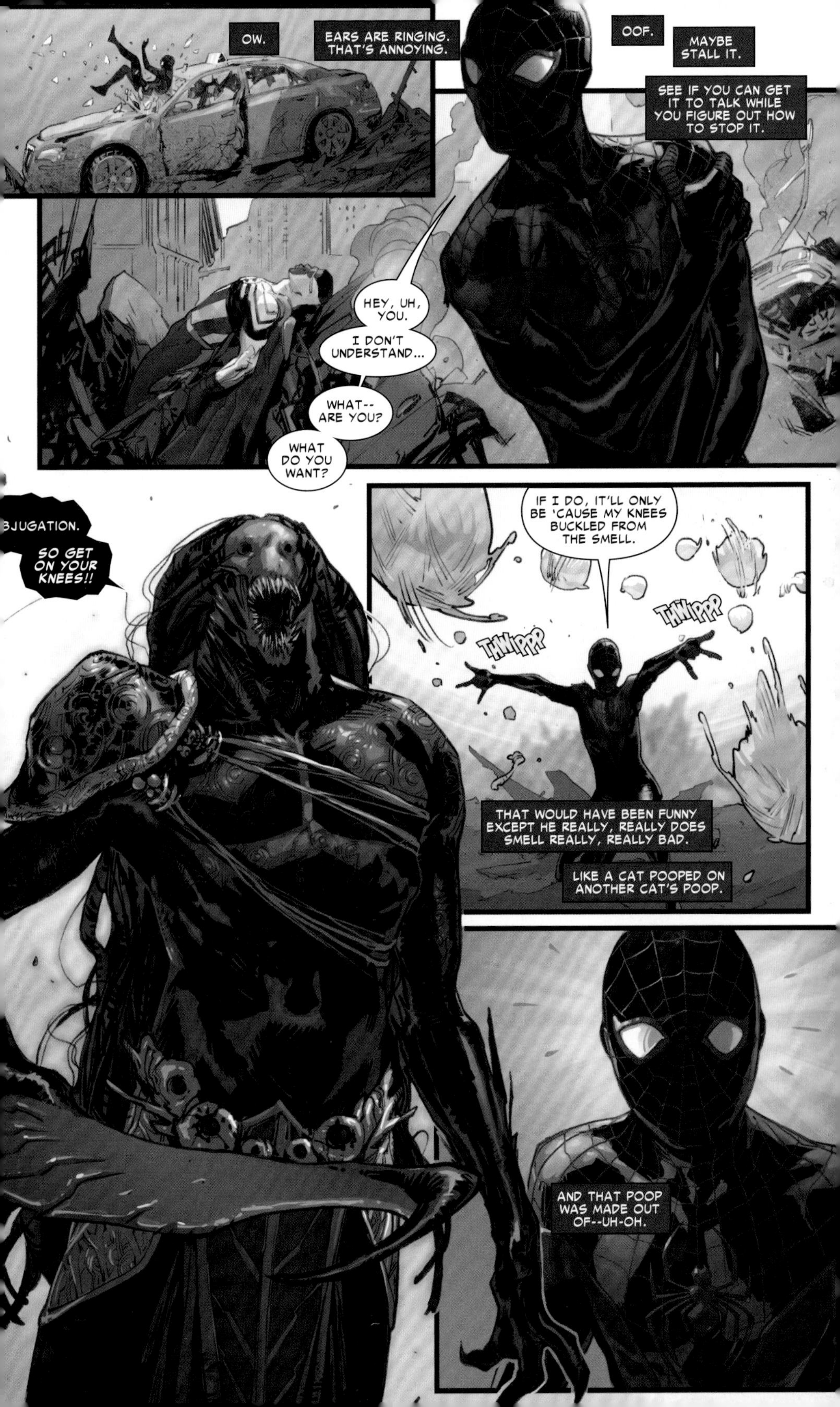

OW.
EARS ARE RINGING. THAT'S ANNOYING.
OOF.
MAYBE STALL IT.
SEE IF YOU CAN GET IT TO TALK WHILE YOU FIGURE OUT HOW TO STOP IT.
HEY, UH, YOU.
I DON'T UNDERSTAND...
WHAT-- ARE YOU?
WHAT DO YOU WANT?
BJUGATION.
SO GET ON YOUR KNEES!!
IF I DO, IT'LL ONLY BE 'CAUSE MY KNEES BUCKLED FROM THE SMELL.
THWIPPP
THWIPPP
THAT WOULD HAVE BEEN FUNNY EXCEPT HE REALLY, REALLY DOES SMELL REALLY, REALLY BAD.
LIKE A CAT POOPED ON ANOTHER CAT'S POOP.
AND THAT POOP WAS MADE OUT OF--UH-OH.

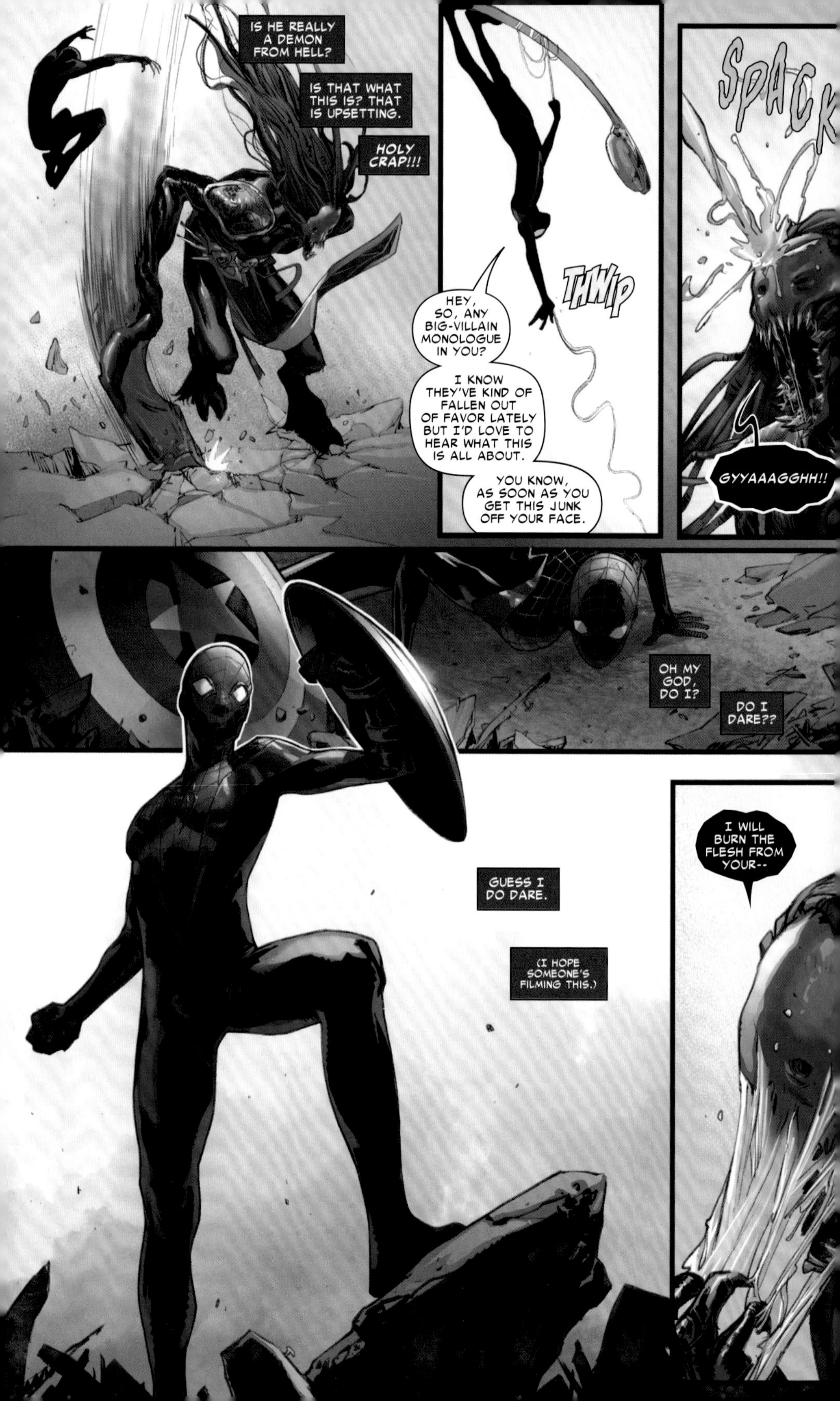

IS HE REALLY A DEMON FROM HELL?
IS THAT WHAT THIS IS? THAT IS UPSETTING.
HOLY CRAP!!!
HEY, SO, ANY BIG-VILLAIN MONOLOGUE IN YOU?
THWIP
I KNOW THEY'VE KIND OF FALLEN OUT OF FAVOR LATELY BUT I'D LOVE TO HEAR WHAT THIS IS ALL ABOUT.
YOU KNOW, AS SOON AS YOU GET THIS JUNK OFF YOUR FACE.
SPACK
GYYAAAGGHH!!
OH MY GOD, DO I?
DO I DARE??
GUESS I DO DARE.
(I HOPE SOMEONE'S FILMING THIS.)
I WILL BURN THE FLESH FROM YOUR--

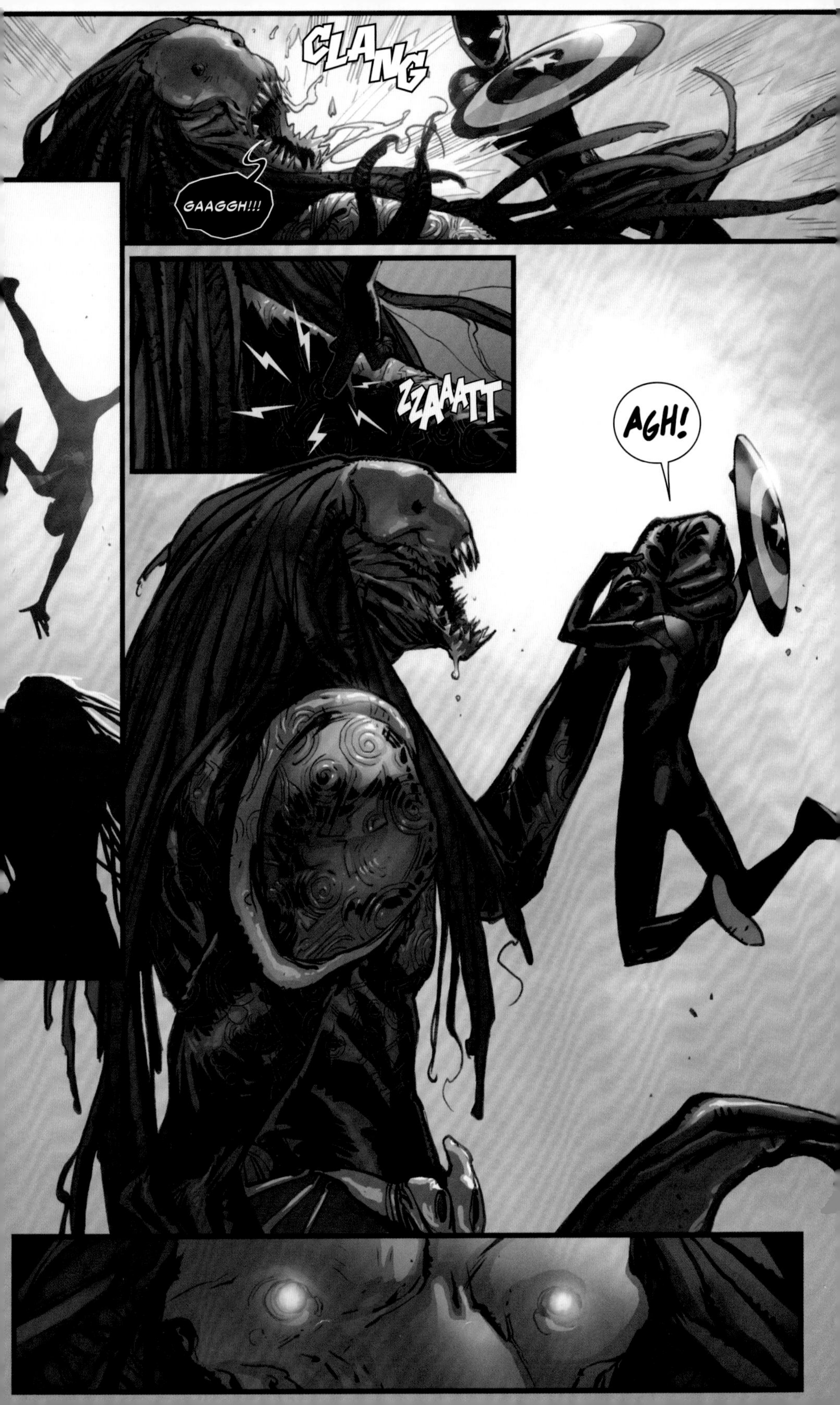
CLANG
GAAGGH!!!
ZZAAATT
AGH!

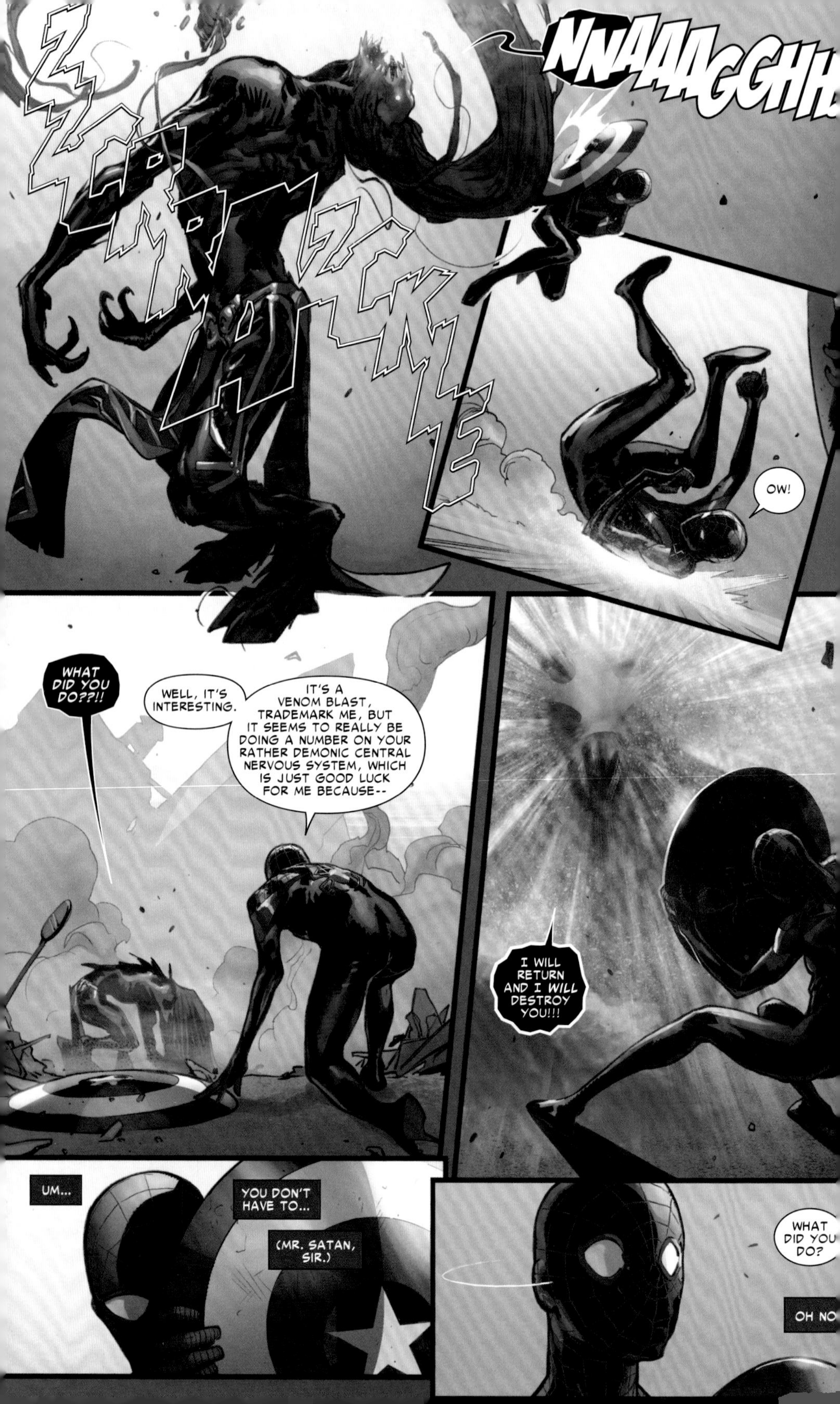
ZZAAKK
NNAAAAGGHH
OW!
WHAT DID YOU DO??!!
WELL, IT'S INTERESTING.
IT'S A VENOM BLAST, TRADEMARK ME, BUT IT SEEMS TO REALLY BE DOING A NUMBER ON YOUR RATHER DEMONIC CENTRAL NERVOUS SYSTEM, WHICH IS JUST GOOD LUCK FOR ME BECAUSE--
I WILL RETURN AND I WILL DESTROY YOU!!!
UM...
YOU DON'T HAVE TO...
(MR. SATAN, SIR.)
WHAT DID YOU DO?
OH NO

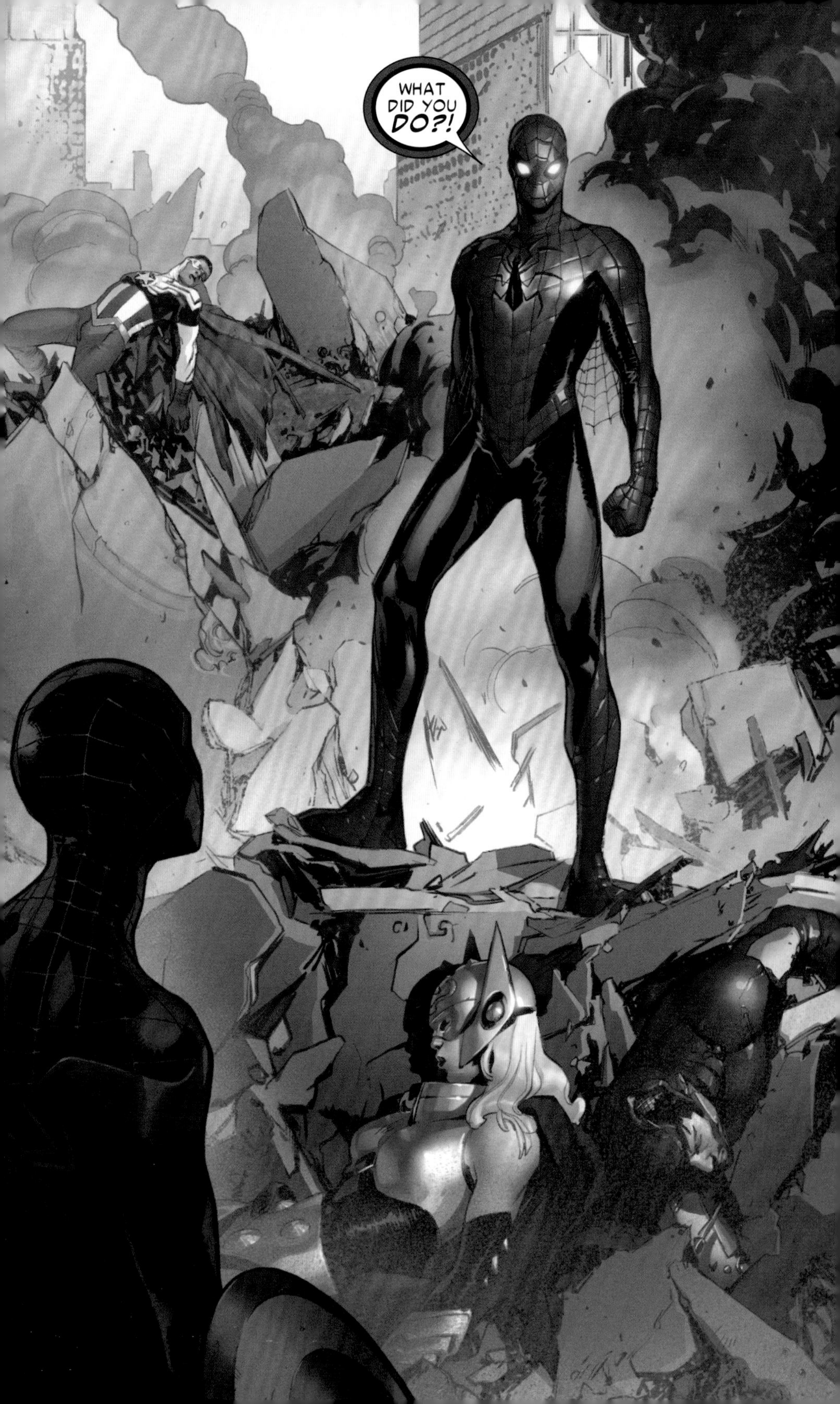
WHAT DID YOU DO?!

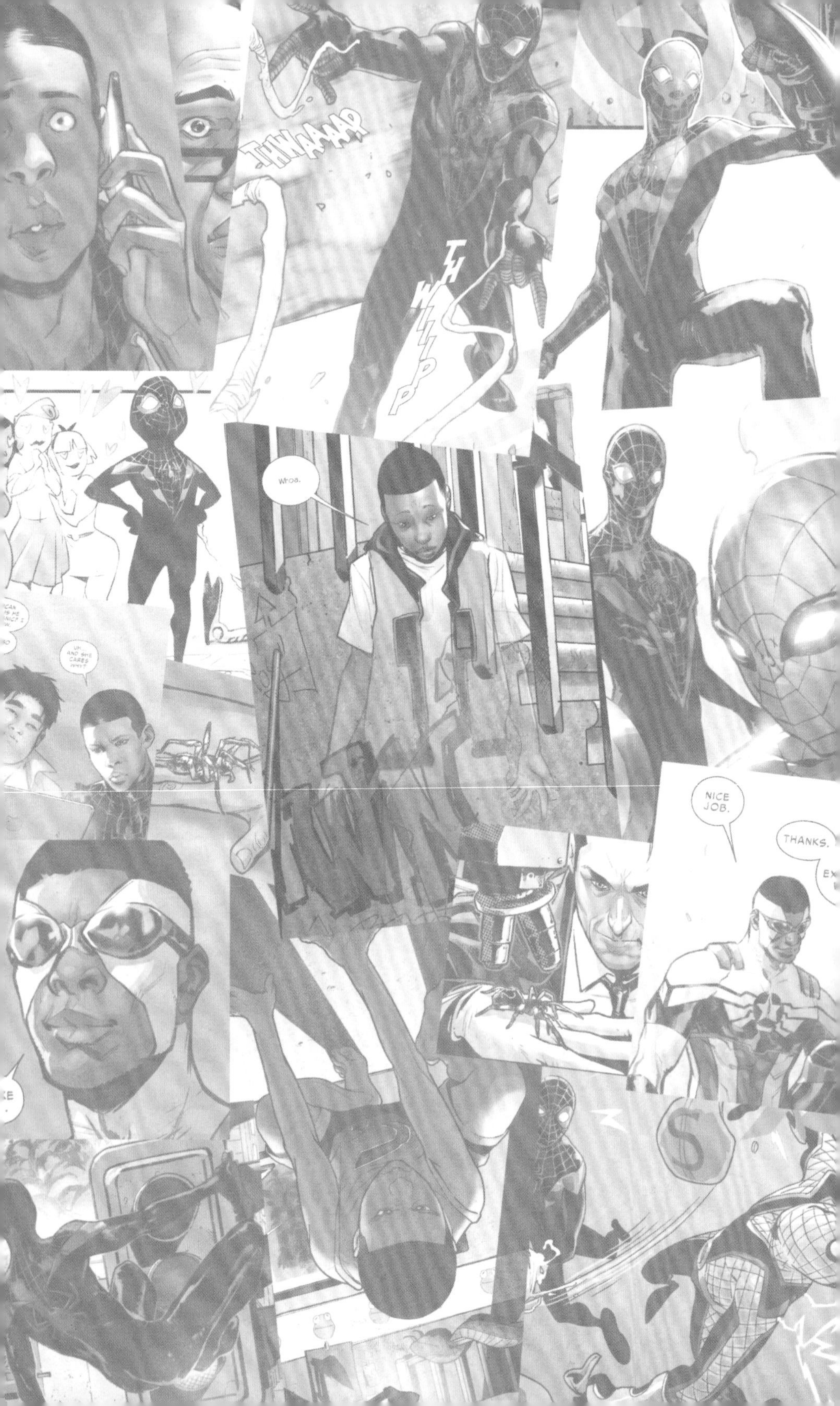
THWAAAAP
Whoa.
UH... AND SHE CARES WHY?
NICE JOB.
THANKS.

SPIDER-MAN (2016) #2

NEW YORK CITY.
REALLY.

DUDE, SERIOUSLY, WHAT DID YOU DO?

I DIDN'T DO THIS.

NO, I JUST GOT HERE. I DIDN'T DO THIS.

OH MY GOD, IT'S-- IT'S HIM.

NO.

WHO WAS HERE?

IT WAS, LIKE, A DEMON OR SOMETHING...

"DEMON?" DID HE GIVE A NAME?

NOT REALLY... BUT HE WAS SMACKING AROUND ALL OF THE AVENGERS AND I JUST GOT HERE AND--

HE BEAT IRON MAN'S ARMOR RIGHT OFF HIS BUTT, BUT THEN HE SAW YOU AND HE RAN?

NOT BEFORE THREATENING ME AND--AND EVERYTHING ELSE.

WHAT COLOR WAS HE? RED?

BLACK.

GOOD, NOT THE RED ONE. (HATE THE RED ONE.)

YOU BELIEVE ME?

TONY?? YOU HOO!!

I BELIEVE YOU.

WHO WOULD (UP A ST LIKE TH

WE TO C AMBL

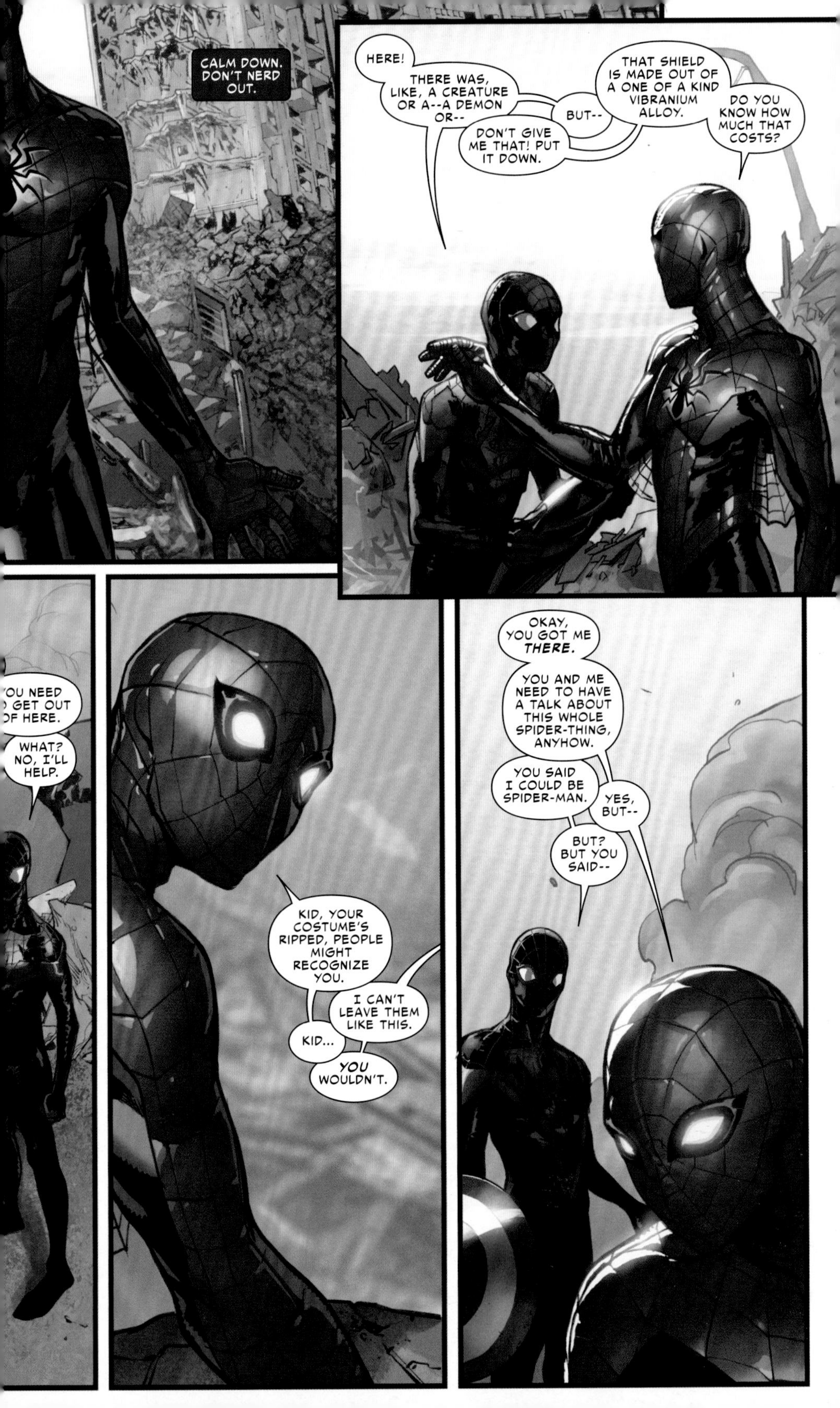
CALM DOWN. DON'T NERD OUT.
HERE!
THERE WAS, LIKE, A CREATURE OR A--A DEMON OR--
DON'T GIVE ME THAT! PUT IT DOWN.
BUT--
THAT SHIELD IS MADE OUT OF A ONE OF A KIND VIBRANIUM ALLOY.
DO YOU KNOW HOW MUCH THAT COSTS?
YOU NEED TO GET OUT OF HERE.
WHAT? NO, I'LL HELP.
KID, YOUR COSTUME'S RIPPED, PEOPLE MIGHT RECOGNIZE YOU.
I CAN'T LEAVE THEM LIKE THIS.
KID...
YOU WOULDN'T.
OKAY, YOU GOT ME THERE.
YOU AND ME NEED TO HAVE A TALK ABOUT THIS WHOLE SPIDER-THING, ANYHOW.
YOU SAID I COULD BE SPIDER-MAN.
YES, BUT--
BUT? BUT YOU SAID--

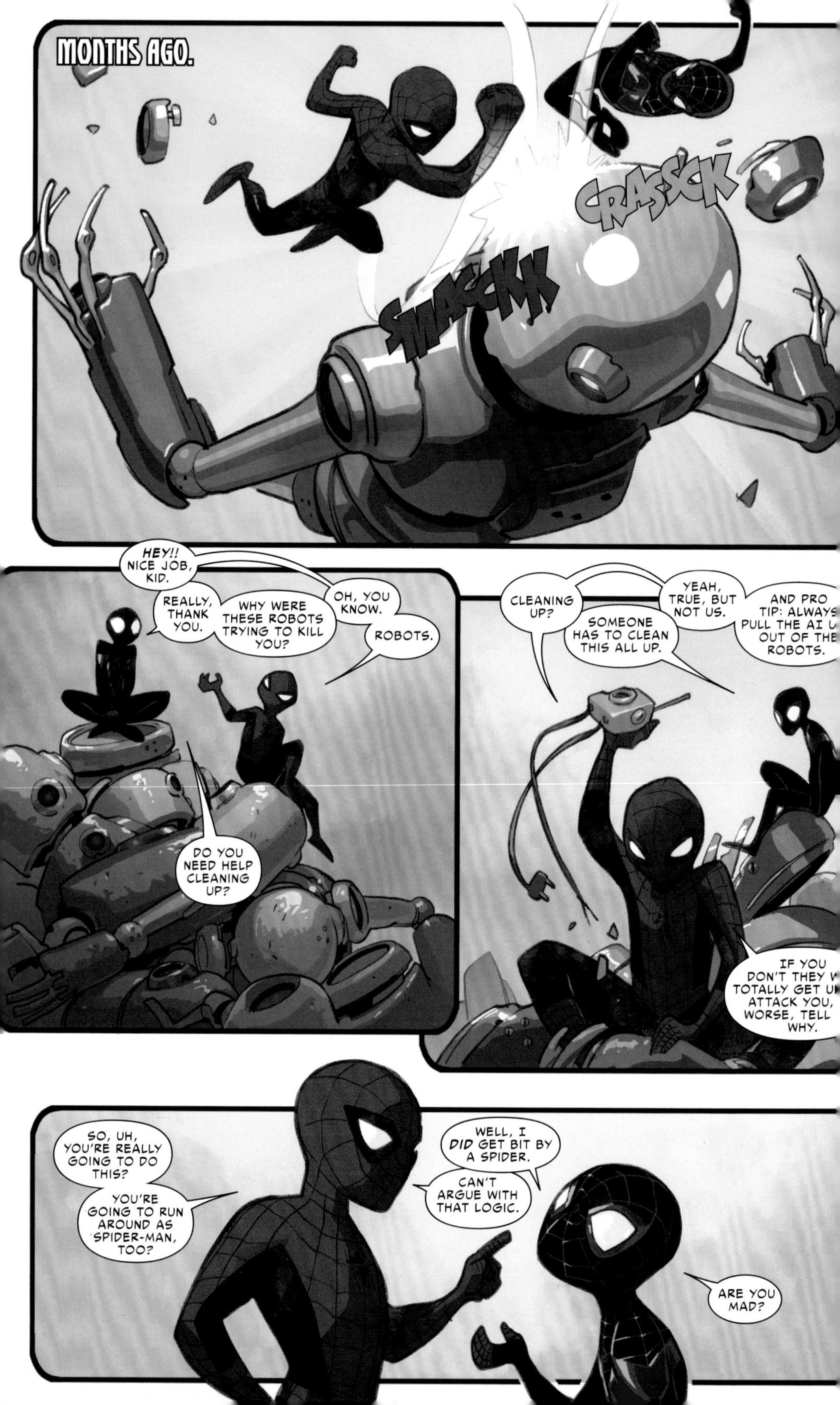

MONTHS AGO.
CRASSCK
SMACCKK
HEY!! NICE JOB, KID.
REALLY, THANK YOU.
OH, YOU KNOW.
ROBOTS.
WHY WERE THESE ROBOTS TRYING TO KILL YOU?
DO YOU NEED HELP CLEANING UP?
CLEANING UP?
YEAH, TRUE, BUT NOT US.
SOMEONE HAS TO CLEAN THIS ALL UP.
AND PRO TIP: ALWAYS PULL THE AI OUT OF THE ROBOTS.
IF YOU DON'T THEY TOTALLY GET UP ATTACK YOU, WORSE, TELL WHY.
SO, UH, YOU'RE REALLY GOING TO DO THIS?
YOU'RE GOING TO RUN AROUND AS SPIDER-MAN, TOO?
WELL, I *DID* GET BIT BY A SPIDER.
CAN'T ARGUE WITH THAT LOGIC.
ARE YOU MAD?

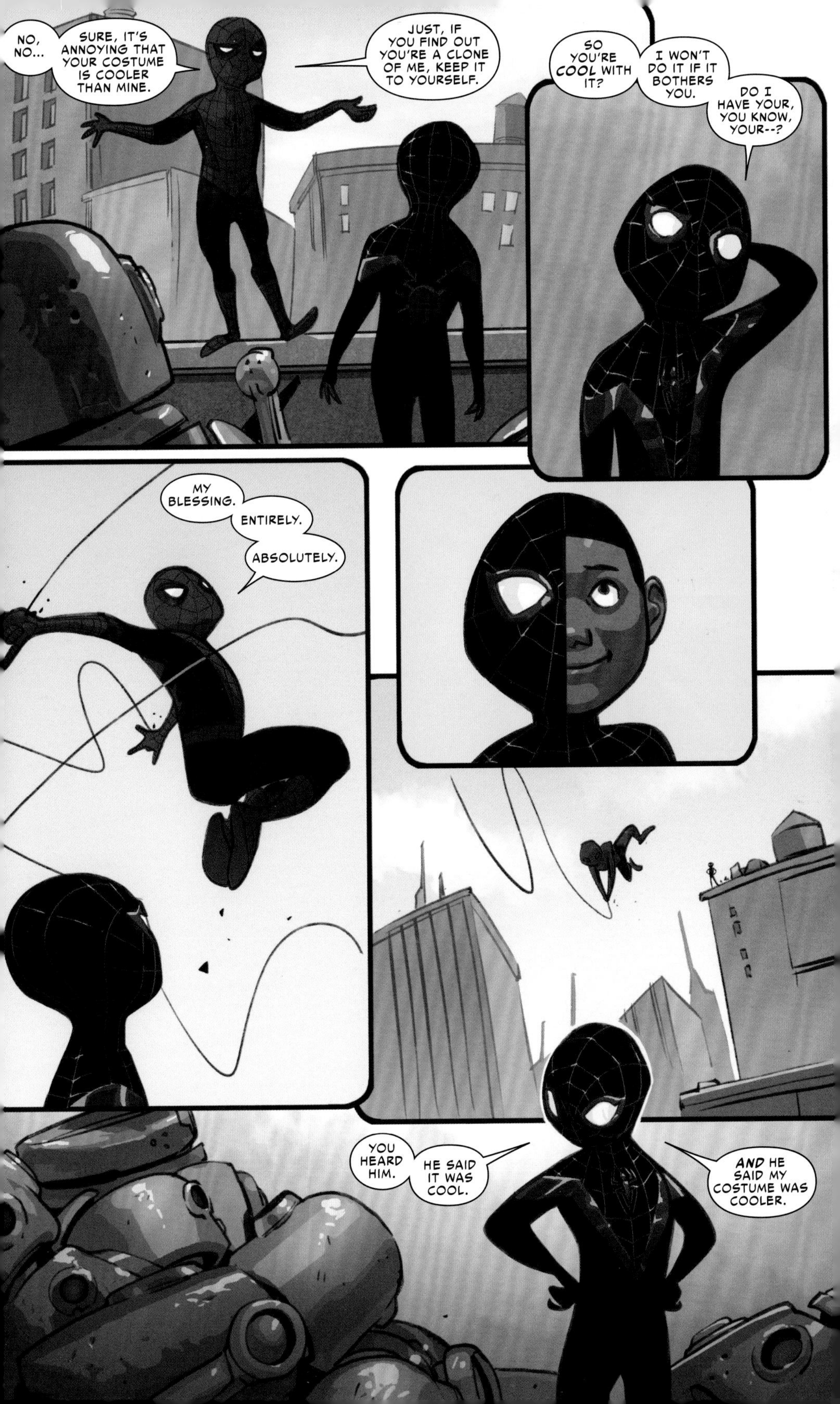
NO, NO...
SURE, IT'S ANNOYING THAT YOUR COSTUME IS COOLER THAN MINE.
JUST, IF YOU FIND OUT YOU'RE A CLONE OF ME, KEEP IT TO YOURSELF.
SO YOU'RE COOL WITH IT?
I WON'T DO IT IF IT BOTHERS YOU.
DO I HAVE YOUR, YOU KNOW, YOUR--?
MY BLESSING.
ENTIRELY.
ABSOLUTELY.
YOU HEARD HIM.
HE SAID IT WAS COOL.
AND HE SAID MY COSTUME WAS COOLER.

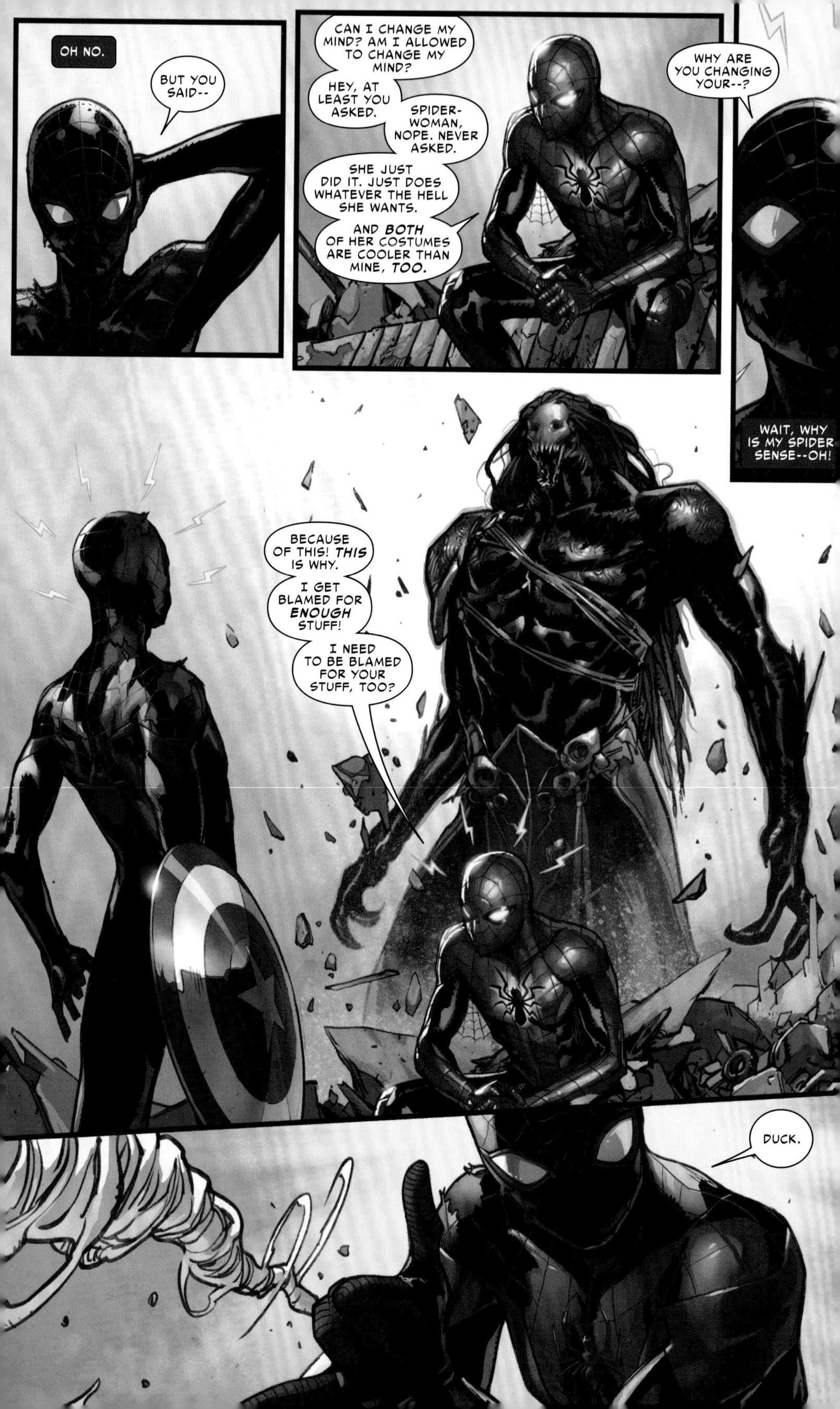
OH NO.
BUT YOU SAID--
CAN I CHANGE MY MIND? AM I ALLOWED TO CHANGE MY MIND?
HEY, AT LEAST YOU ASKED.
SPIDER-WOMAN, NOPE. NEVER ASKED.
SHE JUST DID IT. JUST DOES WHATEVER THE HELL SHE WANTS.
AND *BOTH* OF HER COSTUMES ARE COOLER THAN MINE, *TOO.*
WHY ARE YOU CHANGING YOUR--?
WAIT, WHY IS MY SPIDER SENSE--OH!
BECAUSE OF THIS! *THIS* IS WHY.
I GET BLAMED FOR *ENOUGH* STUFF!
I NEED TO BE BLAMED FOR YOUR STUFF, TOO?
DUCK.

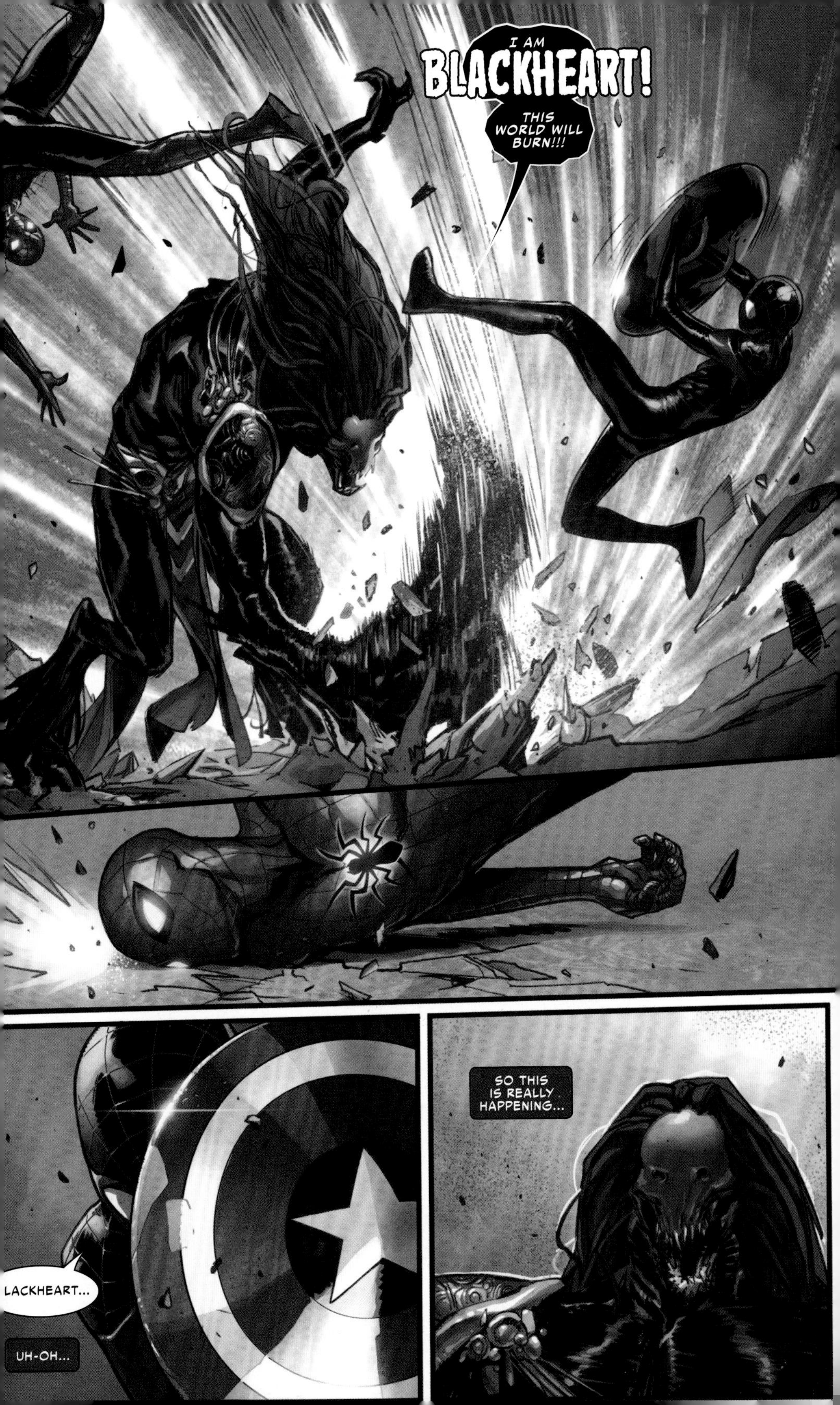
I AM BLACKHEART!
THIS WORLD WILL BURN!!!
SO THIS IS REALLY HAPPENING...
LACKHEART...
UH-OH...

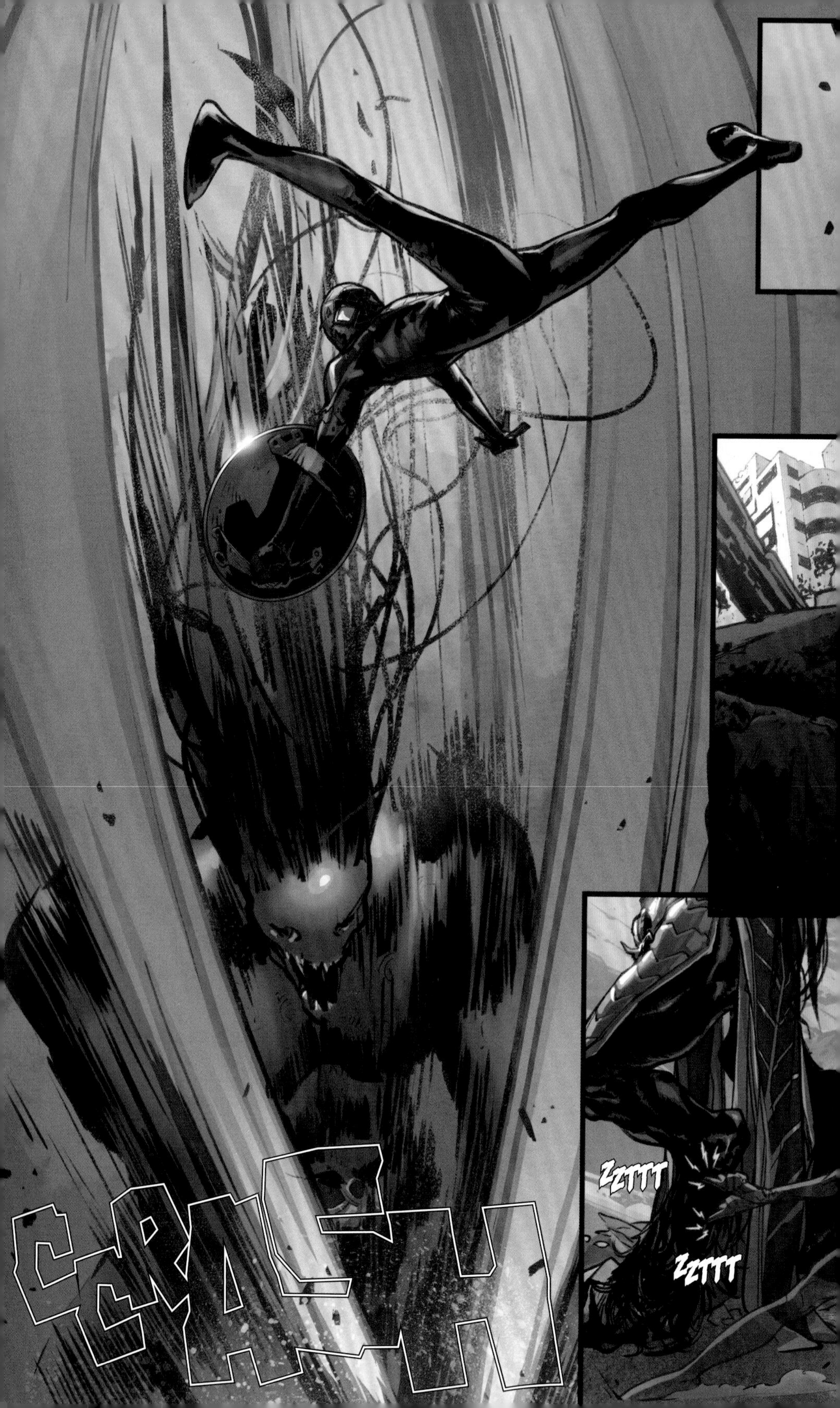
CRACK
ZZTTT
ZZTTT

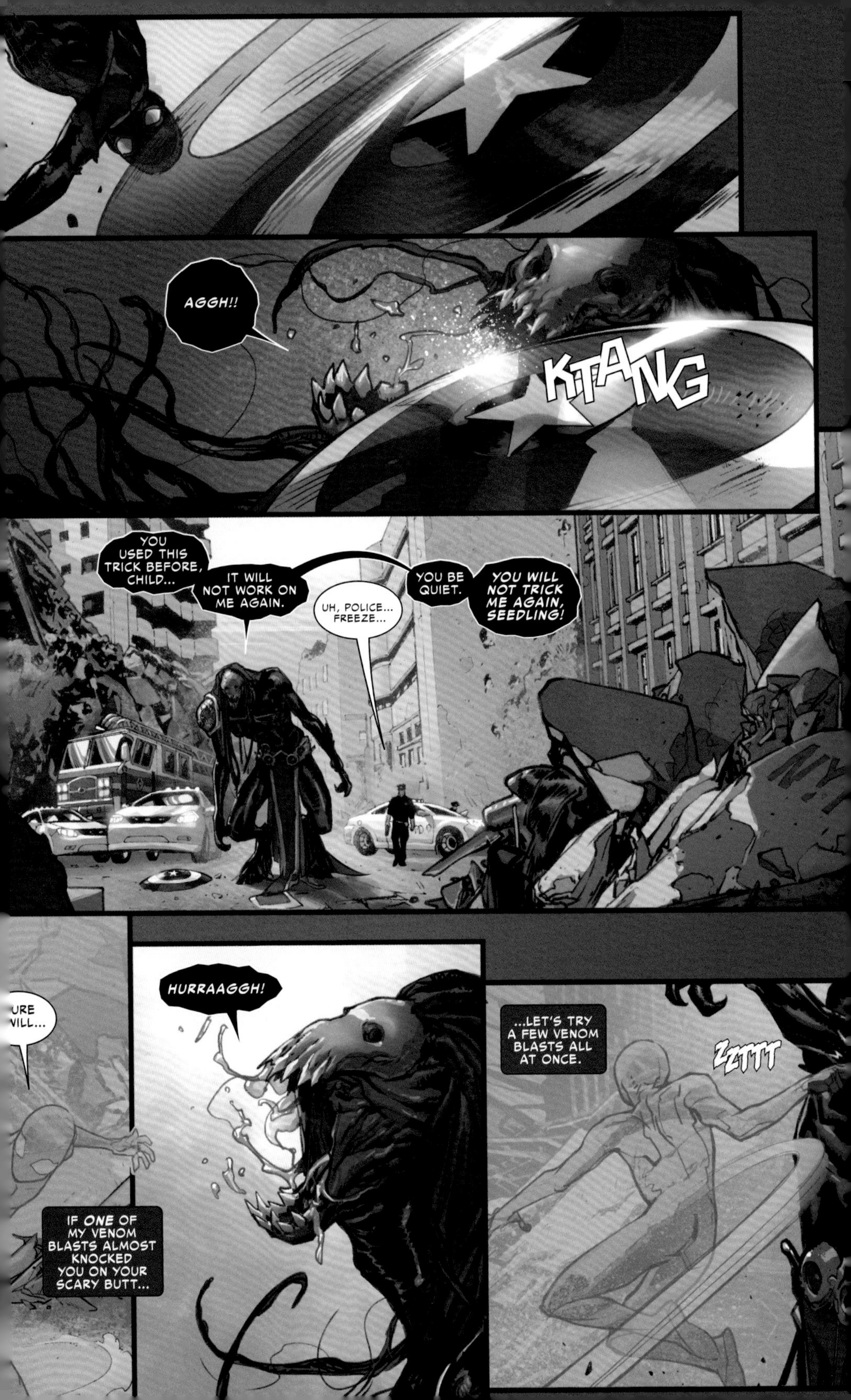
AGGH!!
KTANG
YOU USED THIS TRICK BEFORE, CHILD...
IT WILL NOT WORK ON ME AGAIN.
UH, POLICE... FREEZE...
YOU BE QUIET.
YOU WILL NOT TRICK ME AGAIN, SEEDLING!
URE WILL...
HURRAAGGH!
IF ONE OF MY VENOM BLASTS ALMOST KNOCKED YOU ON YOUR SCARY BUTT...
...LET'S TRY A FEW VENOM BLASTS ALL AT ONCE.
ZZTTT

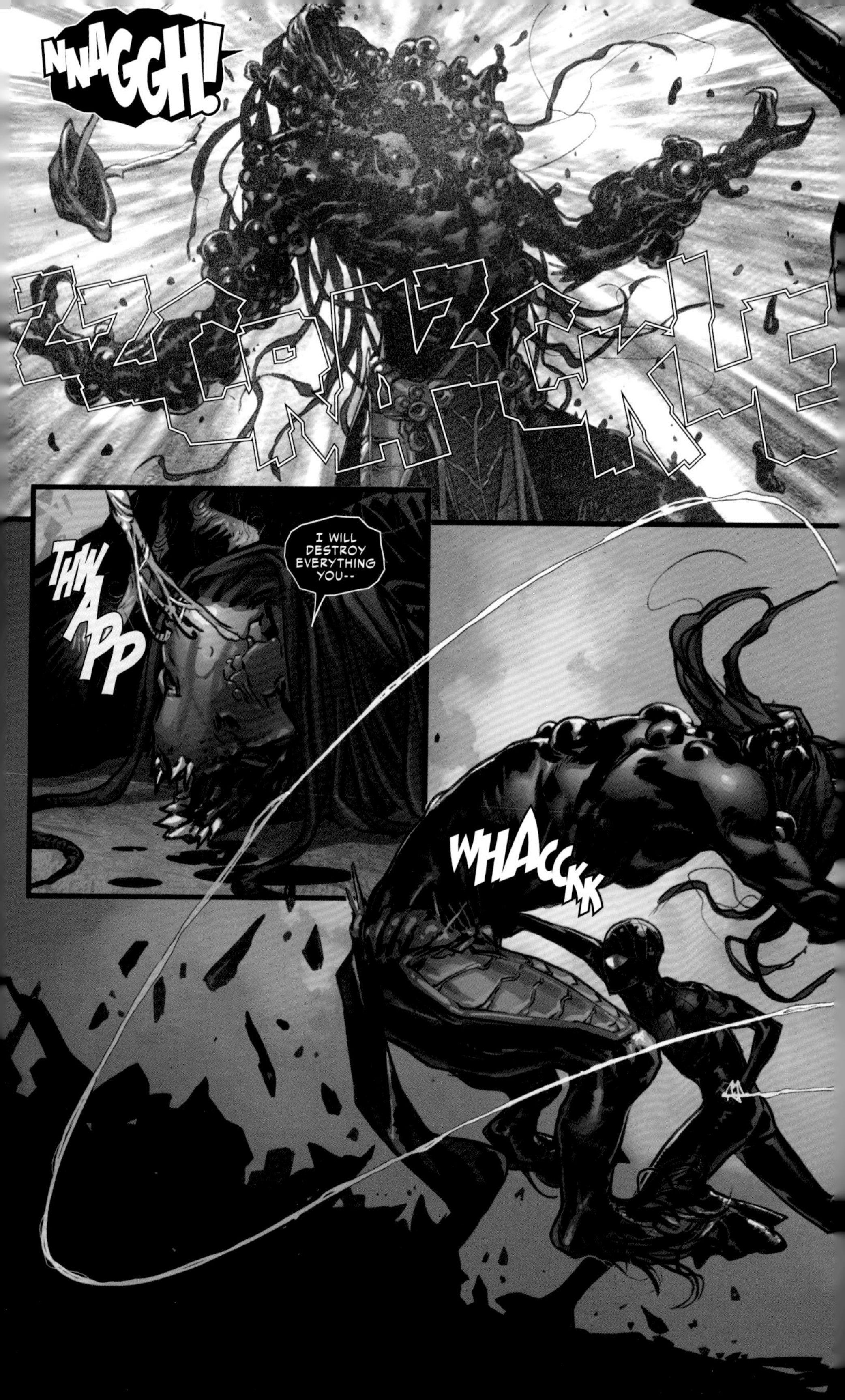
NNAGGH!
THWAPP
I WILL DESTROY EVERYTHING YOU--
WHACCKKK

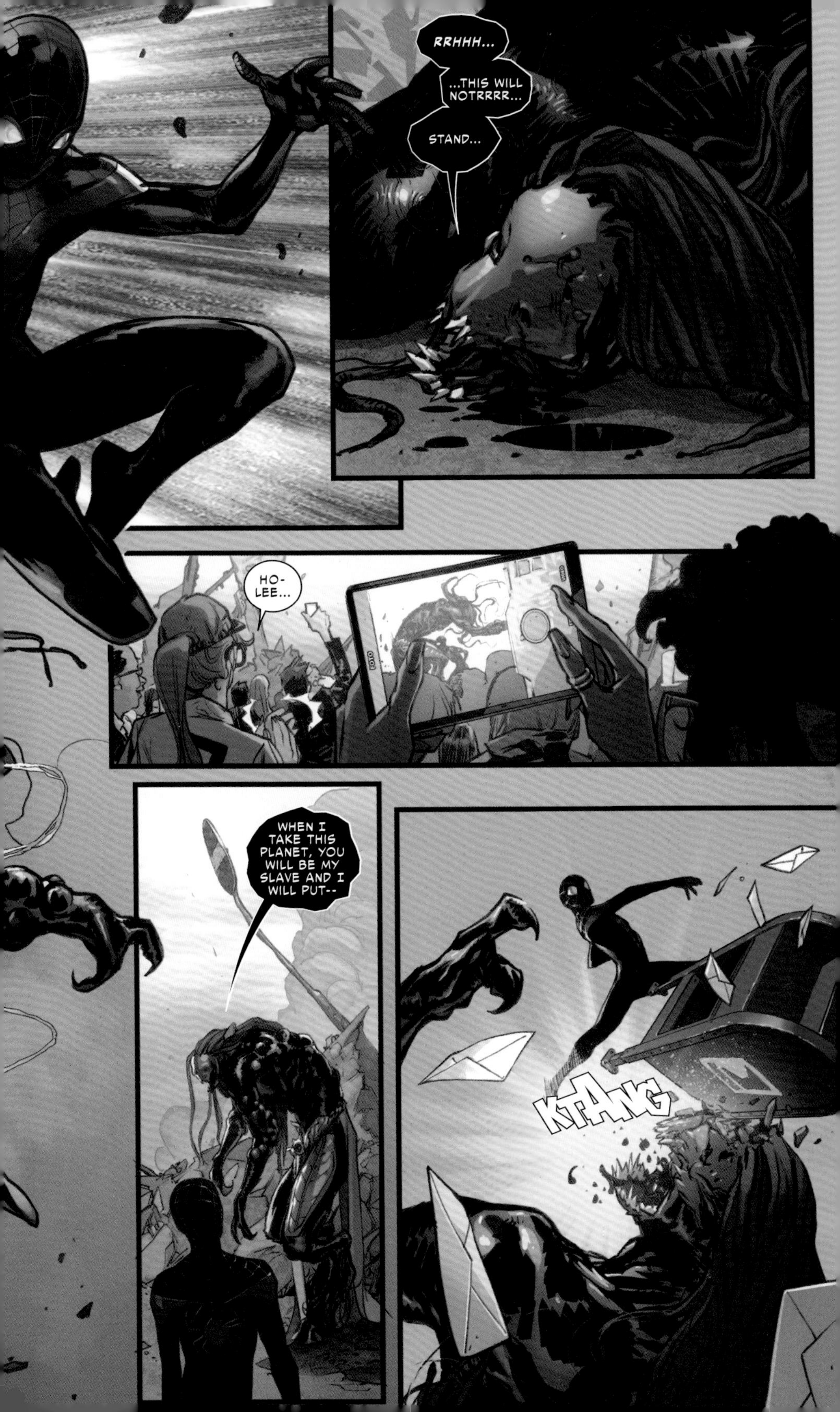
RRHHH...
...THIS WILL NOTRRRR...
STAND...
HO-LEE...
WHEN I TAKE THIS PLANET, YOU WILL BE MY SLAVE AND I WILL PUT--
KTANG

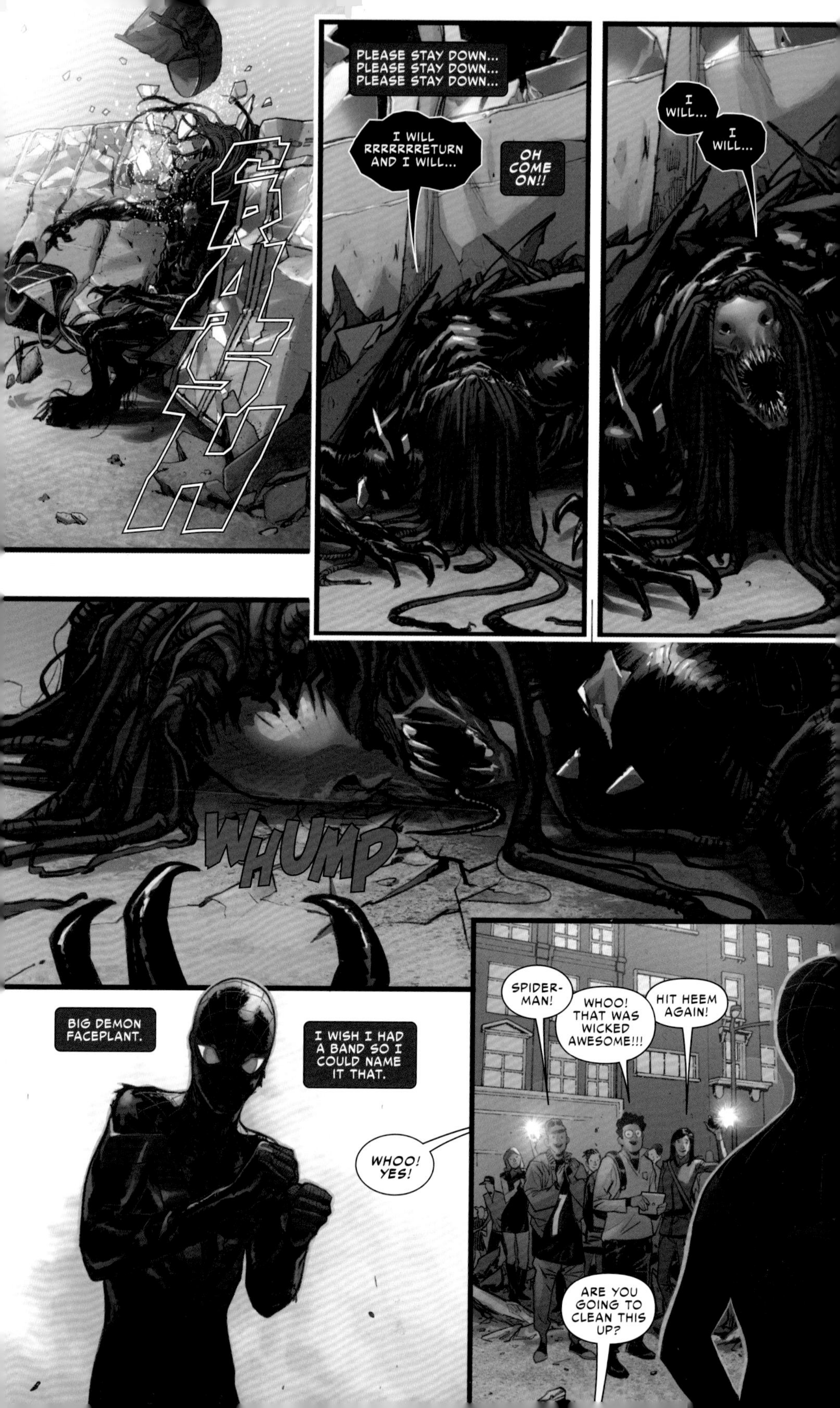
CRASH
PLEASE STAY DOWN... PLEASE STAY DOWN... PLEASE STAY DOWN...
I WILL RRRRRRRETURN AND I WILL...
OH COME ON!!
I WILL...
I WILL...
WHUMP
BIG DEMON FACEPLANT.
I WISH I HAD A BAND SO I COULD NAME IT THAT.
WHOO! YES!
SPIDER-MAN!
WHOO! THAT WAS WICKED AWESOME!!!
HIT HEEM AGAIN!
ARE YOU GOING TO CLEAN THIS UP?

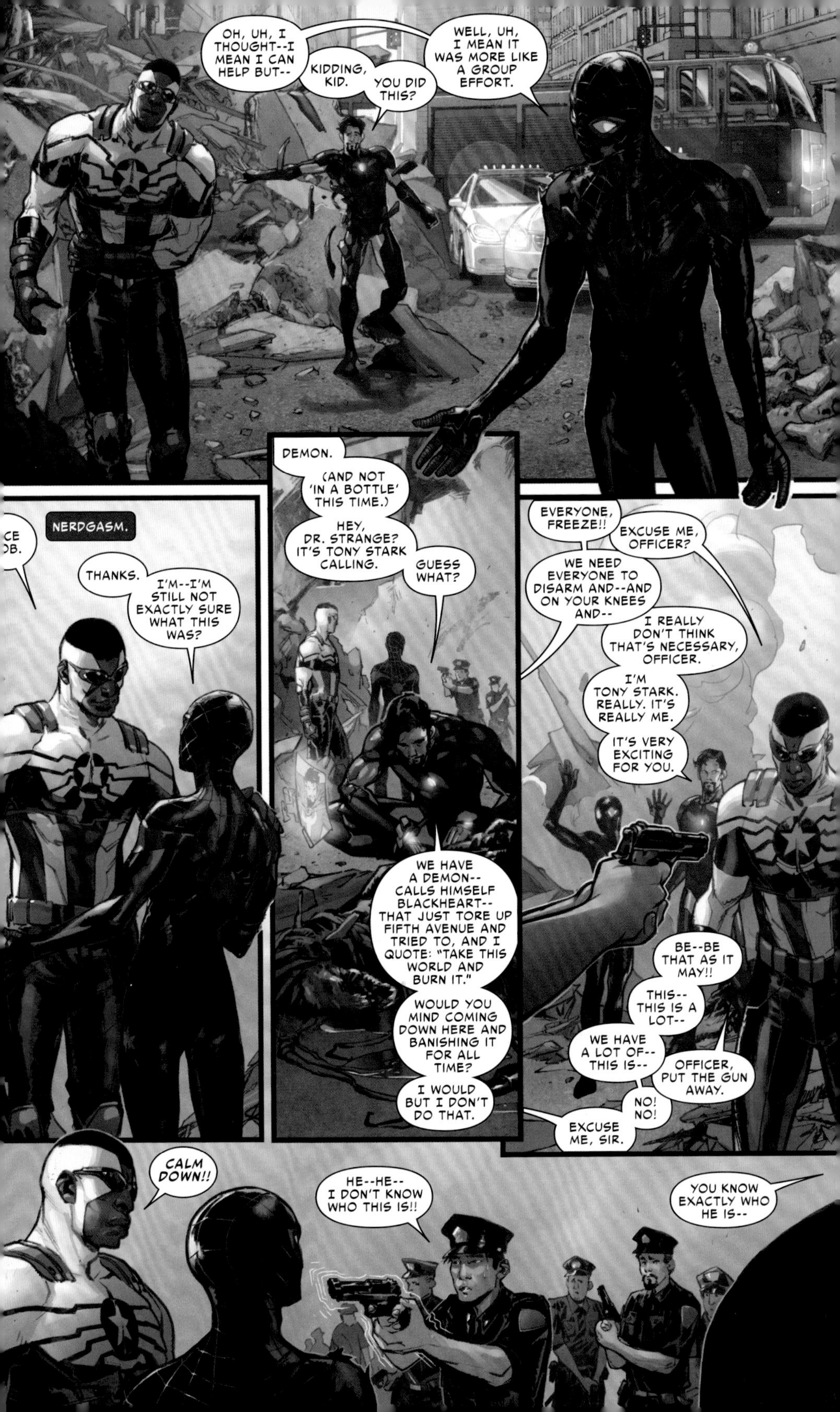
OH, UH, I THOUGHT--I MEAN I CAN HELP BUT--
KIDDING, KID.
YOU DID THIS?
WELL, UH, I MEAN IT WAS MORE LIKE A GROUP EFFORT.
CE
OB.
NERDGASM.
THANKS.
I'M--I'M STILL NOT EXACTLY SURE WHAT THIS WAS?
DEMON.
(AND NOT 'IN A BOTTLE' THIS TIME.)
HEY, DR. STRANGE? IT'S TONY STARK CALLING.
GUESS WHAT?
WE HAVE A DEMON-- CALLS HIMSELF BLACKHEART-- THAT JUST TORE UP FIFTH AVENUE AND TRIED TO, AND I QUOTE: "TAKE THIS WORLD AND BURN IT."
WOULD YOU MIND COMING DOWN HERE AND BANISHING IT FOR ALL TIME?
I WOULD BUT I DON'T DO THAT.
EVERYONE, FREEZE!!
EXCUSE ME, OFFICER?
WE NEED EVERYONE TO DISARM AND--AND ON YOUR KNEES AND--
I REALLY DON'T THINK THAT'S NECESSARY, OFFICER.
I'M TONY STARK. REALLY. IT'S REALLY ME.
IT'S VERY EXCITING FOR YOU.
BE--BE THAT AS IT MAY!!
THIS-- THIS IS A LOT--
WE HAVE A LOT OF-- THIS IS--
OFFICER, PUT THE GUN AWAY.
NO! NO!
EXCUSE ME, SIR.
CALM DOWN!!
HE--HE-- I DON'T KNOW WHO THIS IS!!
YOU KNOW EXACTLY WHO HE IS--

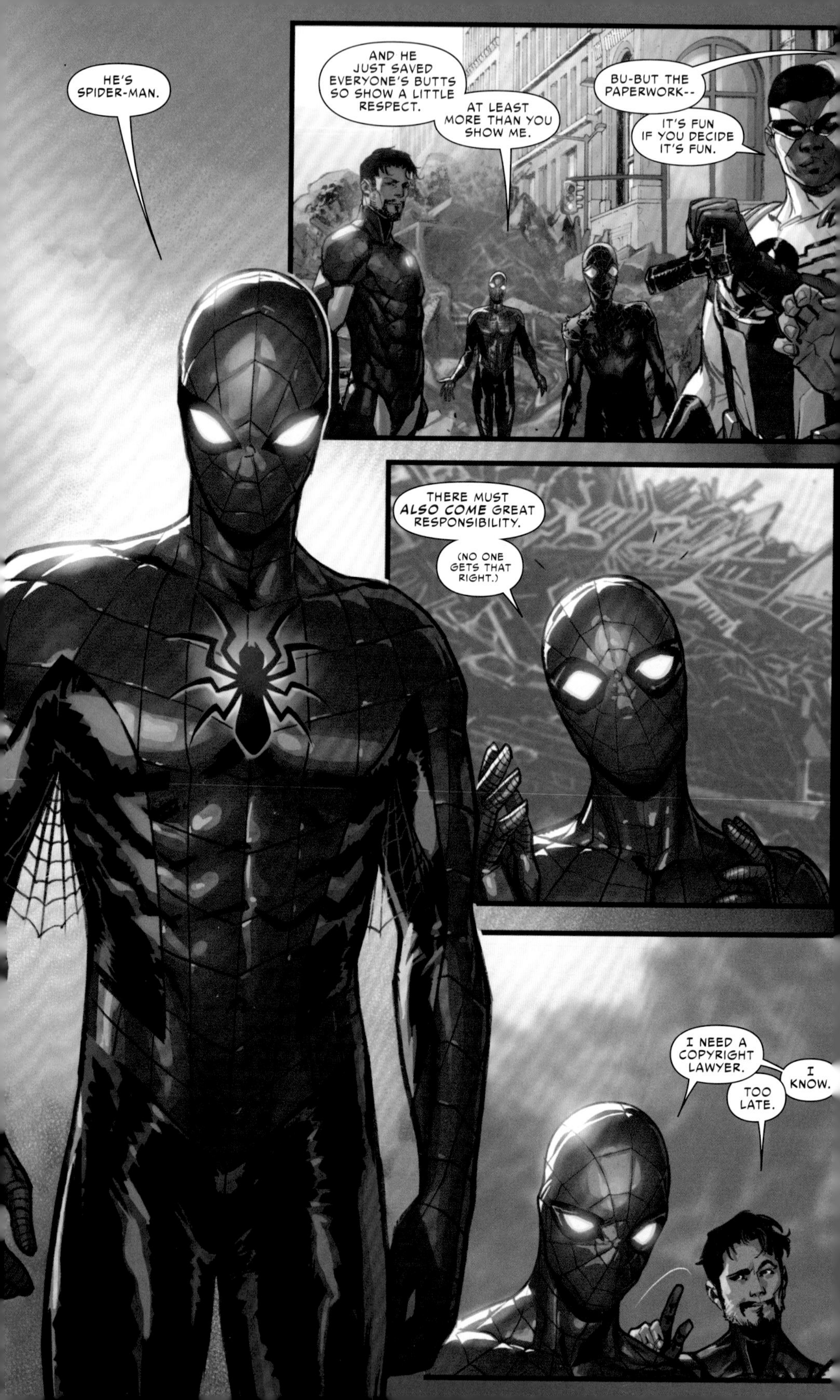
HE'S SPIDER-MAN.
AND HE JUST SAVED EVERYONE'S BUTTS SO SHOW A LITTLE RESPECT.
AT LEAST MORE THAN YOU SHOW ME.
BU-BUT THE PAPERWORK--
IT'S FUN IF YOU DECIDE IT'S FUN.
THERE MUST ALSO COME GREAT RESPONSIBILITY.
(NO ONE GETS THAT RIGHT.)
I NEED A COPYRIGHT LAWYER.
TOO LATE.
I KNOW.

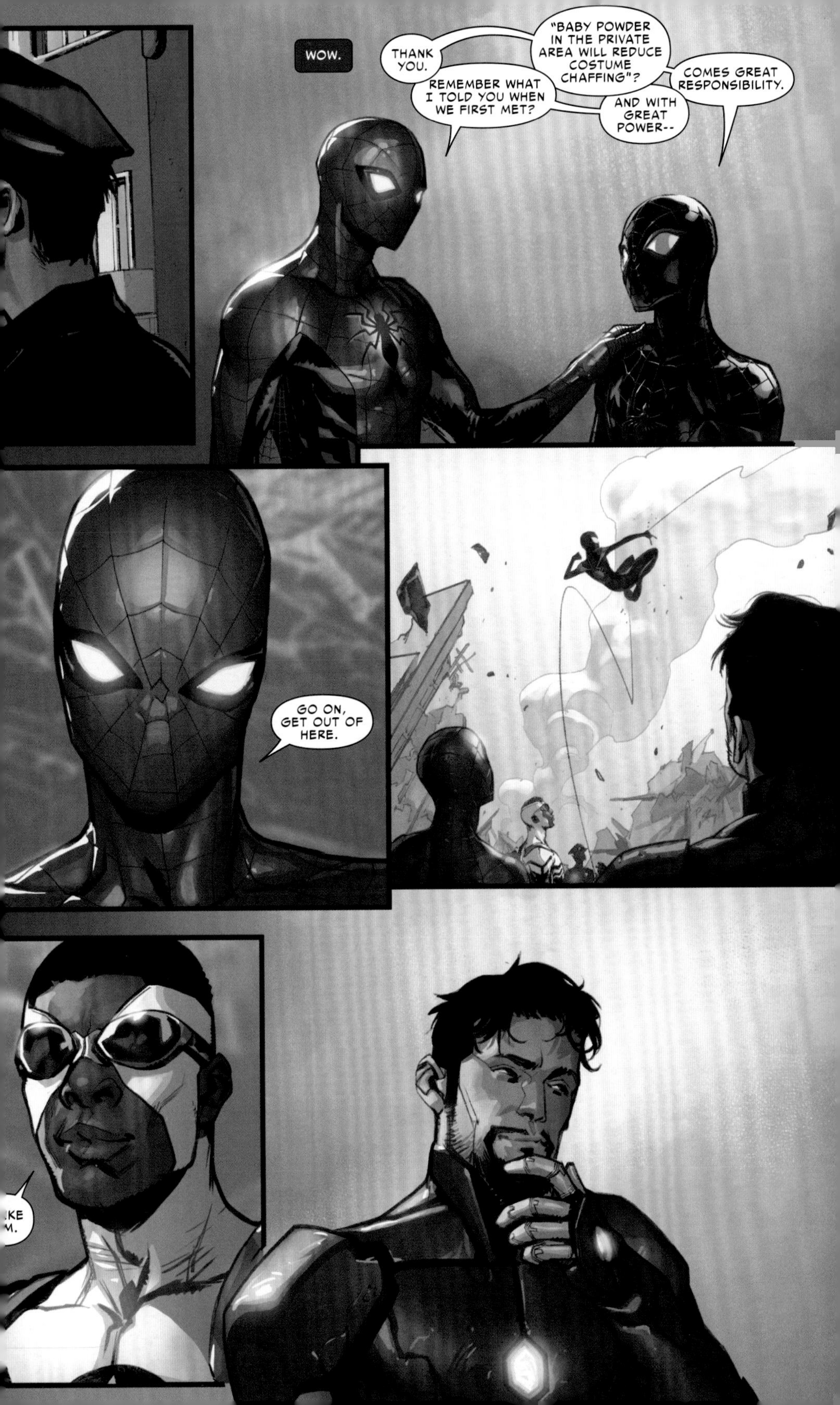

WOW.
THANK YOU.
"BABY POWDER IN THE PRIVATE AREA WILL REDUCE COSTUME CHAFFING"?
REMEMBER WHAT I TOLD YOU WHEN WE FIRST MET?
AND WITH GREAT POWER--
COMES GREAT RESPONSIBILITY.
GO ON, GET OUT OF HERE.

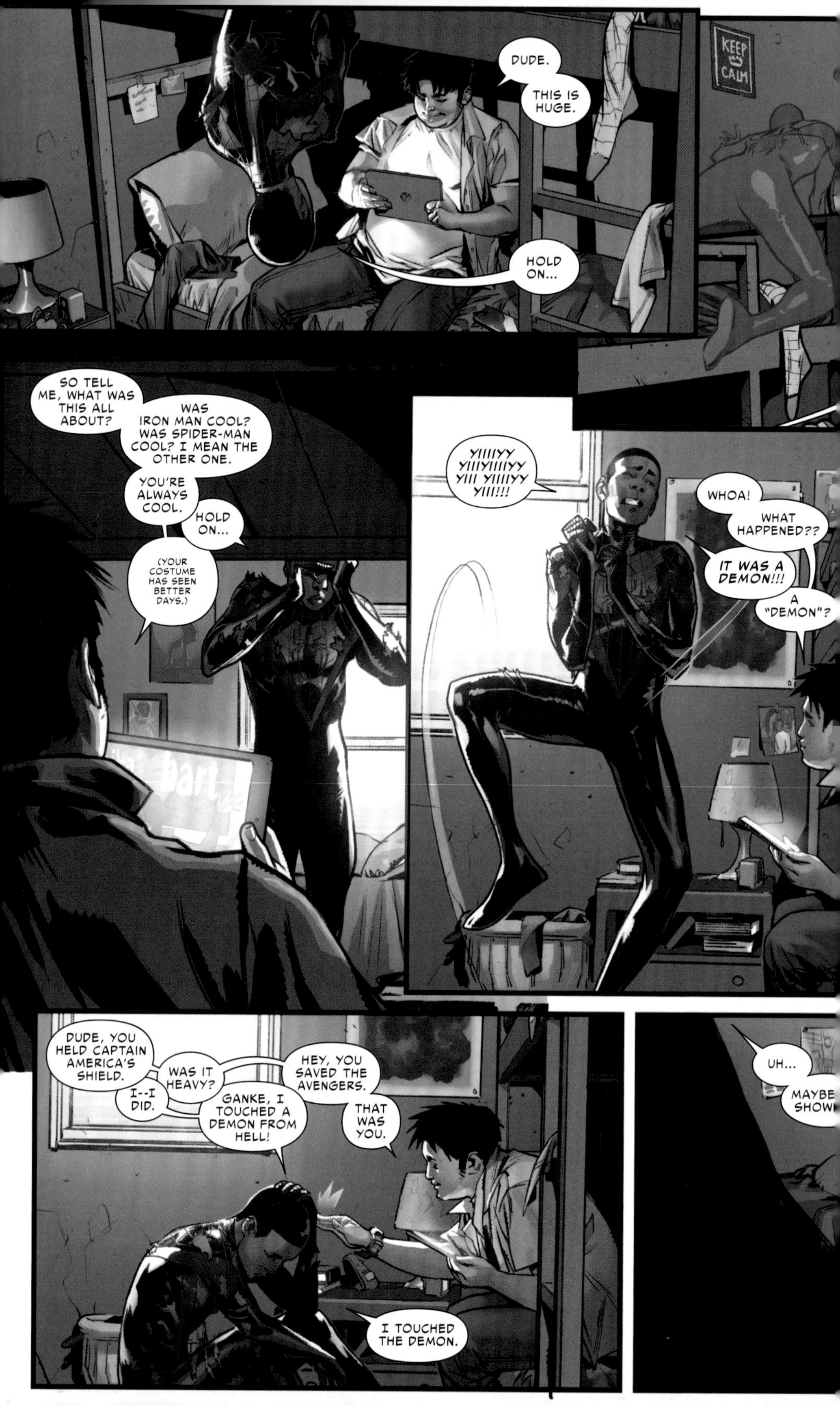

DUDE.
THIS IS HUGE.
HOLD ON...
SO TELL ME, WHAT WAS THIS ALL ABOUT?
WAS IRON MAN COOL? WAS SPIDER-MAN COOL? I MEAN THE OTHER ONE.
YOU'RE ALWAYS COOL.
HOLD ON...
(YOUR COSTUME HAS SEEN BETTER DAYS.)
YIIIIYY YIIIYIIIIYY YIII YIIIIYY YIII!!!
WHOA!
WHAT HAPPENED??
IT WAS A DEMON!!!
A "DEMON"?
DUDE, YOU HELD CAPTAIN AMERICA'S SHIELD.
WAS IT HEAVY?
HEY, YOU SAVED THE AVENGERS.
I--I DID.
GANKE, I TOUCHED A DEMON FROM HELL!
THAT WAS YOU.
I TOUCHED THE DEMON.
UH...
MAYBE SHOW

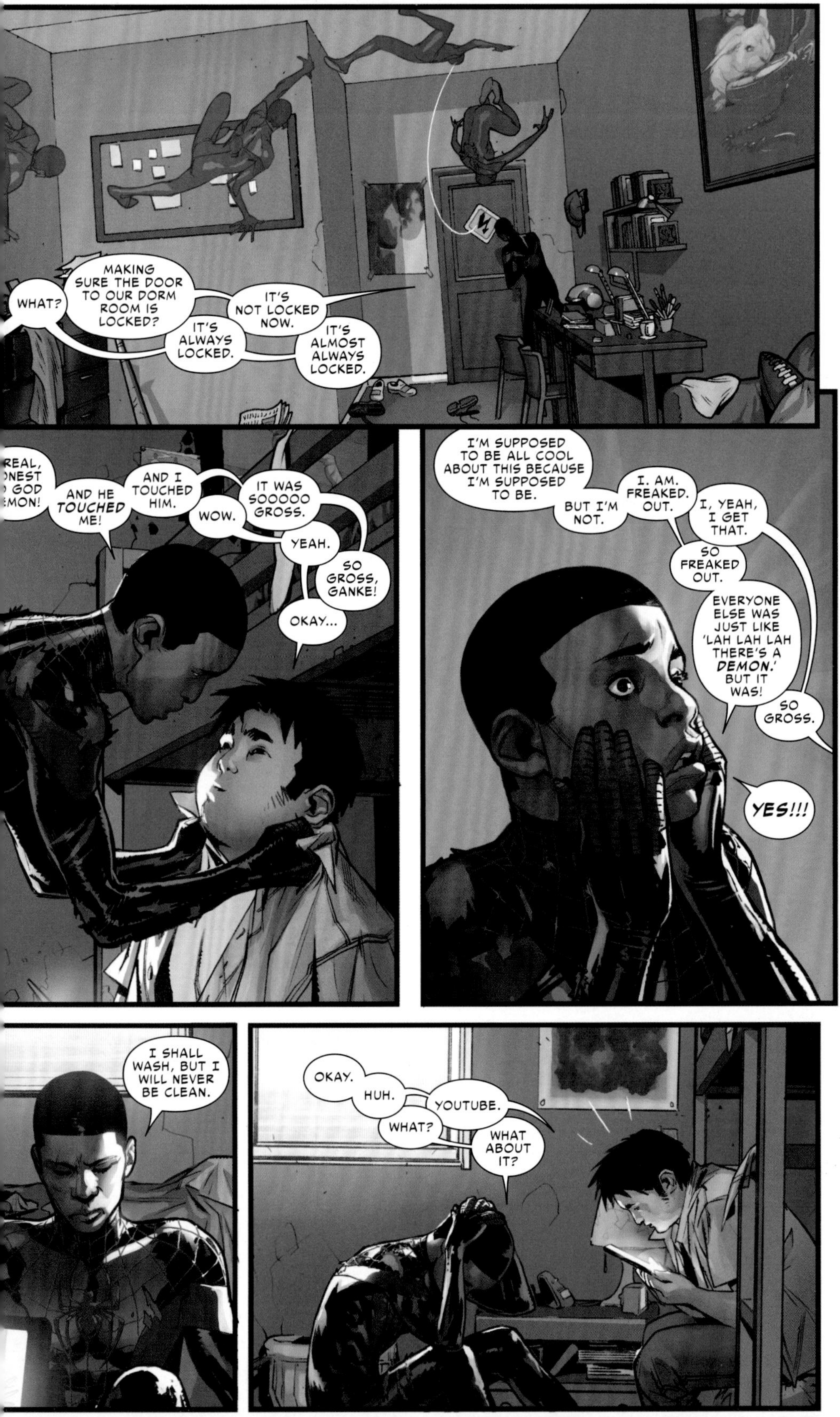
WHAT?
MAKING SURE THE DOOR TO OUR DORM ROOM IS LOCKED?
IT'S ALWAYS LOCKED.
IT'S NOT LOCKED NOW.
IT'S ALMOST ALWAYS LOCKED.
AND HE TOUCHED ME!
AND I TOUCHED HIM.
WOW.
IT WAS SOOOOO GROSS.
YEAH.
SO GROSS, GANKE!
OKAY...
I'M SUPPOSED TO BE ALL COOL ABOUT THIS BECAUSE I'M SUPPOSED TO BE.
BUT I'M NOT.
I. AM. FREAKED. OUT.
I, YEAH, I GET THAT.
SO FREAKED OUT.
EVERYONE ELSE WAS JUST LIKE 'LAH LAH LAH THERE'S A DEMON.' BUT IT WAS!
SO GROSS.
YES!!!
I SHALL WASH, BUT I WILL NEVER BE CLEAN.
OKAY.
HUH.
YOUTUBE.
WHAT?
WHAT ABOUT IT?

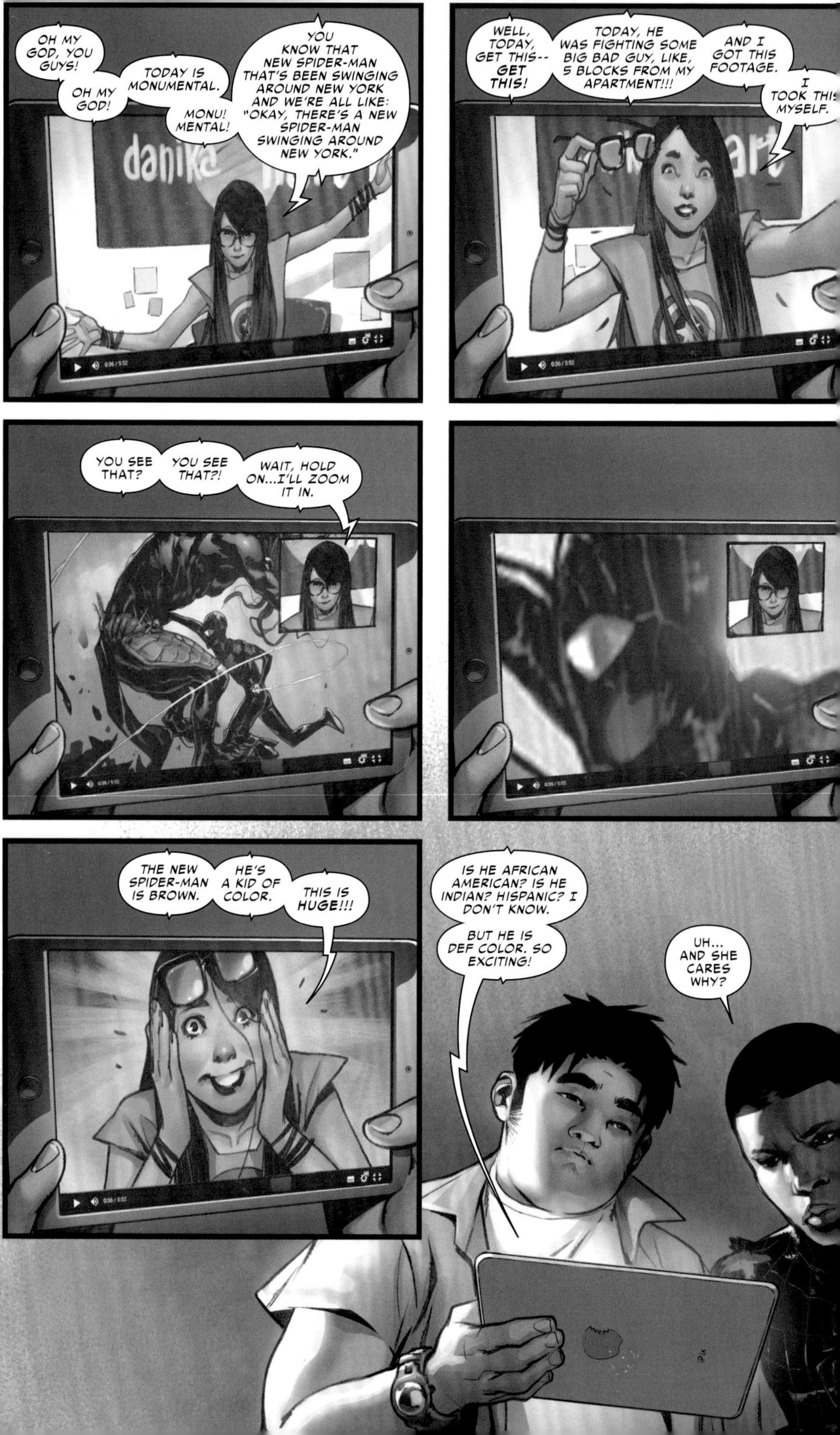
OH MY GOD, YOU GUYS!
OH MY GOD!
TODAY IS MONUMENTAL.
MONU! MENTAL!
YOU KNOW THAT NEW SPIDER-MAN THAT'S BEEN SWINGING AROUND NEW YORK AND WE'RE ALL LIKE: "OKAY, THERE'S A NEW SPIDER-MAN SWINGING AROUND NEW YORK."
danika
WELL, TODAY, GET THIS-- GET THIS!
TODAY, HE WAS FIGHTING SOME BIG BAD GUY, LIKE, 5 BLOCKS FROM MY APARTMENT!!!
AND I GOT THIS FOOTAGE.
I TOOK THIS MYSELF.
YOU SEE THAT?
YOU SEE THAT?!
WAIT, HOLD ON...I'LL ZOOM IT IN.
THE NEW SPIDER-MAN IS BROWN.
HE'S A KID OF COLOR.
THIS IS HUGE!!!
IS HE AFRICAN AMERICAN? IS HE INDIAN? HISPANIC? I DON'T KNOW.
BUT HE IS DEF COLOR. SO EXCITING!
UH... AND SHE CARES WHY?

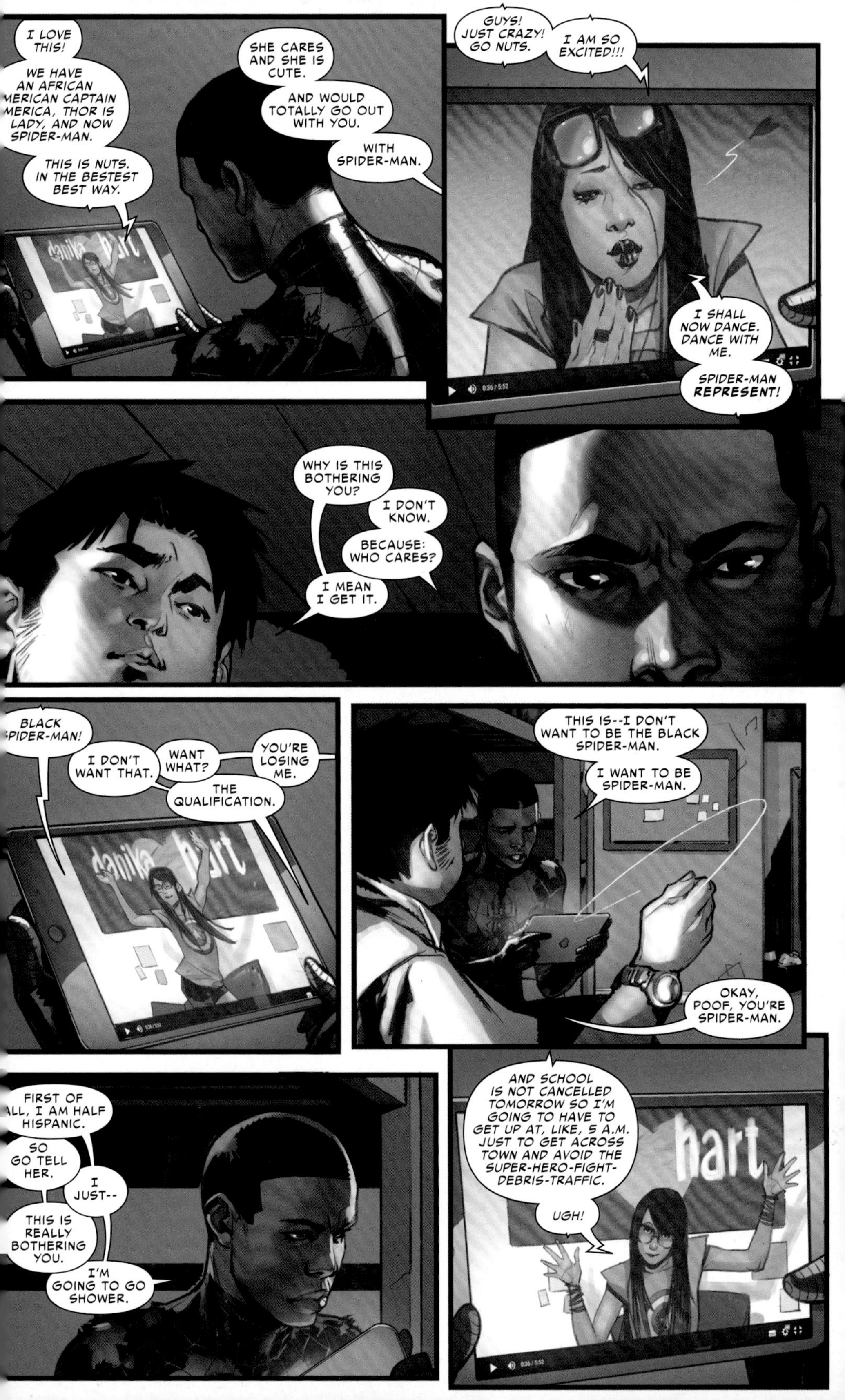
I LOVE THIS!
WE HAVE AN AFRICAN MERICAN CAPTAIN MERICA, THOR IS LADY, AND NOW SPIDER-MAN.
THIS IS NUTS. IN THE BESTEST BEST WAY.
SHE CARES AND SHE IS CUTE.
AND WOULD TOTALLY GO OUT WITH YOU.
WITH SPIDER-MAN.
danika hart
GUYS! JUST CRAZY! GO NUTS.
I AM SO EXCITED!!!
I SHALL NOW DANCE. DANCE WITH ME.
SPIDER-MAN **REPRESENT!**
WHY IS THIS BOTHERING YOU?
I DON'T KNOW.
BECAUSE: WHO CARES?
I MEAN I GET IT.
BLACK SPIDER-MAN!
I DON'T WANT THAT.
WANT WHAT?
YOU'RE LOSING ME.
THE QUALIFICATION.
danika hart
THIS IS--I DON'T WANT TO BE THE BLACK SPIDER-MAN.
I WANT TO BE SPIDER-MAN.
OKAY, POOF, YOU'RE SPIDER-MAN.
FIRST OF ALL, I AM HALF HISPANIC.
SO GO TELL HER.
I JUST--
THIS IS REALLY BOTHERING YOU.
I'M GOING TO GO SHOWER.
AND SCHOOL IS NOT CANCELLED TOMORROW SO I'M GOING TO HAVE TO GET UP AT, LIKE, 5 A.M. JUST TO GET ACROSS TOWN AND AVOID THE SUPER-HERO-FIGHT-DEBRIS-TRAFFIC.
UGH!
hart

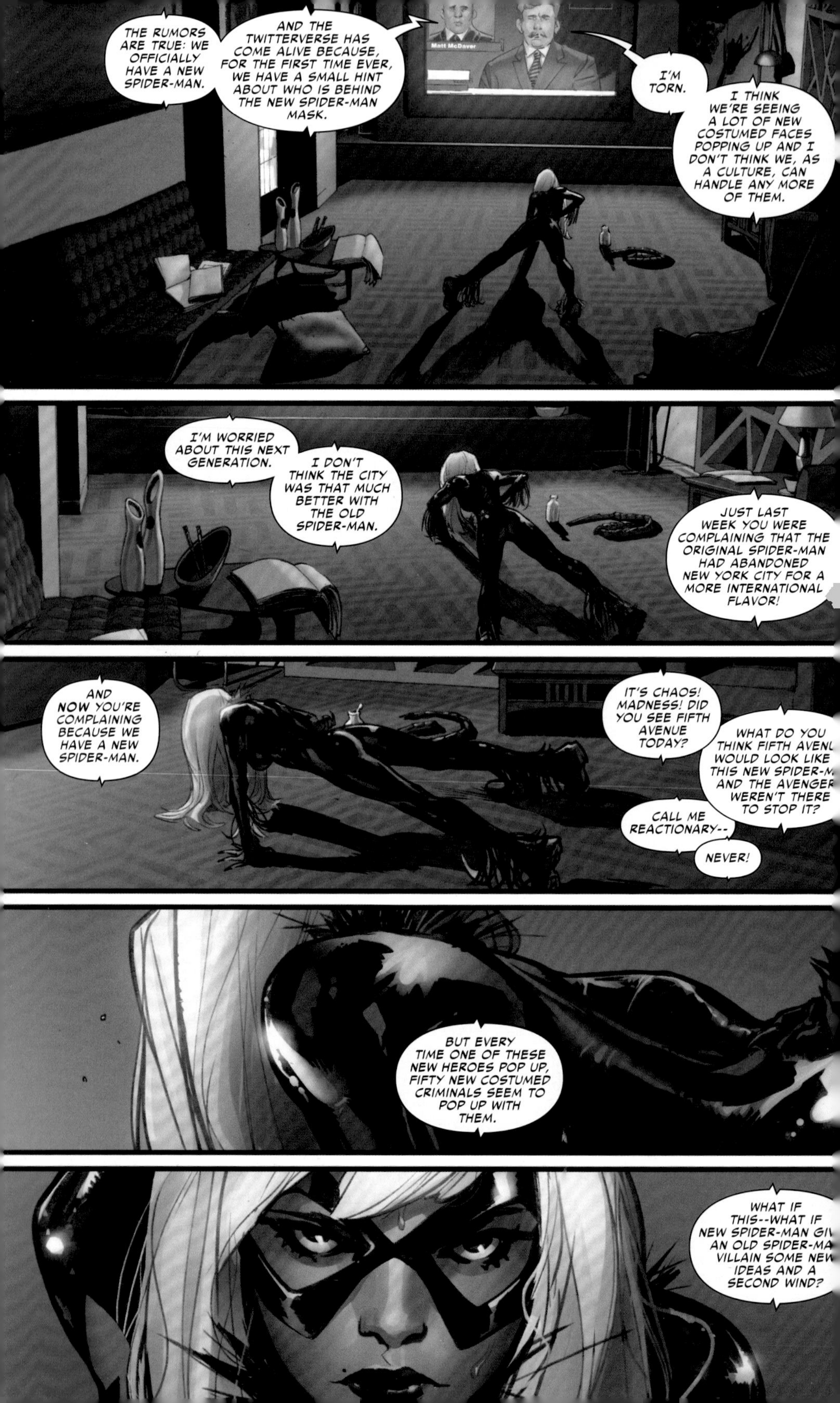
THE RUMORS ARE TRUE: WE OFFICIALLY HAVE A NEW SPIDER-MAN.
AND THE TWITTERVERSE HAS COME ALIVE BECAUSE, FOR THE FIRST TIME EVER, WE HAVE A SMALL HINT ABOUT WHO IS BEHIND THE NEW SPIDER-MAN MASK.
Matt McDaver
I'M TORN.
I THINK WE'RE SEEING A LOT OF NEW COSTUMED FACES POPPING UP AND I DON'T THINK WE, AS A CULTURE, CAN HANDLE ANY MORE OF THEM.
I'M WORRIED ABOUT THIS NEXT GENERATION.
I DON'T THINK THE CITY WAS THAT MUCH BETTER WITH THE OLD SPIDER-MAN.
JUST LAST WEEK YOU WERE COMPLAINING THAT THE ORIGINAL SPIDER-MAN HAD ABANDONED NEW YORK CITY FOR A MORE INTERNATIONAL FLAVOR!
AND NOW YOU'RE COMPLAINING BECAUSE WE HAVE A NEW SPIDER-MAN.
IT'S CHAOS! MADNESS! DID YOU SEE FIFTH AVENUE TODAY?
WHAT DO YOU THINK FIFTH AVENU WOULD LOOK LIKE THIS NEW SPIDER-M AND THE AVENGER WEREN'T THERE TO STOP IT?
CALL ME REACTIONARY--
NEVER!
BUT EVERY TIME ONE OF THESE NEW HEROES POP UP, FIFTY NEW COSTUMED CRIMINALS SEEM TO POP UP WITH THEM.
WHAT IF THIS--WHAT IF NEW SPIDER-MAN GI AN OLD SPIDER-MA VILLAIN SOME NEW IDEAS AND A SECOND WIND?

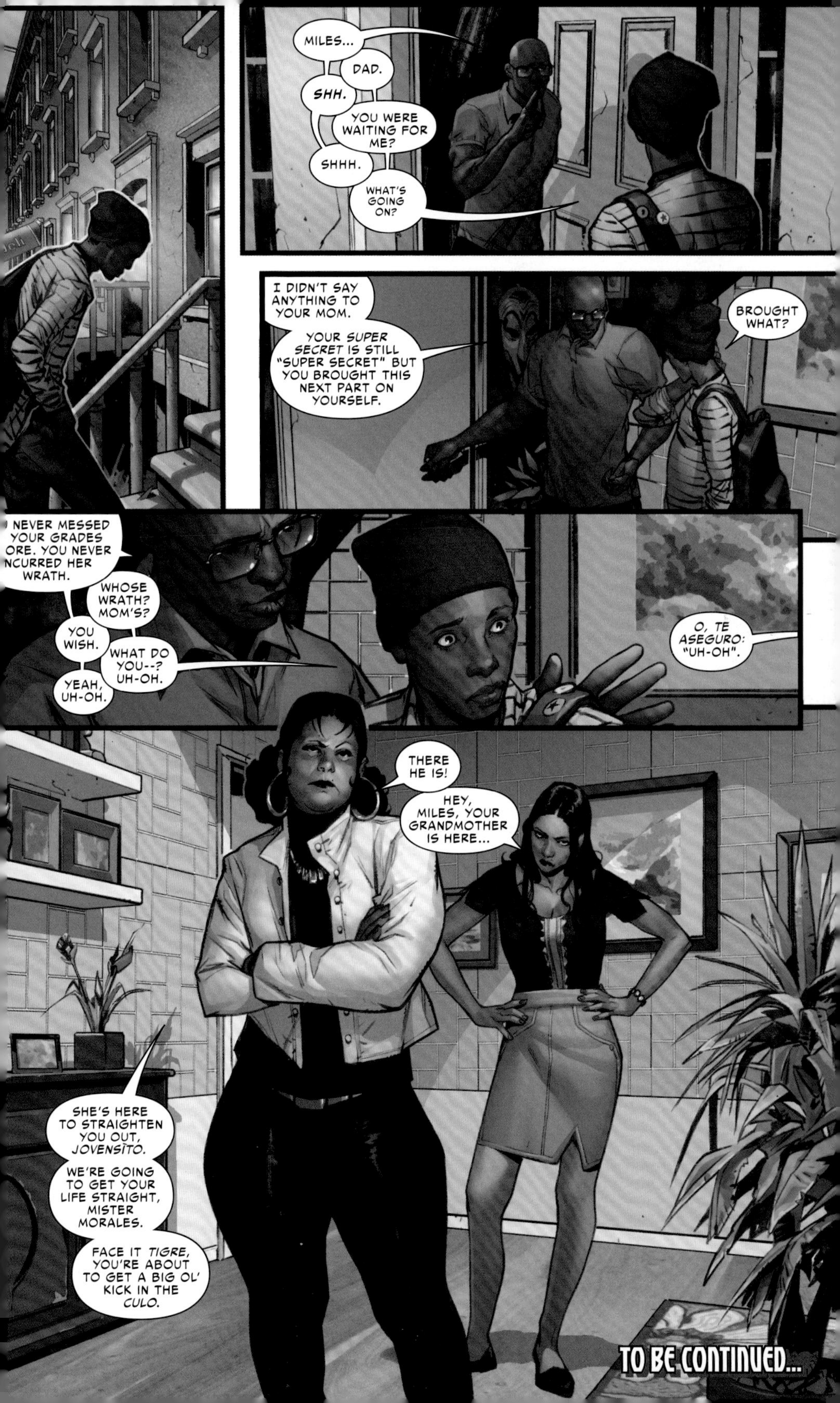
MILES...
DAD.
SHH.
YOU WERE WAITING FOR ME?
SHHH.
WHAT'S GOING ON?
I DIDN'T SAY ANYTHING TO YOUR MOM.
YOUR SUPER SECRET IS STILL "SUPER SECRET" BUT YOU BROUGHT THIS NEXT PART ON YOURSELF.
BROUGHT WHAT?
NEVER MESSED YOUR GRADES ORE. YOU NEVER NCURRED HER WRATH.
WHOSE WRATH? MOM'S?
YOU WISH.
WHAT DO YOU--? UH-OH.
YEAH, UH-OH.
O, TE ASEGURO: "UH-OH".
THERE HE IS!
HEY, MILES, YOUR GRANDMOTHER IS HERE...
SHE'S HERE TO STRAIGHTEN YOU OUT, JOVENSĪTO.
WE'RE GOING TO GET YOUR LIFE STRAIGHT, MISTER MORALES.
FACE IT TIGRE, YOU'RE ABOUT TO GET A BIG OL' KICK IN THE CULO.
TO BE CONTINUED...

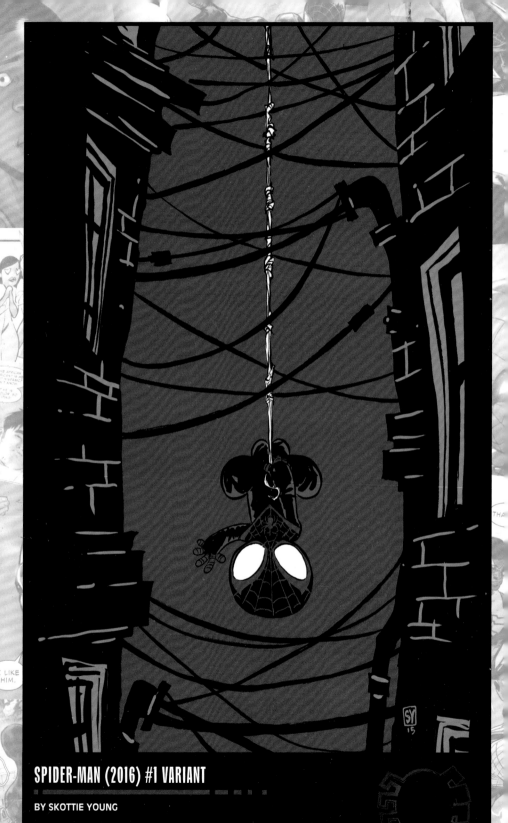

SPIDER-MAN (2016) #1 VARIANT

BY SKOTTIE YOUNG